Shattered Vanilla

Neil Hall

This is a work of fiction. Unless otherwise indicated, all the names, characters, businesses, places, events and incidents in this book are either the product of the author's imagination or used in a fictitious manner. Any resemblance to actual persons, living or dead, or actual events is entirely coincidental.

Dedicated to authenticity.

1

tHe rAnCiD CoPpEr PoT

Opportunity reverberates like a G sharp power chord, crackling deep within us all. Experience is the kick drum of acidic exhalation, breathing promiscuity. Opportunists are the cool mint sleaze preying on the young ears of inebriation.

At the bottom of dusty, scuffed, concrete steps, behind an ominous black reinforced door. The basement of subculture exists. A smoke filled, seedy setting. Dark vinegar ale and stale body odour lick at nostrils. Five pound entry fee, paid in loose grubby coins, exchanged for a smudged stamp on the hand. Red light bulbs cast shadows stretching to anarchic perfection. Glazy eyed, sweaty middle-aged clasped palms, tie knots around the corset trained waists of teenage Suicide Girls. Smouldering cigarettes squeezed between stained fingers, trace the faded outlines of inked pentagrams on pale naked shoulder blades. Leather jackets wiped clean of splashed slivovitz. The free spirited and rejected live shielded from the judgement of conformity. Stomping feet to the mantra: 'Fuck Authority', showcasing two stiff fingers to the 'man'. The club welcomed the disenchanted damned.

'The Rancid Copper Pot', the weekend haunt. For those preferring sordid fantasies to the soundtrack of debauchery. Low ceilings draw closer with hands tickling dark oak beams. A crowded hot box of ecstasy. Treated to live bands. Tonight, the local band 'Animosity' would provide their brand of metal distraction. Unlike the University Union, playing bubble gum cheese music. The hardcore underground folk didn't care about 'All that shit'. At least at the 'Pot', you can throw caution to the stage and feel comfortable padlocked to the scene. Nothing too shiny or clean, the walls drip dirty living. Two fingers inside a stranger, warm hands on the shaft of a penis. The music foreplay, everything desired. Ravaged to convulsive orgasm, vibrating through ankle bracelets, down to tingling tattooed toes. A connection to the DJ, through beat and melody. Songs played only and just for you, matching heartbeats. Jennifer Lost The War, tender caresses from the vocals of Dexter Holland, stroking up the inner thigh. A tongue tantalised. Tracks mixed with female screams from Bikini Kill, The Slits and The Runaways. The beat bounced souls, feet floating free. The dance floor, forever packed with rubbing heated bodies, sweat dripping from spilt ends. Enough shoulder friction for hair-raising static electricity. Rumbling grunts of appreciation for punk. Those that embraced up strumming ska classics from The Specials or skanking to tenor saxophones on singles from The Might Mighty Bosstones. Knees turned from jelly to granite. Some of the scene wore designer trucker hats, different shades of woodland green. Others, more obscure, deliberate in enigma. Those into serene riffs and trumpet introspection from Oingo Boingo. Dedicated followers of fashion. Tight black jeans and lumberjack shirts buttoned up to the collar. A mix of all ages, from teens into Emo and adults into Rage.

"Outta the way," said the Landlord. A bald, burly, punch-drunk, natural born fighter with skin like a pork scratching. Pale eyes close together. The music cut off. "Another brave little soldier, giving it the berries." He pushed through the crowd at the bar. Through gritted teeth. "You'll learn not to dip in my eggs," he added. Poking a fresh faced, stiff shouldered eighteen-year-old's croissant chest. "Don't push your luck with my daughter, bitch."

Salty tears building in the young man's moist eyes. "There's a video of it," he said.

Ruby, the daughter, stood embarrassed, finger twiddling long blonde hair, behind the bar. Arms crossed, hitching smooth, voluptuous breasts into her neck. All eyes of the club cast hyena attention on her, admiring and criticising in no particular order. She smirked, serpent tongue pushing its way between yellowed teeth. Concealing enjoyment, she rubbed her chin on her pointy, bare shoulder. Standing erect, bouncing her body weight. Subdued howls and wolf whistles came from the club as her chest jiggled and wobbled, threatening to overflow.

"Son, you're taking it too far," said Landlord, an inch from the boy's face. "Pushing your luck."

The boy forced flinching eyelids not to blink. "You should tell these people what you're doing here," he said. "Think what they'd do." He flapped his hand. Landlord circled his head, neck cracking. The crowd shuffled, turning away.

"You're on your own." The Landlord's face moved from the shadows, eyes slurry brown. A deep furrow ravine appeared, on his forehead like aged leather. With the explosion of a precise blurred left hook. A stiff, cracked knuckle sucker punch to his glass jaw. The bolstering boy felt a heartbeat shudder behind his ears. Then, a vacuum of silence, crumpling to the floor. Vision Arctic white.

Landlord gripped his gorilla fist around the boy's dyed green mohawk, dragged him limp across the grey, beer soaked slate floor. The crowd cleared an accommodating pathway, bowing to their deity. Shuffling Doc Martin's, sliding sticky Converse trainers aside. The boy moaned, teary eyes fighting to open. Feet kicking out. The back door slammed shut, the fire escape push-bar clattered. The cartoon sound of fists on flesh like cabbage under a hammer. The warp and wobble of metal flexing, the boy's body tossed against industrial bins.

Landlord returned, door clicked shut. A burning cigarette drooping, shaking his right hand, examining bloodied knuckles.

"That kid'll shake my hand the next time he walks through that door," he said, scanning the crowd, all providing polite laughter. Clapping his massive hands together. "What'll it be?"

Pills by the New York Dolls burst into life from the speakers, attacking silence. Arms shot up, trainers shuffled. Studded belts hoisted and adjusted by filed, painted fingernails. Toothy smiles returned. Collective indulgence, grinding dirty dancing, hips crunching.

Until the night becomes lubricated and forgotten. Dylan leaned alone against the cold cellar walls. Not touching shared surfaces. Discreet observations and apologising for getting in the way. Easing with delicate politeness through the rowdy crowd. Jostle jumping and body squashing. Chocolate brown, bell bottom, corduroy trousers chimed against his ankles. Avoiding more shoulders and squeezing sideways. Desperate to breathe in open space. Salvation found in a dark corner. Groups of friends and acquaintances chatted around stained square tables. He yearned to join in with their laughter. If only to be noticed.

"Excuse me," said Dylan.

Gripping his sloshing pint high. Couples embraced. Heads tilted, eyes closed. Breathing heavy through pierced, nose ring whistling nostrils. The fruity stench of Joop turned sour on bitter skin. Tongues shared spiderweb saliva. Averting his instinct to stare, he reached another quiet corner, far out of the way. The music roaring, Ten Foot Pole's, My Wall thrashed out distorted. The walls echoed, bass rumbled with a tremor through warm Converse covered feet. Through the blurred matchsticks of people, he could make out the stage. Clubbers pitching devil horns into smokey air. Sighing with relief, adjusting his glasses, clutching his pint close to his beating chest. His bewildered eyes darted and shifted, taking in the colourful crowd. Scanning from the frowning bouncers, across the elbow throwing dance floor and four deep at the busy bar. Wide mouths shouting into deafened ear lobes. Hands gripping at petite hips. Band posters hanged torn from the damp, chewing gum speckled walls. Afraid to make eye contact with anyone, even the ones with tiger eye contact lenses. He could never be caught staring at fingers tickling under short skirts. Snake groping grips, fondling C-cup bras. Girls in band t-shirts, pinned against speakers, received love bites on teasing necks. The married men removed wedding rings, hidden deep in socks. Dylan could only look down, tapping his foot to the sounds of Millencolin's Bullion. Trying to fit in. Nodding at a scowling skin head who glared at him and said.

"When I walk past. Get the fuck outta the way. Cut yer hair, mop head." He slapped Dylan on the head. "Faggot." Spat at his feet and swaggered off, impersonating Liam Gallagher, shoulders swaying, knees bent to the side. "Mad for it. Mad for it." Chains and metal key rings jangled against his thighs. Some onlookers chuckled, pointing. Dylan focused on the floor, patted and squashed his 'mop-top' hair. A rickety wooden shelf housed his lonesome glass. Glancing up at a wall of Polaroids. Blurred, drunk, tired faces smiled back, band autographs on greyed lacy bras in sprawling magenta lipstick. Tattooed arms wrapped around necks. Cigarettes flopped from moist, silky mouths. Enough to feel a cigarette would be his ultimate saviour. A warming, secure sleeping bag. A way to concentrate his hazy mind and instil misplaced, unrealised confidence. Stretching for an overflowing, chipped glass ashtray, he sparked the cigarette tip. The taste of burnt cherryade warmed his throat. That first drag was the sweetest of honey serenades.

A trio of punks kicked from the wall, cutting a look, as Dylan exhaled, darting his eyes in every direction to avoid theirs. As soon as they made space, light reflected off their leather jackets. Noticing a small green door in the corner, two wooden steps up. He would need to duck to step into what was hidden behind.

He jerked the handle. Locked solid. Yanked it like Arthur from The Sword in the Stone. No movement. Pressed his ear against the cold wood. Listening for life the otherside. Nothing.

2

aDdIctEd tO bAsS

"God damn." Said Dylan with an intake of shallow breath, impersonating Mia Wallace from Pulp Fiction, minus the powder snorting. Moving his intrigued attention from the green door. The cigarette flamed, taste changing from diamond luxury to paraffin bitterness. Second it finished, he'd light another. Never stopping. A perpetual cycle. The glowing cherry was rattling to drop.

Mark, his housemate, landed double footed in front of him. Loose change chattered in his pocket. Hair spiked to perfection, as it always was. Dylan pictured him stood in front of the mirror, running waxy fingers through his hair, applying it front to back, left hand, right hand. Plucking like a conductor.

'The Pot' is Mark's second home. Out of breath and without words, he took a gulp from Dylan's pint glass, smiling through blue eyes, emptying the glass in one proud swallow. Condensation dampened his palm. He thrust the glass back into Dylan's chest, pinching the cigarette from his lips, launching it like a dart into his own mouth. He inhaled smoke deep, swirling within his lungs, blowing it

6

out into Dylan's twitching face, shielding burning eyes.

Mark leaned into Dylan's ear. "Gonna get me some fucky." He said, exhaling smoke through his nose as his beady eyes scoured the club. His voice drowned out by Bad Religion blaring New America.

"This is my tune," he said. Raising onto tip-toes, his tongue flicked as if lapping at rum and raisin ice cream. He eyeballed blonde girls emulating Christina Aguilera, slut dropping and bending at their narrow hips, accentuating pancake bottoms. Running soft palms up smooth, tight thighs, a single finger trailing and teasing over pierced navels. As fast as Mark sprang into appearance, he bounced off, leaving Dylan. Fading to mingle among the many girls. Dylan felt weak as a passenger. A lonely stranger in this new punk land. Tagged along with Mark for most nights, living with the hope, he too, would be discovered. A girl might whisper a sultry introduction, take an interest. Share in longing for intimacy. Mark would forever insist and bribe him with Marlboro's, guaranteeing, in that distracted coercion, that he'd meet someone. A funny girl, cute in Cuban heels, maybe a wild one, happy to explore her perversions. Dylan would forever submit, itching for that promise to become a wet fingered reality. He stood in the shadows, wrestling with jealousy, watching Mark. Intrigued and revelling in the innate ability to seduce 'fit talent', as Mark would describe them. The way he'd work his proverbial magic. Thin lips suckling the end of a secondhand cigarette. Head darting right, a cloud of white smoke. He disregarded goth girls. The last, Holly, into The Cure, slapped off his red DC cap and spat bubbly phlegm in his face. All because he said he couldn't stand The Lovecats. 'Too much piano'. Not stopping his search. He swept his head left, another cloud of smoke lapped free from his mouth. He caught the eye of 'top heavy' Ruby, the barmaid, Landlord's daughter. She dripped absinthe over ice. Mouth open, tongue rolling her lip with concentration. Dylan noticed the Landlord slap the back of her bare arm, breaking her submissive eye contact. Mark stared at her cleavage, confused it wasn't her peachy buttocks strapped to her chest. He scratched his eyebrow with his thumb and chuckled. He eyed up leather jackets.

The girls with Bad Brains scrawled in thick Tipp-ex on their backs. Reminisced about Jennifer, dancing with her eyes shut. The way she tasted like maple syrup or Mikhaila's orgasms sounding like the harmony to Little Surfer Girl by The Beach Boys. He didn't want to deal with that tonight. Her crying, signalling the definitive end to their single bed encounter. He scanned, hoping for someone different. In the mosh pit, elbows thrown. Head banging girls, avoided now too. Polly and Alice, the last two, gave him weeping cases of chlamydia. His usual conceit crumbled behind lips encrusted with herpes blisters. Thankful now, he could show his face again. With a quiver of delicate nostrils, Mark winked back at Dylan. Dropping the cigarette to the floor, it sparked and rattled to a stop next to beige kitten heals. He locked eyes on a blonde, swaying her pencil hips. Her attention his. High cheek bones cast shadows down her teardrop face. Constructed from the straight edge pages of Vogue magazine. Noticing Mark admiring, she parted her fingers against her neck, stroking bright pink, Hello Kitty nails between her flat cleavage, pulling down the handmade cut in her Jimmy Eat World t-shirt. Frayed string bracelets tied around both bare, bony wrists. Her spear tongue flicked the tip of a luminous yellow drinking straw, escaping the nibble from glistening glossy lips. She moved her denim hips in a figure of eight, in time with the music, the crowd clapped and cheered. Her pupils fixed on Mark over midnight purple eyeshadow. His giddy eyes refused to divert, lost in ellipsis. To Dylan, it was as if Mark floated alongside, whispering rose water in her ear. His stubbly cheeks grazing hers. Close enough to sniff her lengthy hair. Fluffy marshmallows mixed with nicotine. Mark fought the desire to lick her chin. She turned toward his warm breath and longed for him to buy a shot of tequila, if only.

"Bass," said Mark. She shivered, as if ticklish. "Like the four-stringed instrument. Turned up to eleven." He covered his mouth, coughing into his fist. "Not like the fish." He clarified. Her baffled face said it all. No clue what he was saying, what any of it meant.

"The fish is pronounced like the shandy," said the blonde. "You'll have to rethink that one."

Dylan wanted to hear. He had to know what made her laugh like Pac-man. Giggling so sweet, from the belly, spraying her drink. He needed that talent, Mark's ability. It was enviable. With analytical intrigue, he continued to study Mark's movements, edging closer to overhear, listening for tips and advice on shady adult living. If only he had a notepad. This was priceless.

Mark banged his chest. "Bass," he said, nodding.

Dylan rolled his eyes, having heard it before. The way Mark introduced himself to everyone. Leaning back into her, he gawked down the front of her shirt, longing to glimpse apple pie nipples. Their hands touched. Only for a moment. She moved as he moved. Heads brushed and palette eyes continued to mingle. Denied each other a taste of tongues, holding lust, loin deep.

The band, 'Animosity' dressed in black leather and flicking loose dyed hair from their faces, jumped on stage. Lifted guitars over necks. Sat at battered, dented drums. The lead singer took hold of the microphone, wrapping the lead around his wrist twice. The crowd cheered, clapping.

"OK Bass." She said, raising an eyebrow. "I'm Tabitha." Cheeks dimpled, sucking on her straw.

Bass stopped clapping for the band. He pulled Tabitha's hand to his lips. "I can see I'm losing ya, pickle." He kissed once, twice, and a third time. She shrugged, pulling away. Dylan snorted. He shifted attention to the band so not to get caught staring.

"Mark," he said, brushing his fingers over her smooth forearm. He flicked her long hair from her face.

"Yeah!" she sang loud and laughed above the thrashing noise from the band. "Ya know." She flapped her arms to encourage recognition. "Mock, like Mark. The song. Mock, yeah. Ing—yeah. The mocking bird song." Tabitha clarified. Shaking her head, "Never mind. I'm entertaining myself, at least."

"Mark's my real name," he said. "I don't usually tell people that. I wanna be honest with you from the start," he stood on tip-toes, to be heard over the melodic chorus.

Tabitha smiled, bewitched by boozy articulation. She giggled, taking another sip.

Getting closer, Dylan shook his head. He wasn't about to make use of fake names as an icebreaker, to get a girl's attention. Couldn't sell out like that. He wouldn't. The thought sickened him. He forever wondered how these girls fell for Mark's arbitrary drivel. Worked for him, every time.

"I think my name is too," he said. Searching for the word. "Vanilla." He put his lips on Tabitha's straw, drew his cheeks in and swallowed. "Bass says; I'm in a band. It's bold, a slap in the face. I even have a hoodie with it printed on."

"Of course you do," she said. She took the straw back with her lips. Defiant eyes seeped into rounded hypnosis. "So," she paused. "Are you, are you in a band?"

Bass would work through the same practised social routine. Name dropping obscure local bands. Random, but familiar enough to be believed. He implied with pride and mimed strumming a guitar. No one would make this up. That's how he thought.

"I don't know if you've heard of Snuff?" he said. She shook her head. "Miss Black America. No?" He encouraged a reaction. "I've played with Howard's Alias."

"I know of him," said Tabitha.

"Played for MxPx." Said Bass, pausing for breath. "They released the album, The Ever Passing Moment. You must know Consumed." He didn't wait for her to answer. "I played drums on Gutbuster."

With the band set finished. The four-piece dismantled musical equipment, loading a van outside, parked close to the fire exit. The DJ spun the last song. I Wanna Be Your Dog, The Stooges. The crowd savoured each moment. Collected jackets and downed dregs of warm drinks, stubbing out cigarettes. Two guys at the bar. One with a bloodied nose. The other, with genuine concern and apology plastered across his worried face, patted the other on the shoulder. Windmill flailing arms, forgiven with a smile and clink of pint glasses.

Bass ushered Tabitha into the cold. Steadied her by the small of her back. Dylan waited, timing his foot on the bottom concrete step so not to clip Bass's heal. The reinforced door slammed closed, the bolt thundered, locked tight. Dylan longed to guide a girl up from the abyss of 'The Pot'. Rescue her to twilight, together from madness, laughing at cars passing. He needed the opportunity to regret. The choice to wrestle with grim decisions and bury some, any memories alive. Experience in the big wicked world would offer that. A painful story to share. One, in time, added to a punchline and laughed at from his future. Being drunk, he held the rusty hand rail. He only thought about the need to disinfect. Staring at open palms, seeing nothing but teeth chomping bacteria.

"You all right?" said Tabitha holding out her hand. Dylan heard nothing but the vision of her eyes and took hold of her warm little finger. "Dylan, isn't it? I'm—,"

"Tabitha," he said.

"All right, you two." Said Bass, jumping between to separate. "Break it up before I have to piss on your feet." He flung his arm around her shoulder, pulling her into his chest. "Marking my territory, like a naughty little pussy."

"Oh Jesus," said Dylan. White eyes rolling. "So crass."

"What's that mate?" said Bass. "Penis envy is an ugly trait, enmenius sleepus." He pushed his lips onto Tabitha's. Her eyes wide with shock. He held her arms tight at her side. She tried to flap like a penguin, but couldn't move. He pushed his tongue down her throat. Gripped her arse in both hands, dragged her forward, thrusting into her. She relaxed into the forceful kiss and crossed her hands behind his neck.

Dylan walked along the pavement, scuffing his heals. Black night sky, hands deep in pockets. The moon shone paranoid inadequacy at his every step. The street lamps glowed blood orange. Whistles blew from mouths unseen. Forever an outcast in the company of wolves.

3

tA-bI-tHA

Tabitha staggered on cheap heals, clipping the curb. Dylan threw his hands out straight, as if ready to break the fall of a cat from a tree. Under her armpits, he caught hold before she toppled into the road. Her mobile phone rang in her clutch back. With no time for awkward appreciation or eye contact. Bass glared at Dylan. Tabitha flipped her bag open, poking her left finger in her ear and answering.

"Not yet," she said. She stopped and circled on the spot.

Dylan and Bass, hands in pockets, meandered the pavement.

"It's too late now. I'm gonna stay at Chrissy's."

"Which one of us is Chrissy?" said Bass, sitting on a low wall. Opposite abandoned industrial warehouses.

"D'you know how old she is?" said Dylan, folding his arms, looking back at Tabitha. "Out here she looks pretty young, ya know, with that squidgy baby face."

"She's a student, mate. It's cool. Give us a fag."

Dylan reached for a cigarette. "You can be a student at eleven," he said.

Bass shook his head, sparking the cigarette in cupped hands. "And you're supposed to be intelligent, the uni goer. You're a student in higher education. That's college and University. You're a pupil in school. She's in college." He was struck with an annoying epiphany. "Like I give a fuck. Anyway, I'm not gonna ask to see her ID."

Tabitha smiled as she approached. Her cheeks red, huffing with annoyance, folding her bag closed.

"Everything good, was that your housemate?" said Bass.

Dylan smirked at his obvious yet subtle attempt at playful interrogation.

She laughed. "It was my mum, wanting to know if I'd be home. She worries. Now it's just us two—,"

"Just you two?" said Dylan, walking on the outside, closet to the road. Tabitha in the middle, between the two of them as they sauntered. Bass considered double penetration, then shook off the fantasy.

"My parents spilt up over money. My dad's a fireman, although nowadays he only seems on strike, and so, not fighting fires. See, money, there's a theme here." She said.

"You'll be home in time for college," said Bass.

"I'm in sixth form, silly." Said Tabitha, smirking. "Don't worry, I'm coming home with you, no matter what." She rubbed her hand up and down Bass's arm like sanding a door frame.

"How does it feel to be the third wheel, mate?" Said Bass, leaning over Tabitha, patting Dylan on his chest with a thud, a condescending clown smile plastered his face.

"I can drop back, leave you two to chat."

"Yeah, do us a favour, mate." Said Bass, winking.

Dylan slowed his walking pace, dropping back behind. He placed a cigarette between his lips. Soft laughter from the pair ahead as he continued to follow, forming a gap. He watched as Bass ran his hand over the curve of Tabitha's arse. He squeezed once. Dylan noticed the thick vein pumping in the back of his hand. The purple vein disappeared. Squeezed again, the blood pulsing. To Dylan, it was obvious the grope was for his benefit, to magnify the jealousy Bass wanted him to feel. Then, his stiff middle bird finger waggled behind her back in Dylan's direction. Wind up merchant, his only thought. He inhaled on his cigarette, shaking his head, stifling a laugh of incredulity.

The trio passed shuttered shops. The odour of bleach, lingering thick in the air. Signs folded, chained to walls with padlocks, advertising halal meats, sold by the kilogram.

"It's all right round 'ere. We've had no trouble." Said Bass, looking back at Dylan for confirmation.

"It's not the best, it's where we live, kind of used to it now," said Dylan, projecting his voice.

Tabitha scanned the street, under the weight of Bass's arm, wrapped around her neck, taking in the fabric shops and terraced houses.

"All you'd have to say is, 'Allahu Akbar' and they'd forgive you," said Bass.

"I wouldn't suggest you try that though," said Dylan, re-joining them. Tabitha giggled, her shoulders shaking.

"We're like Green Day," said Bass, pointing at their reflection in a shop window. "Look, that video for When I come Around."

"What's Green Way?" said Tabitha.

"It's a good job you're fit." Said Bass, planting his lips on her forehead.

Dylan continued to drop back and catch up. Laughing when invited, providing coughs in agreement. Tabitha and Bass bumped shoulders, giggled like kindergarteners. She shivered each time Bass interlocked his icy fingers in hers. She could see in his dark pupils that he wanted to devour her. His tight grip made her apprehensive, having second thoughts about the inevitable conclusion to the evening. They stopped at a corner junction. Waiting for cars to pass, Bass forced two fingers between her legs, up under her denim skirt.

"Not here." She said, pushing his hands away, squeezing her knees together. "Easy tiger." She grabbed for Dylan's arm, pulling him closer. They walked arm in arm. Bass scowled, insulted she grabbed Dylan for obvious protection. Shook his own arm free of hers, picking up his pace, stomping up the hill.

Tabitha scowled at the semi-detached house. Number '72' spray painted on bare bricks. The front door to the shared, musty smelling house banged closed. Their trainers dragged across the worn, hard wearing paisley patterned stained carpet. Dylan snapped on the small travel kettle in the kitchen, a student housewarming gift from the shelves of Woolworth's. Now used as the only communal beverage maker in the grimy, sparse, outdated kitchen. Bass dragged a pale faced, and now quiet Tabitha into the living room. The door left ajar. She appeared to have lost all confidence. Bass flicked on the fourteen inch TV sat atop a flimsy wooden table in the corner.

"You can't even see the picture," said Tabitha.

"We don't pay for a licence," said Bass. He pushed a black videocassette into the VCR. "We won't be watching TV for long, trust me." Bass slumped next to her on the sinking brown sofa.

Tabitha sat side legged, her thighs locked together. Bass tickled his fingertips over her right knee.

"I love what you've done with the place." She said, pointing at empty Foster's lager cans stacked on top of each other and empty Lambrini bottles decorating the non-functional gas fire place. "That's quite the collection. I've never even tried Lambrini."

Bass tutted. "Lambrini is only for lubrication. It's cheap." He moved closer, hooking his finger over her t-shirt. "Anyway, I didn't notice you liked Jimmy Eat World." He glimpsed at her bra. "I had no idea how much I liked them." His spider like hands cupped her left breast.

She pushed it away. "Dylan's only in the kitchen." She said, adjusting her t-shirt.

"Let's go upstairs then." Said Bass, thrusting his hips forward, pushing himself on her. "I wanna eat you—,"

"Here it is." Said Dylan, nudging the door open with his elbow, concentrating on not spilling the three mugs. Bass backed away from Tabitha, huffing. She exhaled, almost relieved. Bass took hold of one mug, clutched in a triangle in Dylan's hands. Tabitha smiled at Dylan, taking hold of the handle of a second mug. She breathed a concentrated breath through pursed lips, distracting herself from a panic attack.

"You good?" said Dylan.

Tabitha sat and contemplated the question. She nodded.

Dylan sank into a stained floral sofa opposite, resting his mug on the floor at his feet.

"Can I use your toilet?" said Tabitha, setting her mug down.

Bass tutted. "Up the stairs, door right in front of ya," he said.

Tabitha clutched her bag to her hip and made her way upstairs. Step by step, the stairs creaking.

"Mate. I'm gonna roger it 'til high noon." Said Bass, dry humping the air. "You see her tits?" He tweaked his own nipples over his hoodie. "Perfect size."

Dylan scoffed, looking out at the dark hallway. Expecting Tabitha to be standing there, arms crossed in the shadows, disappointed. She wasn't. She wouldn't get to hear who Bass was.

"I hope she doesn't want a shower. I wanna taste that girl from the crack of her clinkered arse to her pussy." He said, slurping on tea, shuffling his caterpillar eyebrows.

"You sure she's up for that?"

"Why else is she here—? It's not to watch Bill Hicks." Said Bass, pointing at the TV. Taking another gulp from his mug. "I'm tellin' ya. Glad I sniffed her out. If the red bull doesn't give her wings, she'll be flying soon." He clutched his crotch over his loose skater jeans. "Shove my face in the abyss of her sex." He lapped his snake tongue, miming being between her thighs, eyes closed tight. Making noises like slurping udon noodles. "Soft chicken lips—, You got any smoke?"

"I've got some left, yeah."

"Skin up, bruv." Said Bass, leaning back on the sofa, listening out toward the bathroom to hear for movement. "Share the wealth. We'll have a blifta before I come in her face. Might relax the bitch."

Silent floppy heads. Red squinting eyes, stared at the TV. All three of them squeezed, slouched together on the sunken brown sofa. Bill Hicks on VHS continued to play.

Bass mumbled. "This is some funny shit."

"Relentless. One of his best." Said Dylan, as he leaned on his elbow. Bass passed the pound round blazing joint to Tabitha, sat between them. She flicked ash into a three dimensional Rasta inspired novelty ashtray on her lap. She took a deep breath in. Dylan watched the tip glow flame orange. She rolled it between her fingers. Losing sight of Bill's head on the TV through thick white smoke as she exhaled. The sound of audience laughter muffled in their minds. Tabitha coughed from her belly, red faced covering her mouth, holding the joint out for Dylan to take. He patted her on the back. She caught her breath, giving him the thumbs up.

"I need to lie down. I can't feel my feet," she said.

"You go up. I'll be there in a bit."

Tabitha struggled to stand, staggering. She used the sofa to balance, shuffling her feet.

"Where you going?"

"Upstairs, I did just say that, didn't I?"

"You did," said Dylan.

"Thank god, I thought I was spinning out." She stood still for a moment.

"I meant, where are you going without a kiss for Daddy?"

Tabitha stopped, forced a smile, as if holding back a mouth full of vomit. She pecked Bass on the lips. He slapped her on the arse. She avoided walking into the door frame and shifted upstairs, using the bannister for support.

"Choker," said Bass. "You get a girl with a choker. You can tie 'em up." He passed the joint. "Handcuffs, rope, whatever you've got. They love it. We'll have to find you a girl like—," he clicked his fingers for inspiration. "A girl like—,"

"Tabitha."

"That's it, a girl like Tabitha. Fisting pink."

"Just remember, Tabitha. Like the girl from Bewitched."

"C'est la vie, Ta-bi-tha, Ta-bi-tha." Bass enunciated, drilling the name into his memory. "Once I'm done, you can take over. Give you a go on my sloppy sopping seconds."

"I'm good, cheers," said Dylan. "Whenever it's supposed to happen, it'll happen. Ya know whenever it's right."

"You've gotta stop with all that Charles Shakespeare shit. Get involved, man. Nice bit of a three-way."

Dylan's eyebrows jumped. He exhaled a cloud of smokey euphoria. Sinking back into the sofa. His body suspended in a metaphysical bubble. Time now could have been stationary. His fingers swimming dry earth across the surface of a dripping canvas. Green eyes flashing, nails dragged over a rib cage. His eyes opened to reality at the sound of Bass's deep voice.

"Seriously." Said Bass, swiping the joint from Dylan's fingers. Taking a drag, blowing smoke into his wide open mouth, almost close enough to touch lips. Close enough, Dylan could feel the warmth of his breath on his tongue, as if they were kissing.

"Get out of here," said Dylan, batting him away.

Bass laughed and flipped backwards over the sofa, landing on his feet, tongue flicking like a viper. "Get it done, and we'll have some fun." He said, high-fiving Dylan. "Time for pickle." He slid his hand between his flat stomach and his belt, grabbing his crotch.

Dylan dabbed his sleeve across his lips. "You'll have to remember their names,"

"Pickle, Tabitha, whatever. Pickle is safer. Plus, they think it's cute. Remember this," said Bass. He backed into the doorway, pointing to the ceiling. "When you've seen their bra, they'll see your come face. I guarantee it."

"That a hard and fast rule?"

"It is for me, mate. See the bra, you're in. You can straddle their shoulders, stick your dick down their throat and shove a Tabasco thumb up their arse." He clapped his hands together. "Pickle, I'm coming to dine, baby."

"Go easy on her."

"What d'you care?"

"I don't. Something tells me she isn't prepared for what you'll do to her."

"We're gonna make sweet, passionate love, mate."

"No doubt."

"Just give us five minutes if you hear screaming. " Said Bass. Laughing and bounded up the stairs, two steps at a time.

Dylan readied himself for the slam of a bedroom door. It rattled the framed animated elephant artwork on the wall above the TV. He read the slogan 'I won't forget', shaking his head, used his lighter to spark loose hanging Rizla from the joint, watching burnt paper land on his jeans. He brushed the ash off and inhaled deep, down to the cardboard roach. Loud, thrashing punk music kicked out from upstairs. Dylan clicked on the remote control, increasing the volume. Bill Hicks shouted a punchline. As the audience roared, Dylan chuckled to himself. His head flopped back, and he stared up at the yellow stained Artex ceiling, listening out for sounds of intimacy from upstairs.

4

nIhiLisM

With the door to his box room closed, tight like an airlock. Vitriolic punk music blared out from a portable stereo. Hooked up via a phono adapter to a bass guitar amplifier. Bass riddled tunes, with glass thrashing drums, rumbled through the foundations of the shared house. Double-glazed windows shook, the buzz ripping through your chest. This evening's selection of a soundtrack to sex, NOFX, Leave It Alone.

Yestin, with the largest room, shared a wall with Bass. He looked up from his desk. A frustrated, night owl frown, his red hair illuminated by a lamp. He drew three-dimensional designs of ergonomic office chairs on A3 sheets of white paper. Swapping between a tooth marked HB pencil from his mouth, with a 2B he was sketching with. Drowned out the noise from next door, using headphones blasting Ice-T's Home Invasion. It muffled his dislike for punk, and any orgasm escaping moans. Noises he didn't wish to hear.

* * *

Bass's DC branded belt buckle unclasped, rattled against his ripped jeans, pulled down over smooth, hairless legs, unravelled and bunched to his ankles. Fat, black, scuffed Etnies trainers kicked off against the cream panelled door. Tabitha's scrunched denim skirt and lime green thong decorated the floor.

"Are you leaving the light on?" She said, trying to be heard over the rattling music. Laid on the unmade bed, naked from the waist down. Right wrist shielding her eyes from the glare of the bare light bulb above.

Bass crawled like stalking prey, hunting, hovering over her body, blocking the light with his silhouette head.

"I wanna see every inch of you." He said, leaning down, touching his lips on the tip of her silver skin nose and imagined her head in a fridge.

She cupped her hands against his soft cheeks. Feeling hope bubble to laughter. She smiled a wide, bright, toothpaste advert grin. Their lips skimmed, saliva strings pinged. Nibbled her on the chin. Falling back on his knees between her legs. Tabitha giggled as his Dax Wax ruffled hair tickled her thighs. Her hand pressed on his head. Warm wet lips in the crease of her knees. Left, then right, alternating at speed. Pale, fleshy legs pressed hard against his ears, pushing his cheeks into his teeth. He noticed fresh, red lacerations, sliced high up the inside of her thighs. Tabitha tried to conceal them with firm hands. He peeled them free, like pulling at a plaster. Dropping limp arms to her side. Exploring her tight body from fluttering eyelids to the mole on her shoulder, in the shape of a daisy. He thought, how impressive her small breasts were, still defined, despite being laid flat on her back. They held their shape like concrete trifle. Bass read, 'Jimmy Eat World' again, printed across her t-shirt. He scoffed, thinking just how lame he considered the band to be. Not able to recall a song, except Lucky Denver Mint. He rocked his head to NOFX and bit her tidy belly button. Her knees thrust into his shoulders, almost a hit and run. He forced her legs wide open with his elbows like a crowbar. Head deep, shoving his beaky nose inside her. He sucked, sniffed, and licked until she squirmed. Bass became a pig for a moment, tickling out truffles.

Her fingers collected up the stale grey duvet, forcing it into her mouth, biting. Eyes rolled back. She writhed, flicking the hair from her face. Paralysed with numbness, like cloudy levitation. She gasped for breath, her vision blurred. The band posters and flyers pinned to the wall cleared into focus. Scanning from Husker Du to The Pietasters. She couldn't hear a thing, except a ringing in her ears.

"Holy shit." She said, her words hushed and breathy. "What the hell was that?" Bass lifted his head.

"What do you mean?"

She scratched her nose, fingering the tip like it was a sun-drenched strawberry. "My nose is tingling," she said. Her hungry stomach rumbled. She put her fingers between her legs. Bass looked on with a smile as he stroked himself. "Wow, she's swollen." Her fingers traced herself, she smoothed her palm over her shaved pubis and took a deep, airy breath into her lungs.

"That wasn't even the main event," said Bass. His head disappeared, eyes peering up at her. He dragged her band t-shirt, stretching it over her navel, revealing a black and white checked bra. His finger hooked, yanking it down, revealing her pink breakfast club nipples. The left inverted, the right standing proud. She hoisted her knees wide as he pushed himself inside her.

"Go slow." She said, leaning up to find his lips, wrapping her legs around his cold naked buttocks. "Did you put a condom on?"

"It's fine, Pickle," said Bass. "I'll pull out."

Tabitha's belly trembled as he pumped, his pelvis cracked against hers like a splintering glockenspiel. Hips moving fast to the tempo of the music. Track three kicked out, Dig. She winced as he pounded. Her eyes closed tight. Teeth clenched. She saw herself dancing as a child. The smell of bubbling brown sugar and hot butter caramelising on a Sunday. Spinning barefoot on sun-drenched grass, blonde hair sweeping her face. Throwing her legs over her head, her skirt flowing.

Handstands to silent applause. Being dragged up from her shoulders, reminded she wasn't wearing underwear. Slapped across her legs as her parents lured her to discipline. Conscious of guilt. Forever guilty. Then, the warm sensation of her bladder filling with broken glass brought her back to reality, romance devoid. Her eyes watered, staring at the dusty ceiling. The music thudding in her head, wanting to vomit. Fighting the urge to force her feet together, locking them chastity belt secure. Looking up at Bass, as his tongue wriggled loose, eyes shut, abs tight. He pounded harder. She planted her hands on his shoulders, attempting to slow his pace without speaking. Her face strained, scrunched like aluminium with uncomfortable hot needle pokes, rattling through her bones, spiking her flesh. Bass felt a wet warmth around his testicles. He glanced with apprehension and saw the red blood sticking to his shaved white skin, resembling the Rorschach test. Watching a single red drop roll down his stiff shaft, creating a trail for itself. The sight of her blood made him harder. Tabitha closed her eyes, her cheeks round as she held her breath. Close to climax, he mouthed along to the lyrics, repeating the distorted nasal chorus over and over as he closed his eyes. He wrapped his forearm under her neck. Her eyes pinged open. Seeing blurred hair at the side of his head, he pushed four fingers into her mouth, deep down her hot throat. She gagged and spat for air. A sizzle of bile pushed to escape. Bass's body clenched. He gripped his stiff penis from inside her, scrunched her t-shirt in his fist. A red trail of blood dripped over her bare belly button, filling like a bloody rock pool. One hand on his shaft, the other on her naked breast. Stroking himself, he whistled like a boiling kettle and ejaculated on her blotchy neck as he scrunched her dry hair in his hand, like a sheet of gritty newspaper. He laughed, smacking his lips on hers, shoving his tongue in her mouth. Wrenched free a corner of the bed sheet from the stained mattress and wiped his bloodied penis. He leaned forward and powered off the amplifier. It popped as the power died and the red light flashed off.

Click!

A loud whirling noise came from the bedside table. Muffled by a black Snuff, branded band hoodie.

"What was that?" said Tabitha. She covered her naked legs with the duvet, dabbing her neck clean.

"Nothing." Said Bass, jumping on clicking knees to the floor. His jeans tying up his ankles. He shuffled forward and flipped off the power to the plug at the wall, letting go with a relieved breath of panic.

Tabitha admired the thigh muscle in his naked legs, comparing it to a chicken's. She traced the cable from the socket, leading to the open drawer of the mismatched bedside table. The black cable disappeared under the hoodie. Bass pulled up his jeans, clasped his belt closed. Tabitha didn't smile as she followed his tight abdominal muscles. She admired the defined V shape over his hip bones, that cover model physique.

"How many sit-ups do you do for that?"

"None." He said, pulling on the first t-shirt he could find. "Super noodles and string beans." The Marquee Moon t-shirt dropped over his torso. He kissed her hard on the mouth, teeth clanking together. "Won't be a minute." He said, and grabbed for the hoodie, bundling it up into his arms.

"Where you going?"

"I gotta give Dylan his hoodie back."

"Can't it wait?"

"Give me a sec," he said, shovelling the hoodie to one hand. He leaned down, guiding his hand under the duvet. His fingers fumbled. "Then we can go again."

Tabitha forced a smile, holding his hands in place over the duvet. "I'm still quite sore," she said.

Bass shrugged, pulled his hand free and backed out of the bedroom, pulling the door shut behind him.

Tabitha heard the creak of the stairs as Bass descended. She sat up on her elbows, felt like the room was spinning. The snapped luminous green thong caught her eye. She heard her mother's voice again, saw the scene in the lingerie shop. 'My baby's growing up. If this is the one you want. I've got nothing to worry about. This thing is hideous, it's radioactive.' The thought of her mother made her feel alone. She wanted to be held in her arms. The blotted, dry, smudged blood, symmetrical, resembled a butterfly. She balled herself into the foetal position, her shoulders shuddering as she stifled acid tears.

5

sAnYo sEx tApE

Dylan's cold, stiff nocturnal fingers tapped like dripping water at the keyboard. Wearing only black boxer shorts, his naked back and clammy thighs pressed into a leather desk chair. A blank Word document, the setting for an evening of writing. He had noted all that he witnessed, everything he could remember at least. The night thrown into a blender and a story splutters out. The delicate way Tabitha nibbled her front teeth on her glass like a cartoon rabbit. Bass hooking his little fishhook finger in her back pocket with ownership. Dylan was stealing it, owning it with artistic merit. Characters with fictitious integrity, including the disclaimer of any resemblance to actual persons, living or dead, are coincidental. He made the world spiky, slick, knockout dramatic, with firecracker insults and anal sex in public. Anything to spice up mediocre insignificance. The space bar thumbed like a jackhammer on granite. His hands clasped tight behind the back of his head, as he studied his small square room. A pathetic single bed, a flat packed bed-side table, housed a TASCAM four track cassette recorder, never used. Guitar chord books for Oasis and The Stone Roses. A red and white Squire Strat guitar occupied another corner, now a dusty ornament. The crappy TV, always on. It lived on mute, a visual distraction. A large leaning wardrobe contained the few clothes he owned: flared jeans, band t-shirts and hoodies. On top were empty boxes, a small suitcase and piles, of what he himself considered pretentious novels, screenplays, and volumes of charity shop poetry. The spines pristine, never pressed open against a thigh. No accidental coffee spillages. They existed to convince himself he was bookworm intelligent, well read without reading. Deserving of cultural respect.

Like the other rooms in the house. Obligatory student posters donned fading walls, bought from the poster fair in the Union. As if an A5 poster of Pulp Fiction or Jackson Pollock, three for ten pounds, would help with the completion of a dissertation, or the tick box understanding of the Studio System. Dylan too, sucked in by the sales pitch, his loan burning a hole in his pocket like everyone else's. He leaned back in his chair and studied the scary black and white nuclear mushroom cloud poster, the plume over the Pacific, palm trees in the foreground. That duality between nature and man; ruined beauty. Alongside, tacked to the wall, is Hal Morey's Sun Beams Into Grand Central Station. The Christlike shafts of light breaking through the massive windows over Vanderbilt's dream. The last of the special offer, poster three, was The Stone Roses, Ian, John, Reni and Mani, covered in blue paint. Then there were the Live Band flyers and ripped pages from NME magazine. All considered necessary for the ever enlightened student. Blu Tack secure, personality purchased and hanging from walls.

Watching the cursor flash on and off. He paused his personal CD player, track eight. The Hardest thing in the world. Realising the riotous punk music from upstairs had stopped thumping, removed his headphones. Stared at a small mirror on the desk. Pulled Plasticine expressions to inspire facial description. The early morning light cracked through the holey net curtains. He begged his muse for thunder storm inspiration. Performed a toxic squint, eyelids narrowed like a line of cocaine. It would end up recreated in a sentence. Minutes passed, day became brighter. The light never on, the room glowing blue from the computer monitor. Again, he glanced at himself in the mirror, following the outline of his zigzagging face. Losing concentration in thoughts that, although nineteen, he could pass for younger. Little wonder he still gets asked for identification at clubs, as embarrassing as that remains. It's the smallest details that keep him awake. He warmed his left hand under his boxers, pressed firm between his thighs. Staring at the ceiling. Flopped his head forward and read aloud, in a fake Texan accent from the screen.

'The future. They hated the thought of it. Too many people to please. Life is not a slip and slide. That twelve-year-old innocence, now faded and lost. Nothing exciting about education. A shattered door slammed. It got crystal cold. The darkness fizzled to a burden. Bare feet pacing the floor. Flaming lights became blinding. Thou shalt dare to rifle for motive. Defined in life by nightmares of discreet, hidden touching. Disappointing failed careers, scorched shopping lists, and tears from both ends of the dining room table. The interest piles on, despite over payment. You wish to be aborted. Pay rent, commute, get cancer and die.
Forever, Amen.
I am grateful. I am blessed.'

He stopped reading, and grabbed for a roll of toilet paper from behind the mirror, blowing his wet nose. He swallowed a mouthful of copper tasting water from a litre bottle. Filling up on liquids meant he wasn't hungry.

Bang.

Bang.

Bang.

The bedroom door almost rocked from its hinges. Shoulders crumpled into his neck. He spun round in his seat, facing the closed door.

"Dyl," whispered Bass.

"What you doing, knocking like 5-0, man? Jesus." Said Dylan, steadying his heart rate.

Bass cranked on the handle, poking his smiling head inside. His short body soon followed through the crack in the door. Carrying with him his scrunched up hoodie.

"Shit man," said Bass. "It ran out of tape again." He checked over his shoulder before he continued. "She heard it." He unfolded the hoodie. Dylan's Sanyo 8mm camera wrapped up inside, held out at arm's length.

"Did you take that from in there?" Said Dylan, pointing at his closed cupboard.

"You saw her," said Bass. He bit his bottom lip. "What she can do with her tongue is biblical." He mimed fellatio, the tip of his tongue flicking and flopping from his mouth, lapping at air.

"One day," said Dylan. "They'll catch you doing this shit."

"They haven't yet. They all want a bad boy, mate. What can I say? I love watching myself fuck."

"I'm sure it's a beautiful thing."

"You need to watch one with me. Doggy all the way. Her parents would be so proud."

"I'm not watching your hairy man arse humping anyone."

"You don't know what you're missing," said Bass. Distracted, he grabbed for a glossy brochure on top of the computer monitor, flipping it open. "You're doing it then. Leaving me for the U S of A?"

"Yup, finally finished my personal statement. That's my Sleepaway America application done and dusted. Summer to remember and all that shenanigans. I thought it was gonna be a piece of piss. Took me hours. Queuing for a bastard, free computer in the library. June can't come around quick enough."

"Good story, bro. Chat rooms, that's all I used the library computers for. You know they don't give a shit about that. Waste of time. Personal statement. Bollocks. They just want your money."

"Maybe it's procrastination. I should be doing research for my dissertation, anyway. If America happens, I need to get a head start for next year, 'cause I won't have the summer."

"I'm so thankful I dropped out. That bullshit is boring, man." Bass flicked through the brochure. "This is proper fromage," he said. Studying the glossy pictures. "You still planning on travelling after?"

"If I can afford it, yeah. I just wanna spend Autumn in Georgetown. Even if it's only for a couple of days." Dylan stretched his arms wide, yawning. "Then, back here to depressing reality."

"Whatever. Listen, I've got a date tonight."

"It went well then, you and Tabitha?"

Bass smiled. "Not her. What's her name? That blonde thing from work."

Dylan scowled, cheeks blushed red. He knew, without asking, who Bass was referring to. "That Saturday girl you mean, Laura?" he said.

"That's the one. She's the only reason I agree to work weekends. Wrong not to, I can flirt with the virgin angels and their tank top wearing friends. We're going to the cinema."

"You couldn't help yourself, could ya?" said Dylan, shaking his head. "The cinema though, she looks too classy to enjoy the cinema."

"I don't plan on watching the film, mate," said Bass, rolling the Sleepaway America brochure into a cone, tapping it against his temple. "Lights dimmed, back row, my dick in the popcorn. Help yourself, sweetie, if you know what I mean."

"I should've kept my mouth shut."

"What d'ya mean?"

"Nothing. I kind of liked her. She just looked so majestic."

"She is. I didn't see it at first, until you said."

"Well, I'm ecstatic I could help."

"You're not pissed are ya, that I asked her out?"

"Nah, do what you want. You will anyway."

"She's fair game, mate." Bass tapped the brochure on Dylan's shoulders, like he was knighting him, and dashed it on the desk. It fanned open. Make sure you have more tape. He held up the camera. "I'll bring her home. Add to the collection. Anyway, Tabitha's waiting." Bass wiped his two fingers under Dylan's nostrils. "Stiffy Sniffy. Round five."

"Round five?"

"Hey, it's me. She'll limp back to Sixth form on Monday and write in her think book how she lost her virginity to a real man. A story shared over a Capri-Sun."

"What were you listening to up there, Black Flag?"

"Black Flag." Bass scoffed. "You need to stop listening to your indie shit and get a punk education. It's a lifestyle, mate."

"I've still got your list." Dylan scrambled on his desk amongst loose papers and flapped a scrap piece of handwritten paper in front of his face. "Minor Threat, The Misfits and Social Distortion." He read aloud. "I'll listen to them first. You could always romance them with a bit of Sade."

"Who the fuck is Sade?" Said Bass, batting away the suggestion with loose wrist ignorance. "Whatever. Enough of this shit. You got another tape?"

"I shouldn't be encouraging this. There's another one in the camera bag," said Dylan. "Help yourself. You seem to know where everything is."

"Cheers dude, nice one."

"Pop a bit of Sweetest Taboo on." Said Dylan, swaying from side to side. "Light some candles."

"Too late for tenderness, mate," said Bass. He retrieved a plastic sealed 8mm cassette tape from the bag. "Shit hot," he rattled it against the side of his head. "Laura seems like a prude, though. It won't be a late one. You wanna go to The Pot after?"

Dylan shrugged and slumped in his chair, facing the computer screen.

Bass put the tape in his mouth and massaged Dylan's bare shoulders, squeezing his neck between his finger and thumb.

"You're tense," said Bass in a mumble. He karate chopped at Dylan's shoulders. "I'll love ya and leave ya." He reached and tweaked Dylan's nipples, chuckling to himself, leaving the bedroom door wide open behind him.

Dylan shook his head, circling his thumb on his chin, jabbing one finger into his closed eye. Scratching his head for inspiration. He pinched a clump of nasal hairs, pulled and examined what he had harvested, dropping the wiry hairs in a small pile on one corner of his white desk. The flashing cursor interrupted his vacant creativity. Laura's blonde hair, being freed from her collar, shifted into his thoughts. He wanted to claim her without knowing her sensibilities. Find out who she was. A snarl to himself, not bearing to imagine Bass in the cinema's darkness. Too painful to consider.

Teasing him with misplaced inspiration, forever interrupted. Flitting between open Word documents. One being his dissertation, another a screenplay entitled Cinnamon. Making notes, handwriting subtexts and themes, character arcs. Playing with genre, everything he sees as a restriction when writing. Considering critiques more for an audience. Procrastination again.

"Why didn't you just go over and speak to her, ya dick?" Dylan asked aloud of himself.

Time spent wasting emotions. That's all he experiences now. He considered smoking less, only for a flash, as he looked at his overflowing ashtray. It helped him to focus. That's how he thought. Especially at night when the rest of the house was in a slumber. Distractions he doesn't do well with. The toilet flushed up stairs. The door to Bass's room slammed shut. Dylan closed his eyes. He hoped Bass would get caught. That one day, the guilt may tremble through him to realisation. He could see the green camera bag open in the cupboard. Reminded of how it was displayed on the shelf in Cash Converters. He saw it from afar, whilst rifling through three pound secondhand video tapes. His attention drawn to the turtle shell case. The 8mm camera brought him an opportunity. He could create home videos, write scripts to film, make stop motion Ardman-esque animations. Brand himself a filmmaker. Practising his Oscar winning speech, manifesting to him, wearing a tuxedo, blind eyed, spot light approval from his contemporaries as he's clapped, holding the golden statue aloft. He begged his mother for a loan, negotiating a payment plan. The camera with infrared remote control was the last special present he received on his birthday, wrapped in plain gold wrapping paper. Feeling it in his hands made him cry. He would disappear for hours, adding voodoo life to X-Men action figures, recreating scenes from Some Like it Hot. Magneto as Private Pyle from Full Metal Jacket, shouting about Charlene, his rifle. Voiced from behind the camera in a passable American accent. The hours he spent using a hand pumped garden sprayer as a cheap replacement for squibs. Attaching metre length garden hose, funnel filling the tube with fake blood, concocted with ingredients from the kitchen, settling on a recipe of two tablespoons of golden syrup to eight drops of red food colouring. It was the most realistic. Those faded memories of pantomime, gunshot mutilation, pieces of torn sponge soaked in makeshift blood, used as brains splattered across bathroom tiles. All tarnished. The camera now used to capture clandestine amateur sex tapes.

The front door opened. Dylan jumped from his chair. "Hello?" he said. A bunch of keys rattled. "Hello," he repeated, imploring a response from the distance.

Mr. Mitra, the Asian landlord, paced into the kitchen, his dark brown skin and bald head glistened, reflecting the fluorescent kitchen strip light. His thick black moustache with greys sprouting through wiggled on his top lip. He filled the door frame to Dylan's room, wearing a waxed rain coat.

He cleared his throat. "Mr. Mark here?" he said, mumbling in his thick Indian accent.

"Mark?" said Dylan. He looked around for a t-shirt to pull on over his naked torso. "No, he's not."

"You tell him from Mitra," he said, pointing. "Him owe me rent."

He held up two fingers, the wrong way round to symbolise the number 'two', instead making use of the offensive gesture. Dylan sniggered to himself. "Two months, he no pay me money."

"I'll tell him." Said Dylan, pulling on a pair of jeans. He backed Mitra up into the kitchen. "Look, Mr. Mitra. You can't just come up here without letting us know."

"It my bloody house." He said with a frown, almost offended.

"It is. But, the four of us rent it off you, you're supposed to give us warning."

"No warning if no bloody rent pay."

"Mark isn't here." Said Dylan, ushering him toward the door. "I'll pass the message on. Thanks for coming, yeah."

Mr. Mitra leaned for a stack of mail on the windowsill, grabbing it in his dirty hands.

"Good point. Can you redirect your post too, please?"

"My house." Said Mr. Mitra, standing in the open front doorway, his foot stopping Dylan from closing it.

"You tell Mr. Mark, he owes rent." He fanned through the white and manilla envelopes in his hand. He turned on his heel, descending the front steps to his car.

"Will do, will do." Said Dylan, as he shut the door with a click behind him.

"Was that Mitra?" Said Bass, whispering, cowering at the top of the stairs, edging his head around the bannister, taking a seat on the top step. He pressed a single cigarette between his lips, sparked it, and inhaled. "I don't owe him shit." He said, tossing the cigarette packet toward Dylan. Catching it against his chest, removing one.

"Whatever. Don't give him a reason to be here unannounced."

Bass tossed a lighter.

Yestin's bedroom door creaked open. Yestin stepped out with a peach coloured towel wrapped around his pale waist. Running his fingers across his loose red chest hair.

"All right, bud. What was that noise, Mitra?" He said in his Welsh accent, pinching his nose, sniffing.

"Yeah, complaining about some shit," said Bass.

"Anyone using the shower?"

"Nah mate, you're good."

"Sweet, bud." Said Yestin, closing the bathroom door behind him.

"Morning." Said Florence in her chirpy Sri Lankan accent, appearing from inside Yestin's room. Her black silky hair tied up in a ponytail.

"Oh," said Bass. He looked wide eyed at Dylan down the stairs. "All right, Florence."

"I was helping Yest with chair designs." She said, smirking, pushing her thick-rimmed glasses up to her eyes. She banged the door shut to her own room.

Bass held his eyes on Dylan. "I told you." He said, in hushed tones. "What did I say? They're banging."

Dylan exhaled smoke, dismissing the suggestion. "They're friends." He said and walked away, back to his room.

"Hey." Bass called out, looking between the white balustrades at Dylan in the kitchen doorway. "I'll sort his money."

"Make sure you do," said Dylan. "Don't get kicked out."

"Aww, would you miss me?"

Dylan chuckled out of sight.

"It's OK." He said after him. "Everyone does. You can never have enough, Bass."

6

tHe rUbY mOoN

"Thank God, he's gone." Said Laura, sweeping her golden, shoulder length, fine hair behind her delicate pixie like ears. She glanced, peering over her slight shoulders, double checking Bass was out of earshot. He leaned over the long, narrow bar, ten-pound note folded in half, ordering another round of drinks. Dylan admired Laura's tight body over her elegant white blouse, with a ruffled collar, from the opposite side of the table. She reminded him of an Edwardian socialite.

"Nightmare?" said Laura, flopping in her chair. "Are you kidding?" she laughed. "Honestly, no subtlety. Back row, two seconds into the trailers, before I could even sip my Fanta." She swilled her almost empty pint glass between the tips of her slender, manicured fingers and sipped the rest of the alcohol. "Jammed his sausage hands between my legs. I was like, 'easy big man. You're not laying a patio now,' Jeez." She shook her head.

Dylan leaned forward in his seat. It creaked beneath him, resembling rumbling flatulence. "That was the chair." He said, resting on his elbows. "The romance of it all." He took a gulp from his own pint glass, setting it down on the wooden table, tracing the wood grain with his little finger.

"I know, right?"

"Well, you agreed to go out with him." He said, putting a cigarette to his mouth, closing his eyes as he exhaled smoke.

"All right, we're supposed to be flirting here, making the most of him being at the bar." She said, with a smile she couldn't hide. "Since you killed that intimacy." She paused, as if thinking. "He's got nice hair. Hollywood good looks. Thinks he's a punk. Beyond that, nob head. Plus, he works full time at Argos. He would never meet my parents." She said with a squint, examining the cigarette resting between Dylan's fingers. "You don't strike me as a smoker. It's hard to think of you depending on anything. Still, I've never tried it, may I?"

Cause and effect crossed Dylan's mind, that he would be the one facilitating her first cigarette. He would forever remain a memory, a story told if she was to reminisce. He nodded, passing the burning cigarette. Laura clasped it tight with two hands, like a clarinet and inhaled, her blue eyes tentative. She coughed and spluttered.

"Jesus!" She said.

The cigarette dropped, sparking and rolling across the table, ash spilling through the cracks to the carpet.

"That's vile." She said and snatched for Dylan's pint glass, taking a mouthful, holding it in her cheeks.

"You look beautiful," he said.

Laura smiled, her cheeks full and puffy, round, eyes squinting and narrow. Dylan laughed, he wiped the table free of ash with the back of his hand. Laura swallowed, still gasping for air.

"Better?"

"I thought I was gonna drown," she said. "Much better." She forced a cough, her hand covering her mouth.

"Life is one big habit. You wouldn't want to become dependent on it."

"Darling, that's rough," said Laura. "Not sure how you do it."

"Practice." He said, flicking his cigarette three times on the rim of the ashtray. "Ya know, when you speak, I can't help but picture that BBC show—,"

"The Demon Headmaster?"

"The Chronicles of Narnia," said Dylan. "You talk like the kids in that."

With her pristine eyebrows peaked to attention.

"That's a compliment. You're sort of proper," he said. "Oh Lucy, for goodness sake, don't go in the wardrobe."

"You're aware my name's Laura."

"What? Lucy is from—,"

"I know, I'm joking, I read it in School," she said. "Whilst I dissect that. I wouldn't say I was posh. My dad has his own business, sure. Something to do with cars. That doesn't mean we're rich. We live in an affluent area. Any money I'm getting is held in a trust fund, anyway. You know, I rarely go for smokers. I could make you an exception. It's like we've practically kissed already, anyway."

"Me and you?"

"Yeah, my lips have been all over your glass." She said, running her little finger around the rim. "Before I forget, you haven't dropped out of uni, have you?"

"Nope, still doing film," said Dylan.

"Good, with the hope of what?"

"I don't know."

"Lack of direction, attractive." She said, exaggerating a huff, flopping back into her chair.

"It's not a lack of direction, more, I don't wanna think in terms of absolutes. It restricts ya."

"Enunciate. The word is you. But astute suddenly, aren't we? Nothing wrong with knowing what you want."

"But, equally, nothing wrong if you don't."

"David Suchet,"

"Poirot, what's he got to do with it?"

"Suchet, like Touché. You'll get used to me." Said Laura, winking.

"Clever. But I'll probably be involved in the industry somewhere."

"Like a best boy or key grip? You could end up making porn."

"Needs must and all that." He said. Silence for a moment, as he searched to continue the conversation. "Punk music your thing too, then?"

"Not necessarily. I like what I like. Mark kept harping on about Desperation Ivy—,"

"Operation," said Dylan interrupting. "Operation Ivy."

"Sure, that too. I go crazy for a mohawk. The music is… meh to me. I like the scene. I'm more open-minded than indulging in just one genre. Not being allowed to listen to Kate Bush, that's not punk. Who decides?"

"See, restrictions. Forever restrictions. We should open our minds." Dylan ran his hand through his hair. "A mohawk though?"

"Oh yeah, seriously, whatever the colour. I love 'em and a pierced lip." Laura rolled her eyes, curling her lip, stimulating breathy arousal. "Oh," she added. "Has to be a ring, not a stud." She leaned across the table, pushing her finger into Dylan's mouth, gripping the left side of his bottom lip. "Right here." She smiled, holding her eyes on his, and removed her finger, sitting back.

"I'm shocked you did that. Wait, Bass hasn't got either."

"Neither did my ex. It's so you know what I like." She said, smiling. "For the future. Makes me wild. It's edgy. You've got magnificent hair, too. Rockstar hair, brave." She held her soft blue eyes on him. "Talking of romance. What did you think when he called you? Tell me."

"Well, I thought he was gonna say we're going down The Pot."

"The Pot? What's that?"

"How long you lived here?"

"Hey, I don't live in the town centre. I'm from the posh bit, don't cha you know?"

"Indeed, little lady, Narnia." Said Dylan, dabbing his cigarette in the ashtray. "It's a live music venue."

"As you can see, whilst I daintily drink from my empty pint of lager." She lifts it to her lips and drips the last drops of alcohol into her mouth. "I'm your wine bar type."

"Evidently. When he told me to meet you two. I thought it'd be nice to see you again."

Laura's eyes shot wide. "See me again?" she said, confused. "When have you seen me before?"

"Last Saturday, while you were working."

"I didn't think you saw me."

"You're all I was seeing."

"Sweet. I bet I looked fabulous in my red uniform."

"You certainly had my attention, still do." Said Dylan, excited, his dimples faded to a frown, realising with a hot jolt, this was not his date. "I'm sorry."

"What for? You worried about Bass? God, even I hate calling him that. Who calls them self, Bass? Makes him sound like a right dick."

"He thinks it's cool. I thought he'd try to shove you in my face. How well you're getting on. Really rub it in, ya know?"

"To hurt you? Well, that's lame. He's lame. Mel Gibson may know what women want, but Mark, Bass or whatever. We went on one date and it was mediocre. Until, his friend, that turns out to be the same guy I was admiring from afar, showed up, then it got infinitely better."

"Are you messing with me? I mean, has he put you up to this?"

Laura placed her hand in his and squeezed. "I don't know which is more sad, that you don't believe I could like you, or that you think I could be that cruel." She turned around, the chair creaking. "Look at him. Who wears a hoodie on a date?" She looked over at Bass leaning on the bar.

"I'm always his tag along, chum."

"You could be in luck this time."

"When I saw you, I heard that song, Venus."

Laura leaned in, her index finger stroking his palm. "More of this, please. What songs that?"

"The one that's all angelic." He said, enjoying the tickling silk touch from her fingertip. "I felt hypnotised or something. I had this cloudy mix of swirling confusion. Uncontrollable excitement smacked me between the eyes."

"I bet you say this stuff to all the girls."

"Only the vulnerable ones," he scoffed to himself. "I'm really nothing like him, ya know?"

"I can tell. His tricks might work if you've got four GCSEs, but it ain't working on me."

"It's OK if you only have three."

Laura tutted. "You're hilarious."

"He'd probably prefer it more, if you were still sitting your exams."

"I've heard that about him. At least that's the rumour."

"All I'll say is, he doesn't ask for ID at his bedroom door," whispered Dylan, dragging his hand free from hers. "Shhh—,"

"Did you just shush me?"

"He's coming back." Said Dylan, under his breath, sitting up straight, trying to act natural.

Laura shook off her beguiled smile.

"I read the book. That was good. Leonardo made a good Richard." Said Laura, a deliberate clandestine conversation point, throwing Bass off the scent.

"Three chuffing pints of piss." Said Bass, holding the sloshing pint glasses, three in a triangle, pinched between his closed fingers. He shook his damp hands dry of spilled lager. Laura sat back, avoiding the spraying droplets and eyeballed Dylan, laced with suggestion and now stifled intimacy.

"Yummy." Said Dylan, holding his eyes on hers.

"Let me propose a fucking toast," said Bass.

"No offence, Mark. I mean, Bass." Said Laura. "I don't mean to lead you on and I wouldn't make this public, but you know we're not seeing each other again, right?"

Bass glanced over at Dylan, looking for reassurance. "What are you talking about?" He said, taking a seat next to her, leaning on the armrest of the wooden chair.

"I wouldn't usually do this. I don't plan on seeing you again. Unless I'm in the company of this fine fellow." She said, smiling a coy, white, toothy smile.

His face flushed red. "You don't want to do this again?"

"With Dylan," she pointed. "I'm malleable. You, not so much."

Dylan couldn't help but smile. He caught the dark pupils of Bass glaring at him and dropped his head.

"You're gonna ditch me in front of him, in this pub?" said Bass, pushing his elbows deep into the armrests.

"Not just in front of him." Said Laura, adjusting her blouse, as if uninterested. "I'm ditching you, for him."

"Ditching me for this virgin?" Bass jumped up, his fist banging on the table. Nearby patrons looked on to investigate the commotion. Bass grabbed for his pint, slung his head back, gulped the contents. "You coming?" he said, snapping at Dylan.

"I think." Said Dylan, looking across the table at Laura. His eyes focusing on her. He couldn't resist smiling. "I'm staying."

"You clearly don't know the rules." Bass burped, no attempt to conceal it. "Bro's before ho's."

"They don't use expressions like that in Narnia. We wouldn't work," said Laura. "I have a friend, Sofia. You and her would be perfect together. You might kill each other, but you'd have fun doing it."

Bass shook his head. "Unbelievable."He said, jerking his head toward Dylan. "That, over me. You make sure that Sofia girl calls me." Bass slammed his chair into the table and bolted toward the door, pulling his hood over his head. Eyes from the tables he passed watched, mouths wide, as he smacked the front door open.

"He'll get over it," said Laura. "Sofia will give him a run for his money."

"I'm impressed you said that, right here, right now."

"Why waste my time? I'm gonna get you, baby." Said Laura, crossing her legs. "Don't take this wrong, now. I know I'm younger than you. You're 19 right?"

"I am."

She leaned in. Dylan copied. "But are you, are you, a virgin?" She said, whispering.

"How do I answer that?"

"The same way you've answered everything else so far, honestly. Which I'm more than thankful for."

"As pathetic as it may sound, yeah. Yeah, I am."

"Far from pathetic."

"It's not like I haven't tried. Trust me. Just never happened. It hasn't been right. I was seeing this girl. I really liked her. Good taste in music, funny too. Hannah, in the first year. I went down on her but couldn't get it—,"

"It's fine," said Laura. "No need for details." She rested her head on her wrist. "Where are you taking me on our next date, then?"

Dylan cleared his nervous throat. "Billy Bragg is playing at the Potoo," he said.

"The Potoo? Last time I went there was to watch Cleopatra, comin' atcha! Who the hell is Billy Bragg?"

"He's a singer, kind of political, protest type songs. He's good. I have his CD with me." He said, reaching into his deep pocket retrieving his personal CD player, unravelling the headphone wire.

"I didn't think you meant you had it with you now."

"Yeah, of course I walked here alone. This thing comes everywhere with me."

Laura nodded, a perplexed smile humoured him.

Dylan passed the now untangled headphones over the table, perched forward, covering her small ears. Laura guided his hands with hers.

Their connection almost tingled, like a tongue on a nine volt battery.

"Ready?" he said.

"Hit me."

Dylan used a straight, stiff finger, poking down like a slow motion pile driver. The CD rotated, building up speed, spinning. No longer able to read the writing printed on the orange and silver CD. He could hear the first G chord strum out from across the table, loud enough for Laura to drown out other sounds in the busy pub with Billy Bragg's vocals. Everything was blurry surrounding her. Everything but Dylan. The pub filled with friends at tables, men crowding the fruit machine. She couldn't see them, she wasn't interested. She smiled at Dylan as he sat smirking at her with pride, an unexplainable warmth kindled within him. He hoped she enjoyed the sound as much as he did. Capo, first fret. G D Em D C D Em Bm7, simple strumming. Dylan leaned in, pressing his patient fingers against his bottom lip. Trying to conceal his moist mouth for hers. Laura giggled, dropping her head. She closed her eyes and rocked as she listened through the harmonica solo, the last word of 'brunette' and the Am7 outro.

"I like it." She said, removing the headphones. "Wonderful, lived in voice, great songwriter. What time we meeting then?"

"The gig doesn't start 'til eight o'clock."

"Is it a sit down thing?"

"It's seated, yeah."

"How civilised." She said, sitting straight-backed. "Six then. Meet me by Clark's in the Hexagon. That'll give me time to get home and change. Look all pretty for ya."

"You, you mean to say, you. Enunciation."

"Oh, very good. We're learning, I see."

"I try." He said with a smirk.

"God, you haven't turned into one of those pretentious pricks. Now you're at uni?"

"It's my second year. But, I certainly hope not."

"All that Malthusian theory will screw with your mind."

"There's still time, I guess. I must admit, I thought the whole thing, being a student and all that jazz, would be more than it is. It's sold as this chance to be yourself, grow and experience life. It's hardly life changing. I must have two hours of lectures a week, then I just sit in the Union, getting pissed up. Everyone dresses the same, same hair, listening to the same music and if you don't, you're forgotten. Bowling for soup were right."

"Right about what?"

"High school, it never ends."

"Life is a popularity contest, darling."

"Until you die."

"Ah yes, the sweet release of death." Said Laura, leaning for her clutch bag at her feet. "I have to get the bus. I'm having driving lessons. Not far off, but no transport. I hate relying on my parents. Student bus pass it is for me." She flashed a photo card in front of his eyes, flapping at the air.

"I can walk you home, if you'd like."

"Do you have any clue where Penn actually is?"

"I don't mind a good walk."

"It's too far even for Forrest Gump. I'm getting the bus, sweet cheeks. The time apart will do you good. That way, you'll think about me until you next see me. I won't keep you waiting for two days, playing it cool. None of those board games."

"I do enjoy Kerplunk."

"Who doesn't?"

"I've always found it cold here, even with the sun blaring. It's just got a lot warmer."

Laura chuckled. "Dylan, you're an outrageous flirt. You've got the skills to pay the bills."

"Thanks, it's the poet in me, you see. Often, I'll look to the sky, see it's filled with heavy dark clouds covering the valley, edging to invade. It's bleak and depressive. The whole town feels like my Harlaxton Manor."

"You're such a freak. I love it. Your vulnerability is so beguiling. Are you trying to impress me, or is this how you always talk to all the girls?"

"Weird question, but this is how I talk, I think."

"It's different," said Laura, standing. "A requiem for lost words. Now, sir." She poked her arm from her side like a winged dove, inviting Dylan to interlock his arm. "Accompany me to the bus station, darling."

7

pLayStAtIoN fOrGivEnesS

Bass shoulder barged the front door, head bouncing off the rotten, chipped wood frame. Cracking a single pane of glass as the door popped open. He stumbled over the step, flapping his arms to regain balance. Squinted, concentrating on yanking his key from the lock, clicking the door closed on the latch. The house felt freezing inside. Breath smoked from his mouth, turning from gas to liquid with the stale cold. Standing silent for a second, looking off, up the stairs, listening out to understand if he was alone. An exhalation of misplaced relief, tranquillity interrupted as he heard a glass clank on wood from Yestin's room above. He hopped from the doorway, over the sofa, flopping into the cushion claiming it as his own. The heal of his trainer powered on the PlayStation 2. Pro Evolution Soccer 2 sprang to life on the TV with a soundtrack to Queen's, We Will Rock You. A boisterous crowd erupted. Leaning back into the hard backed sofa, his afternoon, relaxed position. He stared up at the cigarette smoke stained ceiling. The floorboards upstairs creaking under barefoot movement. He remained still, quiet. Followed the instructions on screen and hit the start button on the black, crumb filled controller.

"Why you not just lay still with me?" said Florence, as she perched herself on her elbow, the duvet covering her bare, dark-skinned shoulders.

"Babe, I needed a drink." Said Yestin, bending over at the waist. Naked except for loose boxers.

"You always have an excuse to jump out bed."

"I was thirsty," he said.

"I was thirsty. I need shower. I hungry. Always excuse. Can you get me drink?"

"It's just there," he said. Nodding at a glass of rose coloured water on the desk. Hand drawn images of chairs strewn across the surface of his desk, others stuck to the walls with drawing pins.

"Will you pass it me?" said Florence. She forced a playful, sad face, lip upturned and eyes soft, lashes fluttering. "Please, pretty please."

Exasperated, Yestin grabbed the glass, presenting it to Florence with a curtsy, "Here you are, oh great one," he said.

Florence swiped it from him, sloshing the contents. "No need to take piss." She said, putting the glass to her mouth. "Thank you," she swallowed. "That was easy." She stared, wide eyed, at the water. "How many squash is in this, it taste like tap."

Yestin huffed. "I can't buy Vimto until my loan comes through, plus I put my last tenner on the gas."

"And still I'm freezing my chuddies off," she said.

"Never happy, are ya?"

"I let you do the come inside me and you scowl me for a glass of water. Why won't you do anything for me?" she said. A vein throbbed in her neck as she reached out for her glasses, holding the duvet in place, covering her naked chest. She plucked the mint green frames, sliding them up her nose, over her cockleshell ears.

"First, the word is scold. And, babe, I do everything for you. We don't need another argument."

"You scowl at me,"

"Scowled. I may have scowled at you. I'm not angry though. It's like you don't understand sarcasm or something."

"You English people are—,"

"I'm Welsh." Said Yestin. "Two very different things."

"Cold nose English, that's what we call you."

"I passed you the water already. Can I get you anything else, my love?"

"Me and you fall out."

"Just a normal day then." Said Yestin, cracking his neck. "I need a shower."

Bass hit start on the controller, pausing the computerised commentary. He sparked a cigarette, held it in the corner of his mouth, with his left eye closed, the smoke drifting in front. He resumed the game. Trevor Brooking commentating.

'Four minutes to half time. They've got a corner.'

The digital clock stopped. The screen went grey. Bass removed his cigarette, exhaled, and replaced it back between his lips. Rumblings of raised voices from upstairs. He shook his head at the simmering disagreement.

"I don't know why you do it to yourselves," he said to himself. Slamming his finger on the start button again. The sound of an Aragon away team blared from the TV. The crowd and referees whistle rang out as Bass scored. He shifted forward, sitting on the edge of the seat, tapping his foot on the carpet. Flinched further forward, standing as if poked with a cattle prod. Crossed his heals, keeping his eye on the ball and continued to play standing, with one hand on the controller, the other pinching his groin. He paused the game, threw the controller on the sofa, leapt over the back. Inhaled on his cigarette as he bolted up the stairs, four steps at a time, smoke billowing like the flying Scotsman from his mouth. He thumped on the landing, spun the bathroom doorknob. It swiped open, a gust of cold air smacked him in the face like running into a wall. His eyes shot wide, heart shuddered in his chest. The cigarette fell from his loose lips. Eyes seeing nothing but Yestin's boxer shorts, scrunched and loose around his ankles, his naked, pale bottom, ginger trail of hair disappearing between the crack of his arse, clenching as he entered Florence. Her legs propped up and wide, heals pushing into the basin of the sink. Eyes pinched shut, biting her lip, suppressing whines and exclaims of pleasure, chewing on her index finger. Her naked breasts rippled like warm fudge and settled with every thrust. Yestin squeezed them in his sweaty hands. She hoisted herself up, uncomfortable, her back pressing into the taps. Bass stood, one hand on the door handle, mouth wide open. Cigarette smouldering a black hole in the pale blue bathroom carpet.

"Oh fuck." Said Florence, breathless, squirming to cover her naked, dark nipples, noticing Bass standing, a lifeless statue in the doorway.

"Fuck yeah." Said Yestin, sounding almost close to tears, his back tense and bottom jiggling. Florence tapped him on the shoulder, her tiny hands flapped like a fish suffocating on dry land.

Yestin stopped thrusting. "What's up?" He took a deep breath. "I haven't come yet."

"Sorry, my bad. Should have knocked." Said Bass, his teeth touching, a forced smile.

Yestin spun, four beads of sweat rolled from his red hairline. His eyes spoke of embarrassment, his smirk said 'I'm getting some'.

"I'll leave you guys to it." Said Bass, backing out of the bathroom, pulling the door closed.

Florence took a sigh of relief. Yestin snorted from his nose. The bathroom door popped back open. Bass was a blur. He lifted the toilet lid. "Sorry guys. I really can't hold it anymore."

Florence looked up at the broken ceiling extractor. Yestin didn't move. Bass whistled, concealing the tsunami wave he was creating in the toilet basin. He shook as he finished, his shoulders rattling.

"That smells like sugar puffs, bud." said Yestin.

"I'm trying my best not to smell anything," said Bass. He flushed the toilet. "I'm spent. Come together."

"Something burning?"

"Shit." Said Bass, as he picked up his cigarette, putting it back in his mouth and thumbed the black scorched carpet, extinguished. "That was lucky." He pulled the door shut behind him. Stifled, snorting laughter blurted from the bathroom.

Bass clambered down the staircase, side footing all the way.

The block framed, pixelated football players ran stiff legged, the ball stuck to their magnetic feet. Bass shook the controller as his designated player over struck a kick. The living room door creaked open.

"Sorry, bud." Said Yestin, sticking his head around the door.

"How long has that been going on? I mean, we knew something was. I just didn't expect to walk in on it, as you were up to your nuts and guts."

Yestin leaned on the sofa. "Early days, but it's more than, well, fucking against a sink."

"In the sink, you mean."

"Fair point."

"You wanna game?" Said Bass, holding the spare controller in the air.

"Nah, Bud. I better check she's OK. Kind of embarrassed, what with you seeing her sex face."

"I'm trying to blank it out, and your quivering arse cheeks."

Yestin chuckled. "Where's Dylan, I thought you were together?"

"Funny story."

"Go on."

"I need to talk to him, figure out his shady ways first."

"Fair enough. Well, you have a good night. See you in the

morning. Sorry again, bud."

Bass waved, as if to say 'no worries'. His finger smashed the buttons and rammed his feet into the carpet as another strike sailed over the goalposts.

"Fucking Dutch orange bastards." He said, tossing the controller across the room. It ricocheted under the flimsy TV table. "Proper bullshit game."

The front door clanked shut. Dylan peered through the crack in the living room door.

"You gonna apologise then?" said Bass.

Dylan spider walked his fingers along the door opening it wider. He dropped his head, teetering around the sofa, and took a seat opposite Bass.

"Did you win?" Said Dylan, pointing at the TV with a red faced smile.

"Look at my face. Does it look like I won?"

"I wasn't sure if that was the game or me."

"But, why oh why Romeo, why art thou pissed at thee?"

"I never intended to go behind your back. It just happened. Me and Laura like each other."

"I'm so fucking happy for ya."

"I'm never sure if you're taking the piss."

"Nah, I've thought about it nonstop. Sure, I feel betrayed. It's not something I've ever done, not to a mate."

"You don't have to make me feel more guilty," said Dylan.

"I will for a bit longer. You owe me that much. But, if that's what she wants. I can't make her want me. I was only going out with her to piss you off."

"Thanks, I think."

"She must be a mong or something. I'm over it. I can't get Yest's arse out my mind."

"Yestin's arse, what?"

"Further development. We were right. They are shagging."

"Florence and Yest?"

"You got it. I walked in on them."

"What were you doing going in their rooms?"

"I was going for a piss, man. He was ramming her over the bathroom sink. Should have filmed it."

"You chatted to 'em?"

"To Yest, a bit."

"No doubt Florence will pull me aside and let me know."

"Why do you think she likes you? Clearly she doesn't. She's up there, fucking Yestin."

"We're friends."

"You've done well there to change the subject. You know you have to make this up to me."

"How do you propose I do that?"

"When you going out again?"

"Monday."

"When am I meeting that Sofia girl?"

"I was thinking the next time we go to the Pot."

"Make it happen. I'm secretly pissed at you, until I'm coming inside Sofia."

"You don't even know what she looks like."

"She's friends with Laura. She'll do for me. Girls like Laura don't have ugly friends. Wanna game?"

Dylan picked up the controllers, stretching for the one that was dashed, handing it back to Bass. They sat, sharing a spliff that Bass encouraged the creation of, and chatted inconsequential hogwash.

"The life of a student," said Bass.

8

dUmBo anD tHe cRowS

Dylan scuffed the heals of his grubby black and white Converse trainers on the worn lecture theatre carpet. The only defiant stimulation he could muster whilst sat alone in the front row. A shaft of white light beamed from a projector on to a large, pulled down screen, cutting through dimmed lights. A PowerPoint presentation hummed out. He squinted at the bold bullet points and scratched his black Biro pen over a yellow legal pad, taking disillusioned notes. At least if his head bobbed, and he attempted to remain enthused and productive. He hoped he would fade into invisibility and the often intimidating Dr. Kilpatrick, with his thick matted dreadlocks down to his waist, like kraken tentacles. This time he would pass him by without demanding he read passages from film text books aloud. The professor droned on and mumbled. The subject, race and gender in Hollywood.

"Nina Mae McKinney, you won't know who she is because she's black," said Kilpatrick. "Not only black, but black in the black and white Al Jolson era of cinema. Paint my face, I'm a caricature. No black actors existed to represent my peoples. Black folk were happy being slaves, the plantation was their saviour. All for the good of the big old white man and—,"

Dylan coughed, interrupting, causing Dr. Kilpatrick to shoot him a white-eyed glare from behind the podium, readjusting the microphone with his fingertips. It popped and cracked through the speakers around the walls of the theatre. As students fanned notepads.

"The difference between you and me is tenfold, characters never centred with beating hearts. My brothers and sisters are only ever portrayed as big lipped, promiscuous children with no intellect or passion for the creative. With not an ounce of grey matter to string a sentence together, other than 'yes sir, boss'." He said. His lisp filled voice popped and spat with every glottal stop as he spoke with precise, forced eloquence into the microphone. His accent from the richest regions of Hertfordshire.

Dylan drew capital L's in the margin of his page, along with a symmetrical heart. He couldn't get Laura out of his mind. The way her eyes softened when she saw him enter The Ruby Moon. He couldn't take his eyes off her. The light made her sublime. The subtle brush of her fingertips on the back of his hand, the way she squeezed so tight. Everything she did made him smile, consuming his hungry thoughts. Her face shimmering with smiles. She had now become his obsession.

"Moreover, worth noting," said Kilpatrick. "When you consider films like the despicable Do the Right Thing. Spike Lee represents my black community as parasites, erupting into violence at its climax and destroying the only place they live and work and can call their own. Filthy looting. Nobility gone in the flash bang of a riot."

Dylan looked up. His pen loose in his hand and said. "Sorry, what?" His bravery lost in gasps from the students behind him.

"You disagree?" said Dr. Kilpatrick. He leaned forward, tilting his head like an in tune canine. "I don't know your name, but elucidate for the benefit of us all, dear boy."

The lecture theatre audience shuffled, uncomfortable. Dylan dare not look behind. Eyes cast fear on his behalf, drilling into his lonely back. Dr. Kilpatrick held his expectant eyes on him.

"It's not that I disagree." Said Dylan, clearing his throat, shuffling in his seat. "It's more that the riot isn't the climax. The climax to me is Mookie collecting those crumpled dollar bills. He may have stopped Sal from getting killed by throwing the bin. But the main reason for the riot was to avenge the death of Radio Raheem."

"You see, folks. What you have here is a white man's interpretation of a black man's film."

"Wait," said Dylan. "Can Do the Right thing not just be a film that captured the essence of a feeling. I'm not sure it's just a black film."

"You don't have to remind me of your privileged skin colour. You're gonna take that from us, too?"

"I don't want to take anything from you or anyone. White or black. They should depict racism in films because films are a representation of society. They don't shape it. I didn't watch Natural Born Killers and want to go out and shoot the place up."

"Many would argue they do and in fact, you must be forgetting. There was a plethora of copycat crimes off the back of Stone's gratuitous film. If I can even call that trash a film."

Dylan, with soft tones said. "Whipped up by the Sunday Times. All of those cases in the States were dismissed. It might influence weak people. It's that thing of, if you're gonna watch the Royal Rumble, you don't start body slamming your hamster. Most sane people don't see a film and it makes them violent. You don't watch Dumbo as a kid and think the crows are a stereotype. They're colourful characters in a cartoon."

"See." Said Kilpatrick, jumping on the spot. "Right there." He pointed. "Colourful."

"Colourful as in, they're drawn that way."

"By a white man. 'I'm not naughty.'" said Dr. Kilpatrick in a high pitched, put on female voice. "I'm just drawn that way." He fluttered his eyelashes. A titter of uncomfortable chuckles resonated around the lecture theatre from the learned students.

"The line is 'I'm not *bad*' I couldn't tell you who drew the crows.

I just don't think it would be any better if you removed them altogether. That, to me, is far worse than being exposed to different cultures. There's never judgement as a kid. Well, I can't remember having any," said Dylan.

"It's taught. Someone has taught you to turn a blind eye. You know what, you can take the stand. I want you to do your presentation, right here, right now." Said Kilpatrick, stabbing his finger into the wooden podium.

"Thought we were presenting in seminars?" said Dylan.

"I'll afford everyone else the luxury of a smaller group. But, since you hold your truths to be self-evident. You have the stage, dear boy." Said Dr. Kilpatrick, holding his straight arm, pointing at the microphone.

Dylan stood, wiping his palms on his jeans. Approaching the podium, carrying with him a pile of printed pages, stapled in the top left corner. His cheeks flushed and blotchy, knee caps vibrating under his jeans. The lecture hall lights cut into his eyes, making it difficult to see the faded faces at the back of the theatre. Which helped him stave off more of his petrified feelings. If only he was stoned right now. What would Jimi Hendrix do? he wondered.

"Wow. This is intimidating." He said, clearing his throat into the microphone. "Public speaking. What fun. Presumably, I'm supposed to picture you all naked." Soft giggles filled the silence from the throng of the theatre. "You quoted the declaration of independence there." He said, nodding at Kilpatrick. "Not that I can recite the whole thing. I suppose if you had continued, you would've got to 'all men are created equal, that they are endowed by their creator'. We have this idea that somehow, unless written in a rule book somewhere of things you can't do and say. That we'll all turn feral and smash the place up. Most of us understand the difference between right and wrong, with no labels." Dylan flicked through his printed pages. "So, originally my presentation was on Douglas Sirk's Imitation of Life. I'm going to freestyle. Could be a disputatious crowd now."

Dr. Kilpatrick frowned, shaking his head and mumbling under his breath. He kicked Dylan's backpack from his feet, sitting in his vacant seat, crossing one leg over the other, flapping his wrist to have him continue.

"As a society, or at least a Western society, we've grown up on the fundamental ideologies presented to us via television, media manipulation, and motion pictures. As children, we develop according to the thoughts dictated to us through cartoons and animation. The Walt Disney Company remaining eminent. We're influenced by those purported to hold authority. It's only when an audience ignores their own reticence to the concepts portrayed and takes an active interpretation of films that they too will discover the falsified tranquillity contained within." He said.

Dylan concentrated on the black foam microphone, comparing it to a pitted olive. His egress to social embarrassment. For many within the audience, the first encounter of his timbre. Words spilling from his mouth, with considered thought to his articulation. Pronouncing each syllable like a children's television presenter. He heard Laura's posh tones, emulating her distinct delivery. He noticed the large wall clock at the back of the theatre, ticking by, the hands almost not moving. His heart beating faster than the second hand. Every cough and lumber from the audience of peers distracted him from his textbook regurgitation.

"I can only wish that one day, like Martin Luther King said in his I have a dream speech, with his poor little children. I will too, one day live in a world where courses like this don't exist, whereby we won't even need to recognise race and the differences that stand between us, constructed by others to exploit our harmony." He took a deep breath. "That's all I have."

Dr. Kilpatrick stood to his feet as a slow, bored hand clap resonated around the theatre. "Not quite ten minutes," he said.

Dylan returned to his seat, red faced and sweating. Squeezing his mouth closed, forcing his shrivelled dry throat to swallow.

"I won't grade that drivel now. But, before you try to change the damn world and expect a Hollywood ovation, start with tidying your own bedroom first. For your information, King said 'Four'." Said Kilpatrick. Holding up four of his thick, black sausage fingers. "My 'four' little children. If you're to quote. Ensure you do so correctly. Yet another example of the white man rewriting history. The truth fades into footnotes."

Dylan shook his head, assassinated by Kilpatrick's words. His dagger like pauses punctuated and twisted into his well-intended confidence.

The flap of Dr. Kilpatrick's limp wrist dismissed the room. Dylan collected his papers from his desk, stuffing them deep into his bag at his feet, keeping his head down as students whispered behind cupped hands and funnelled out through double doors.

A soft female voice said. "What's say we sack this seminar off and get a drink?"

Dylan shocked, his vision filled with bright blue, box new, clean Converse high tops, he followed them up flared fitted jeans, dipping in at tight curved calves, flies zipped almost to the top, three rungs shy from being closed. A Mustang belt, clasped through makeshift, forced holes in auburn leather. Bare, smooth coffee bean coloured arms spouted from under a tight Ramones t-shirt. A smooth, light-skinned black girl, her lips brushed twilight blue. A silver septum piercing stood out against her skin like a dangling teardrop. Thick, blue-rimmed glasses matched the shade of her lipstick and trainers. She flicked her hair, the black bob disappearing to a sharp point on one side with a number one undercut.

Dylan's mouth remained wide open, ravished by her plucky approach. "It's Moira, right?" he said.

"And, you're Dylan." She said, holding out her hand to shake. "Perhaps now more famous than you'd hope."

Dylan fist pumped into her fingertips, fumbling with misunderstanding. Moira sniffed the air with a subtle snigger, dropping her awkward hand.

"I could do with a drink, ya know." He said, finding it hard to disguise his smile.

* * *

They both perched on their elbows at the Union bar, saying very little. Waiting for two pints to be served by an uninterested student bartender. Moira nodded toward an empty table by a window overlooking the staff car park. Dylan followed, scoping band posters covering the walls. Students playing a round of pool. Dylan side eyed Moira's breasts jiggling underneath her band t-shirt as she dragged her back pack free from her shoulders. His eyes shifting so as not to be exposed as a letch.

"Not sure I've ever listened to the Ramones." Said Dylan, pointing at her t-shirt as he mirrored her sitting down.

Moira's chin rested on her chest. "You should. They're more than a fashion statement for me. The pioneers of punk." She said.

"Ya think? What about The Sex Pistols?"

"Overrated. They only released one album. Public Image is where Lydon came into his own."

"That isn't the first time I've heard that." Said Dylan, chinking his pint glass against the side of her's. Before gulping a mouthful to ignite his conversational skills with impassioned conviction.

"Banging the Door has to be up there as one of my favourites," she said. "You're still thinking about that lecture, aren't you?"

"Is it that obvious?"

"You look a little defeated. But don't worry." She sipped from her glass. "Kilpatrick is what we call a bounty."

"A bounty?" said Dylan. His face twisted with confusion.

"Yeah, or, a coconut. Dark on the outside, white in the middle."

"Isn't that racist?"

"Nah, I can say what I like. He's not happy in his life. Wishes he was white. That's what it means. He might flap his gums about black heritage, but I'm telling ya, mi man ain't no soul brudda. He would rather be reading the ten o'clock news."

"Like your namesake, Moira Stewart," said Dylan.

"Funny you should say that. My dad had a massive crush on her. As a result, I go through life baulking each time I tell people my name."

"It's a nice name."

"Thanks. I hate the word 'nice'. But, anyway, Kilpatrick married a white sista so he could torture her."

"I thought he was gay."

"Nah, just bitter. The type who berates his poor wife for serving jerk chicken." Said Moira, sitting upright, shoulders back and in a 1940s radio broadcaster voice said. "Where's my bread and butter, bitch? He's one of those guys, too afraid to ask for brown sauce."

"Well, he's a jerk," said Dylan.

"No." Moira said, pointing her finger to the ceiling. "Say it with me. He's a coconut." She took a gulp of lager.

Dylan placed his pint glass down and readied himself for the newly learnt mantra. "He's a coconut," he said.

"Very good."

"I wasn't dismissing race or anything in what I was saying back there."

"Don't waste your time worrying." Said Moira, waving her hand, dismissing his need to explain.

"How come we've never spoken before?"

"Because I'm like an epiphany," she said. "Plus, I like to test people. See if they squirm in my company. So far, you haven't. Besides, you're like me, always got your head in a book or headphones blocking out the world."

"Three hundred words a minute, longing to be pestered. That's my claim to fame. You not going to ask me what I'm reading at the mo?"

"Nope. Last time I saw you, you were reading A Confederacy of Dunces."

"You read it?"

"Consider that a stupid question, Ignatius. Just be grateful we're talking. You can call me Tiramisu. I'm here to pick you up."

"Is that a chat up line?"

"Depends. Is it working?"

"Could be," said Dylan. Doing his best to suppress excitement.

"Look, a few of my housemates are coming down here for the gig tonight. Chris Helm and that guy from the Inspiral Carpets are playing. You should come."

"You're into indie?"

"Why are you so shocked?" said Moira. She took a swig from her drink. "Because I'm black?"

"Nah, I mean. I'm at indie night all the time, just never seen you there. I'd remember."

"Is *that* a chat up line?"

"Could be."

"Well, I work in the cloakroom. I'm only allowed out for the DJ sets at the end."

"And, I never wear a coat, that explains that."

"I've seen you wearing that Stone Roses money shirt."

"The first track I heard of theirs was Sally Cinnamon. I had no clue what he was singing about, salty cinemas. Almost wore the tape out trying to figure it out." He paused. "I have tickets to Billy Bragg tonight."

"Oh shit, at the Potoo? Cool. I tried to get some."

"You like Billy Bragg?"

"Again, with the shocked face. What's the matter with you? I can like Billy Bragg."

"I know, sorry, you're just throwing me curve balls all over the place."

"Curve balls?"

"You know, like surprises."

"Thanks, I know what it means. You talk with this weird transatlantic vocab. It's sweet but different. Ya know, my ex-boyfriend was a Richard. I used to sing that Billy Bragg song to him all the time. Really pissed him off." Moira sang in tune to the track. "Richard belongs to Moira. You get the idea. Hey hey, here comes

Richard."

"You sing it well. Could be why he's your ex-boyfriend."

Moira laughed. "Could be." She swallowed lager. "Could be."

"I've got his CD with me." Dylan reached for his bag. "Get me in the right mood." He said, thinking better of digging out his CD player again, given the reaction he received from Laura. "I could always come down afterwards."

"You should. We'll be here. I'll keep a snakebite waiting for ya," she said.

Dylan was stunned into silence. Excusing himself to the toilet meant he could examine his face. He smirked and stroked his chin, looking into himself for the origin of this sudden mask of sex appeal. First Laura, now Moira. He let the hot water tap dribble, scolding his soapy hands. The mirror misted with condensation. As he left, he drew a capital 'L' in the middle of the mirror. He stared into himself, pulled the skin under his eyes taut and smiled, pursing his lips. He then traced an 'M' over the 'L'. Smudging his fingers to erase them both as he left.

Moira sat with legs crossed, tapping her index finger on the now empty pint glass, puffing clouds of cigarette smoke above her head. Her blue Converse rocked up and down. She noticed Dylan returning and for the first time; he studied the gap between her teeth. Cute, he thought. Uncertain, it was something he should compliment her on. He searched for the medical name for it.

"Look, I gotta go," she said. "I'm meeting a pair of newlyweds."

"Sorry, you're gonna have to explain that."

"Button face," she said. "I need a side hustle to study."

"Like swinging?"

"Not quite. I'm a part-time wedding planner. Wouldn't have thought that, would ya?"

Moira picked up Dylan's Nokia 3210 from the table with its red fascia. Unlocked it in one impressive finger movement, sliding across the menu, glanced across the star button. Typed something with her thumb, hitting each number to spell the words. Jammed her thumb down, punctuating that she had finished. "You got credit?" she said. "Nevermind, it's sent." She continued to thumb digits. "I've got your number, and you have mine. Check your contacts and call me when you're done tonight. I've gotta sprinkle some Moira love dust." She kissed two fingers and planted them on Dylan's left cheek, pushing her chair under the table.

Stunned. "Bye," he said. Feeling bewildered by the whirlwind conversation. "Diastema," he said to himself. He sat smiling, noticed his phone still illuminated. He looked at the space previously filled by Moira. Then concentrated on his phone. Opening the contacts, arrow key down. Alphabetically, he worked his way through:

Adam
Andy H
Andy Video P
Beena
Big D Smoke
Coconut
Creepy Chris

Not able to control his smile. He scrolled back and landed on *Coconut*. Chuckling to himself, circling his finger on the screen with affection over the name. The phone screen flashed green. Four bars of signal, one bar of battery; *1 message received*. He hit the menu button to read it:

'Hexagon, 6. U & me, Billy Crab. C U l8tr babe X,'

Dylan winced at Laura's inclusion of the word 'babe', shaking his head, ridding initial disapproving judgement from his mind. He gulped at the remaining dregs of lager in his glass. Flicked back to his contacts, scrolled back down to *Coconut*. His bemused smile returned. He continued to scroll until he reached *Little Lady Laura*. Shook his head and scoffed a laugh from his lips, as if he couldn't believe his luck. He composed a reply.

'It's a date. Mwah x'

9

tHe pOtoO

The Hexagon, a bright indoor shopping centre with the smell of chlorine emanating from a rockery water feature Dylan sat beside, salty spray splashing his neck. Shops closing, advertising boards pulled inside by youthful staff. The centre remained open for pedestrians to make their way from one side of town to the other without a two mile round trip in poor street lighting and the possibility of grievous assault. Dylan perched his elbows on his knees, looking off into the distance toward the automatic doors. No sign of Laura. Nerves tackling his impatience. He wanted to be next to her, feeling her touch on his skin. He considered conversation starters. They could discuss her busy retail work. That's too boring, he thought. He checked his mobile phone for the time. She wasn't late. Where was she? Apprehension coursed through him. What if he messes this up? He could say something stupid or not be as funny as he hoped he was. He longed for his CD player. Some music would soothe him, settling his searching mind.

Laura smacked her hands down on his shoulders from behind.

"I hope you're looking for me," she said.

They threw their arms around each other. It felt natural to be so close. The rest of the world was quiet, only they mattered. She smelt of honey.

The foyer of the Potoo theatre was full of firemen, standing behind paste tables, handing out flyers on fair pay and union information, shaking charity collection boxes of coinage.

A booming, loud, familiar fudge voice caught Dylan's attention.

"If only I was here on official business. This is my night off."

"Oh god," he said.

Laura turned to Dylan, grabbing his arm. "Everything OK?"

"I think so," he jerked his head. "I think that obnoxious voice." Laura leaned, subtle to see who he meant. "He's one of my lecturers. Have a look. He hasn't seen me, has he?"

"Doesn't look like it," she said. "You think he'll come over if he —, Oh, yup, he's noticed you."

"Shit."

"Master Dylan," said Dr. Kilpatrick. He swept an elaborate black cape from his side. "It's so good to see you and who's this with you?"

"Evening Sir, this is Laura."

"I see he added no context," he tutted. Taking hold of Laura's hand. "A pleasure to meet you, my darling. We can't rely on these creatures to propel us to the forefront, we do that ourselves isn't that right. It's a pleasure to meet you, my love. Are you both here for Mr. Bragg?"

"Indeed, big fan."

"I had no idea you were this cultured. It's a tragedy that we've got these lovely gentlemen out here having to draw attention to their plight. Poor bastards. I hope you'll be generous with your support, young man."

"I've already donated."

"Good to hear. Well, I won't ruin the rest of your evening.

Especially if this is a date. I'll leave you two lovebirds to it." He tapped his fingertips on Laura's arm. "Take care of this one." He waggled his loose wrist, his cape sweeping back behind him, floating down around his waist.

"Who was that guy?"

"I can't stand him."

"Bit homophobic," said Laura.

"Not because he's gay, there's something about him."

"I'm tellin' ya. He wants a slice of your arse."

"Hush up, the doors are open."

They took up their front row seats in the auditorium. A woman sat next to Dylan, took out a yoghurt pot from her handbag along with a plastic spoon. She peeled back the foil and dug her spoon deep into the bottom. Swirling four and a half times. She tapped it on the rim as if she was mixing cement. She gulped a spoonful and smacked the spoon on her knee with satisfaction.

"We've got one here." Said Dylan to Laura, nodding in the woman's direction.

"Let me know if she touches your crutch."

"Crotch."

"What?"

"You mean crotch."

"Do I?" Laura glared at him.

The lights went out, the crowd clapped and shouted.

"Here he comes," he said.

"Lucky for you," said Laura. Her eyebrows still raised with her face straight.

Billy Bragg, in his cockney accent, told a joke into the microphone, a political punchline. Tony Blair, the subject. Dylan was inspired to want more out of life after seeing him in the spotlight. Beguiled by how talented and funny he was. He welcomed to the stage a grey haired, old guy, revealing him to be the keyboard player from The Small Faces. Everyone seated clapped their hands with recognition. Laura followed and so too did Dylan, clapping. Sucked in by the music. The band strummed the opening chords to Shirley. Laura consumed Dylan's smile, taking him by the hand, squeezing it tight in both her palms against her chest. He smirked, tapping his foot along to the song. Laura spent the rest of the set gazing at Dylan, fighting the urge to hide her happiness. The lights came up. The band bowed to the crowd, rapturous applause. Dylan and Laura merged into the sea of people as they exited.

"Thank you," said Laura to Dylan, interlocking her arm under his as they exited into the cold, dark night outside.

"I thought that was you," said a posh sounding, deep voice. Laura's eyes glanced over, her head dropped.

"You're fucking kidding me," she said in a whisper. Dylan looked up as a dark-haired, studious looking guy with black-rimmed glasses pecked Laura on each cheek.

"How you been?" he said.

Laura inhaled, looking at Dylan.

"Sorry, should I introduce myself?" he said.

"No. No. Dylan, this is Charlie. Charlie this is Dylan."

They gripped hands. "Nice to meet you," they said.

"I didn't know you liked Billy Bragg," said Charlie.

"There's a lot you don't know about me," said Laura.

Charlie raised his hand in the hair, leaning over Laura, waving. No chance of avoiding the natural urge for Dylan and Laura to turn and look toward the automatic doors as a blonde girl, wearing a black, tight dress, clutched a small bag to her flat stomach. Laura looked her up and down. Dylan smirked. "You two could be sisters," he said.

"We do look quite similar. Funny that, Charlie," said Laura.

"Lizzie, over here." Charlie beckoned her. "This is Laura and David. I've known Laura forever. What I don't know about her isn't worth knowing." He said.

"I love your eyes." Said Lizzie, studying Laura's face. She, too, noticed the resemblance.

"I love your dress," said Laura.

"Thanks, it still does the job."

"Oh, and what job is that then, babes?" said Charlie, nudging Dylan.

"Did you enjoy it, the show?" said Laura.

"I'm sure it was good. I wasn't paying attention. My vision went blurry until the climax." Said Charlie.

Lizzie elbowed him in the ribs, rolling her eyes. "He's such a bullshitter." She said.

"I didn't get that. Were you implying she was giving you a hand job?" said Dylan.

"Is this guy for real?"

"It was great to see you." Said Laura. "Nice to meet you Lizzie." She ushered Dylan away, grabbing the back of his arm. "Charlie, always a pleasure," she said. Glaring at him from the corner of her eye. He recognised her familiar scorn.

"You too, take care. Nice to meet you Darren," said Charlie.

Laura and Dylan ambled through the historic market street of the town centre.

"Ex-boyfriend?" he said.

"How did you guess?"

"That hinted at intimacy. Alienation of a private joke, when you're not let in on the punchline."

"I didn't mean to make you feel that way. He is my ex-boyfriend. But, he's an ex for a reason."

"How long have you known each other?"

"He wasn't lying there. Since we were little kids. I mean, tiny. Our parents were friends, still are."

"Should I be worried?" he said. "I'm never sure how I should react in those situations. I mean, am I supposed to crash my jaws together and start gnawing?"

"You did fine. You were cool."

"I could have peed around your ankles, marked you as mine or something."

"No need. I haven't seen your…" She said, nodding to his crotch. "Your man yet, but I bet yours is a grower. He just has massive balls."

"Sorry, what, massive balls?"

"Not sure why I told you that," she said.

"I'm not either. It's weird he seems to 'ave replaced you with your near as damn it, twin."

"I'll admit, that is odd." She said. "Anyway, what did you think? You enjoy it?"

"Yeah, it was all good."

"Is that what you really feel?" she said. "I mean, that was a first for me and I thought he was amazing. For you, being a fan. Tell me what you felt, deep down." Laura patted his flat belly over his shirt.

"It gave me the hope that I could achieve something," he said. "Then I was introduced to your ex-boyfriend, and the world got smaller."

Across cobbled streets. Groups of drunken friends staggered and fell out of club entrances. Arms stretched above heads, urinating in shop doorways. Dylan directed Laura away, avoiding intimidation from late night louts. Hand in hand, they reached rusted iron gates to a churchyard. They ventured inside, dodging head stones. An empty wooden bench pushed up against the stone church wall. They sat, looking out at the sparkling lights of the town. Headstones cast stretched shadows.

"Don't let my past with someone else determine the experiences of the future we share. If you grant him that power, he'll succeed and we'll be over." Said Laura.

"I struggle with that, being able to consider a future. Sometimes it feels out of touch. It might be living here. I don't mind it. It's a nice enough town. If I had my time over, I'm not sure I would've come here, just to feel alone all the time."

"But then you wouldn't have met me. Plus, you're not alone anymore."

"I'm thankful for that," he said. "You make it bearable. I don't like uni and all the obligation. The structure of seminars. It doesn't encourage discussion or open debate. It's always the ones with the loudest voices that get heard. Instead, I seem to buy up Purple Haze and dream about what my future could be, never convinced it'll be a reality."

"Manifest it. That's what they say. What's Purple Haze?" said Laura.

"Nevermind. Isn't all that manifestation stuff just pseudo-science?"

"Could be. I just know it can't do any harm. Don't become a hermit. I still want to see you." She said.

"It's not that. My passion for education may have left me. Last week, I walked in the rain, didn't even have an umbrella. Stopped at the gates and watched everyone waiting outside the lecture theatre. I turned around. Wasn't worth it. I couldn't put up with Kilpatrick rambling on about 1960's, British kitchen sink dramas and William Hague."

"Has anyone ever told you, you're too political?"

"I've not heard that before, no. But, he's the one who tries to push his agenda, when he should be teaching film. One lecture, he recited the speech Hague gave at the party conference."

"He didn't seem that bad," she said.

"Teachers do that, though. They're one thing in the classroom and then they metamorph to a human. You can call them by their first name at parents' evenings. It's a crazy, manufactured institution."

"When you're in the system. It's difficult to shake the comfort and feel the embarrassment of knowing you're not worth anything. Share something of yourself with me," she said.

"What do you mean?"

"Whether I like it or not. You met my ex. That exposed me, gave more context for you. Now, you need to expose yourself to me a little."

"I got it, OK. You show me yours, type thing. I guess in A-level, English, Paul Lenan referred to the pimples on my face as braille. We used to sit next to this Mediterranean looking girl, Jodie. She had a beauty spot on her left cheek, right in the centre." He said, touching his cheek. "She was dark, sort of tanned, chestnut hair, hilarious too —,"

"Get on with it," she said. "Yeah, yeah, Jodie sounds gorgeous."

"Anyway, Paul and I would always squabble over who got to sit next to her. We were pathetic. He got the seat by her side. I sat opposite, looking at her face on. That was the better view. I mean, I could look into her eyes."

"Do I need to say get on with it again?"

"Right. Sorry, anyway. We sketched one another in between learning about the duality of patterning or some shit. We revealed our hand drawn interpretations. I drew Jodie; it was complimentary, an excellent picture. I used my black Biro on lined paper to add dark intensity to her eyes. I flattered her, capturing her positively. She was happy. That made Paul jealous. He scribbled some finishing touches, flicked the paper over, revealing his masterpiece. He included the four obvious spots around my chin. I had squeezed them that morning; still red and angry, ya know. It shattered me. I never spoke to Jodie again. Avoided her for the rest of college, despite her attempts at friendly chat. Through pride, I blew it all away. Thankfully, I've gained more personality with age, I hope. I couldn't laugh it off back then. Knowledge is the only good. Ignorance, the only evil—,"

"That line yours?" said Laura. "Don't answer that. Sometimes, I wish you'd shut up." She grabbed him by the lapels, pulled him in close, and planted her lips on his. Their warm breath mixing in the darkness. Eyes squeezed shut. They sank into one another.

Laura rested her head on Dylan's shoulder, her finger poking at his button hole.

"I can't even think of a soundtrack worthy of that kiss." He said, exhaling cigarette smoke.

"It was magical," she said.

"Champagne with two maraschino cherries." He said, breathless. Staring out over the town.

"Excuse me?" said Laura, sitting up, shaking her head.

"That's what we should drink, or that's what I feel like drinking. You know, to celebrate."

"Celebrate our first kiss?"

"Yeah."

"You're a freak." She said, laughing. "But, I love it." She flopped her head back on his shoulder.

"It's hard. I don't know why I can't just be myself. You know, be more of myself."

"I'd like to know more of you."

"You will. I wanna be me. I feel like I can do that with you. Be goofy, say stupid shit. I've just always been so scared that the world is gonna judge me."

"Masugar," she said. "I'm not gonna judge you." She grabbed his hand and kissed it. "I'm willing to know you, if only you'd let me."

Dylan's phone vibrated in his lap, making Laura Jump, dropping his hand. The green light shone bright.

1 message received

"Do you need to read that?" she said.

Moira's blue neon lips against perfect chocolate skin flashed into Dylan's mind. Laura's hand squeezed his, he saw his reflection in her pupils.

"No. I'm good," he said. "What were we saying?"

10

lOvE cOmEs iN sPuRtS

Laura explored Dylan's bedroom for the first time, still wearing her tanned corduroy jacket, holding a chipped purple cup, almost empty. Now she had finished the tea Dylan had poured. More to warm her hands inside the cold shared house. Her fingertips brushed over the iconic posters tacked to his wall, her eyes wide, sweeping the room, scanning the boxes on top of the cupboard.

"You really like the Stone Roses." She said, peering, distracted into the full-length mirror on the inside of the cupboard door, running her fingers through her blonde hair, flicking it behind her ears. She moved hoodies and t-shirts along the cupboard clothes rail, metal hangers screeched. Her stiff index finger rolled over the spines of his stacked books. Dylan heard her muttering the titles aloud to herself. She sauntered beside his tiny white computer desk, held up the round mirror and smiled a toothy grin. She caught him smiling, his amused reflection, and stuck her tongue out, returning the mirror to where she found it.

"What are all these pages?" she said, flapping a wad of paper in

74

the air. She let the pages fan, thumbing through them.

"I'm writing a book." He said, turning the TV on, hitting mute on the remote.

Laura snapped her head up. "A book? What like an autobiography?"

Dylan sidled over to her, taking the pages in his fingers. "I suppose there's an element of me in it." He said, looking over the lines of printed ink. "Write what you know and all that." He tapped the pages together on the computer monitor.

"Dylan, the writer." She said, plucking a small piece of white fluff from his hairline. "Am I in it?"

"You're not, not yet anyway. I can always squeeze you in somewhere."

"What's it about,—? Your net curtains don't match." She said, pointing at the window. "That horrifies me."

Dylan shrugged. "It's a student house. They were already here," he said. Laura nodded, as if humouring him and not impressed with the explanation. "I don't know what it's about."

"Don't you need to know, to sell it?" She said and sipped from her mug, placing it on the corner of the desk.

"Who's saying I wanna sell it?" He said, moving the pages, aligning them along the edge of the computer monitor.

Laura flapped her shoulders, shaking her jacket off her arms. "Why else would you write it?"

"I find—," said Dylan, stopping himself as he took hold of her collar, helping to slip it from her back. "I'm not in control of my desire to sit and write. I need to do it."

"Alright, you artist, you." Said Laura, rolling her wrist like a melodramatic thespian, knuckles to her forehead. "One must write, otherwise I dare not breathe." She chuckled to herself. "I'm joking. Don't look so scared. I'm jealous. I'm not creative. I do like water colours, just never have the time to paint."

"You need to find your bliss." He said, resting his fingertips on the paper. "It's a love story. They all are, I suppose. Cassia's the main character, sort of my Holly Golightly."

"Holly Go-whatly?"

"Truman Capote—,"

"The Truman show?"

"Nevermind. As the pages print, I live vicariously through my characters' hopes and dreams," he said.

Laura sat in the leather desk chair in front of the computer. "Weirdo. Well, if you don't have a dream." She said, kicking her feet off the ground, spinning in the chair. "You got a title for it?" Her eyes closed as she spun.

"Cinnamon," he said.

She stopped, her eyes steadying, attempting to focus. "Spicy." She said, lacing her enunciation with sultry innuendo as she swept her delicate pink tongue across her bottom lip.

"Like your name, Lauraceae."

"What are you talking about now?"

"Cinnamon, it's from the Lauraceae family," said Dylan.

"How do you even know that?"

"I don't know."

"You're special, aren't you?"

"I'm waiting for you to include *needs*," he said.

"No need. You did it for me."

"Sometimes, though, I feel I'm wasting my time with it. There's none of that immediate reward. It's so difficult to convince people to even read it, and I suppose who the hell am I?"

"You mustn't think like that. Printing the pages has to be some kind of reward. At least you've got a goal."

"I guess."

"No, you have." She said and jumped up. "Don't let anyone, not even me. Ever tell you otherwise. One day." She grabbed for the pages. "You'll be taking these." She flapped the pages above her head. "Jamming them into a leather shoulder bag and delivering them to a grateful agent. The world will catch up. They're just late to the

Rodeo."

"That's a lovely thing to say."

Laura set the pages down. "Didn't you notice?" She said, flopping and spinning the chair one rotation, stopping. "I'm bloody lovely, me." She crossed one stiff, outstretched leg over the other, emulating Kenny Everett.

"You know, I'm not sure what type of writer I'll be. It took me an hour to find pusillanimous in the dictionary."

"What does that mean?"

"I can't remember. David Dimbleby used it on Question Time."

"At least you looked it up."

"What good is that without retention?"

Laura's attention shifted to the desk, picking up a pocket dictionary. "P - P- P-u. I can't find it," She said. "You sure it's a word?" She ran her finger down the columns of the small pages. "Here we go," she looked up. "Cowardly."

"That's what it means?"

"According to…" She flipped closed the book, her thumb marking the page, and read the front cover aloud. "Collins."

Dylan stabbed his finger in the air, as if struck with inspiration. "The Wizard of Oz. I remember, I associated it with the lion."

"I thought the lion had no heart."

"Nah, that was the tin man. Lion wanted courage. He was *pusillanimous*."

Laura grabbed Dylan's hand, patting it with condescension, in both her hands. "You feel better now?"

He closed his hand on her soft skin and pushed his fingers between hers.

"Did you know the Wizard of Oz is about communism?" he said.

"The film with the midgets?" Laura stood up, wrapping her free arm around his waist, kissing the back of his hand, clasping hers.

"They're munchkins, but yeah. King Vidor. No, Victor Fleming included two roads for Dorothy to follow; one, the yellow brick road to Oz and the second was a red brick road to communism."

"Didn't one midget hang themselves from a tree?—, You think studying film has sucked the life out of it for ya?"

"Having to analyse them can do, I guess. But, it's The Wizard Of Oz. You can't ruin that."

"Analyse this," she said. Laura leaned in, eyes closed, and kissed Dylan on the lips. He felt himself disappear into secure familiarity. His thoughts were mutual with hers.

"What's this music?" She said, opening her eyes. Slow and considered, as if she was trying to stabilise her giddy self.

"The Stone Roses. You like it?"

"Makes sense, what with all these posters. They're no Norah Jones, but it'll do. I'm just grateful it's not that Santana track. They play it all day at work.

"Oh, Smooth, you mean. Worse would be that track, Wherever you will go."

"Way up high, blah blah blah." Said Laura in melodic, weary articulation.

The room became a spinning blur. Their lips warm, eyes closed tight. The Stone Roses playing low from the stereo. As their eyes relaxed open, orientating themselves, the room shone yellow bright. The bedroom light above their heads beamed, casting shadows over their connection. Laura, with her hand in Dylan's, tiptoed over to the light switch, snapping it off. Removing her shoes, standing on each heel, her ankle socks gracing the grubby carpet. She pulled closed the stained cream curtains, barely attached to the rail. Dylan perched on the edge of the bed and untied his Converse laces. Laura crawled behind him, placed her cool palm on his chest, lips on his neck. She exhaled deep warmth into his ear.

"Your ticklish." She said, biting his earlobe as they rolled back, their heads landing on two flat pillows, eyes shooting to the ceiling.

"This bed spread is garish." She said, running her hand over the surface of a pale blue stripped duvet cover.

Dylan's brown corduroy trousers tight around his crotch. Laura grabbed for his hand, guiding it to unbutton her jeans. He fumbled, swallowing icy air. She laid flat, her hand on the inside of his thigh. He pulled his knees closer to his body. Fighting the urge to squirm, and flinched as Laura's tongue pushed its way into his mouth. She nestled into his chest, their noses clipping. The next music track chimed in, All Across the Sands. Almost in time with the music, as Reni's drums kicked off and Ian Brown rattled his vocal chords. Laura rolled over, higher on Dylan's body, nibbling on his bottom lip, before forcing her tongue into his mouth again. She tickled her fingers up the inside of his thigh. Without warning, his leg clenched and they head-butted. She laughed. He couldn't. Instead, grimaced. His stomach contracted, a damp sensation on the inside of his leg. A sticky warmth between his thighs. He couldn't ignore the pungent aroma of instant mash potato filling the air around his sensitive nostrils.

"Excuse me for one second." He said, rolling from underneath her, jumping to his feet.

"You OK?"

"Just need the toilet." He said, avoiding eye contact with her. Dylan bolted out of the room. Laura laid back, smiling, exhaling as the door closed, suppressing a giggle.

Standing in front of the bathroom mirror. Dylan dropped his corduroys to his ankles, splashed lukewarm water on his thighs, cleaning his gooey, matted hair, using a handful of toilet tissue to pat himself dry. Shaking his head with red-faced embarrassment, he examined his reflection in the dirty mirror. He dropped the tissue in the toilet basin and flushed, grabbing for a can of Lynx Africa from the windowsill and sprayed a blast on his thighs. Hoping it would conceal the smell of semen.

Closing the bedroom door behind him with a click.

"Don't worry." Said Laura, leaning on her elbow.

"I'm sorry."

"Don't be. Come here." She said and patted the space on the bed. "I once gave this guy a hand job. He came on my knee. I wanted to die. My God. But his goofy come face smile made me forget it all. Sometimes, you have to wipe the jizz away and laugh." Dylan's shoulders shook with laughter. "I guess. I just wanted everything to be right," he said.

"Whatever our journey." She said and dragged Dylan's cheek toward her, turning his face with her finger. "It'll be right from the start." She kissed him on the tip of his nose. "Seriously, don't think about it. I'm not."

"I really like you."

"I really like you, too. Why else would I be here? It's not for your politics," she said.

They both chuckled, the tension evaporating. She straddled his lap, taking his face in her hands. She placed her cool lips on his closed eyes. Their breath danced and intermingled as their tongues writhed for fleshy contact. Arms wrapped around one another. Cool palms on the back of each other's hot necks. Dylan lifted Laura's shirt over her head, sweeping her golden hair from her pale face. A modest, plain white bra covered her breasts. Dylan pressed his lips against her chest, pecking at her collarbone. Laura pushed her groin into his. He plucked at the clasp of her bra with one hand. She recognised him struggling, almost spat whilst kissing, trying to suppress her giggles.

"Let me." She said, throwing her arms back. "It's complicated." She smiled, pushed her lips on his and pinged the clasp apart, letting the bra drop to the floor. Dylan's eyes stared at her pert, fuchsia nipples. He was mesmerised.

"32 B's," she said.

"That means nothing to me." He studied the curve of her breasts. "You're utterly perfect."

"Put your mouth on the girls," she said. "My nipples, suck my nipples."

With the pace of tentative nerves, he edged in and suckled soft. With no clue about accepted pressure.

She pulled his head into her chest. "Gently, don't bite."

"Sorry."

Laura slapped the back of his head. "Don't apologise,"

"Sorry."

He graced from the left nipple to the right and repeated the lip soaked greeting to the right. She pushed him back on the bed and dragged off his corduroys, tugging them free from his ankles. She unclasped her jeans, began swaying her hips to the music. Dylan noted to himself she was out of time with the beat. It didn't matter to him. He was concentrating on controlling his bubbling belly, his loins solid, a pang of concrete excitement deep within him. She stood naked, confident, her bare feet standing on student carpet. She jumped onto the bed, pulling the duvet over her goose pimpled body. Nestling herself against him, she shuffled her feet together.

"Why is it so cold in here?" she said.

"We've probably run out of gas again." He said, pulling her close to his hairless chest. "We have to top up a key."

"I don't know what that means."

"We have to take a plastic key to the shop—,"

"I don't want you to explain. You're gonna have to keep me warm."

Dylan gave an upturned smile and planted his moist lips on hers, rolling on top of her as she helped to slide underneath him. The duvet lifted like a tidal wave as he prepared himself to enter her. He thrust once, shuffled on his knees, slumped forward on his elbows, assumed a press up position and raised himself back off the mattress.

"You OK? You want me to help?"

Dylan nodded as Laura took hold, guiding him inside her.

"Wow," he said. "It feels so good."

"Quite the reaction. Not sure if I'm disappointed or complimented."

Dylan smiled, then squinted, inhaled deep like a vacuum, then blew hot air in Laura's face. His hips moving faster.

"Easy tiger." She said, grabbing his bottom. "I don't want you running to the bathroom again just yet."

"I don't want it to stop."

"I'm in for the night." She said, turning her head as if speaking to an imaginary friend. "What the hell is this, comedy sex?"

"This might just be the best night of my life."

A hollow bang at the bedroom door. Both their heads jolted at the sound. The handle squawked. Laura gasped, pulling a corner of the duvet over her naked shoulder. The door opened a crack. Dylan remained motionless. A shaft of light cut in from the kitchen.

"Don't worry. I'm not coming in." Said Bass, with a laugh. His straight arm poked through the gap, Dylan squinted at a DVD sized case he was holding in his hand. "Dude, I got us this," he rattled the case.

"What is it?" Said Dylan, cowering under the duvet.

"We can play it when you're done." Said Bass, his voice sounding more distant.

"When you're done," whispered Laura. "Dick." She rolled her eyes.

"OK. Yeah, cool man, maybe later," said Dylan.

"Leave you guys to it." Said Bass, shutting the door. "Row, row, row yer boat."

Laura glared up at Dylan. "Well, you won't go forgetting your first time in a hurry."

"Hey, you said it. Whatever our journey." He kissed her on the forehead. "I wouldn't forget tonight for anything, and nothing could spoil it for me. Nothing has."

"When do we have that chat about whether we're together?"

"Which chat's that, the item chat?"

"Bang on," she said. "Although, I may have tossed some guy off on a wall outside Mr. Brown's geography lesson. When I have someone inside me, a guy that I like, if we're at this stage, then he's more likely my boyfriend than he is some booty call. Plus, I'll always be your first."

"My first everything."

"Have you come?"

"Oh, long time," said Dylan.

Laura covered her mouth with her hand, concealing a cute laugh. "Continual improvement, that's all I can ask for," she said.

"I don't care what you say. I just had sex."

"We, we just had sex."

"Shall I pull him out?"

"Him?"

"Yeah, you know."

"You can leave *him* there. You'll probably fall out anyway, if you keep making me laugh."

"It wasn't that funny, was it?"

"It's more the thought of your penis having a personality. They're usually so angry." She said with snarling teeth. "All veiny, or pathetic and weeping. A grower, not a shower." She screwed up her face and forced her tongue between her lips, inflating her cheeks. "I'll buy you your first Big Mac."

"My first Big Mac, what? You know I'm a vegetarian. Have been since I was seven."

"Don't waste your time. Get a Big Mac down you. I can see your hip bones." Laura ran her fingertips over his body, wandering like braille.

Dylan looked into the darkness under the duvet, studying his stomach. "You can see my hip bones?"

"Yeah, you need to eat more."

"I had a lot of puppy fat as a teenager, or as my Mother would say, 'I was covered'."

"Well, you're not anymore—, Please, don't mention your mum whilst you're inside me. You can wolf down a burger. You haven't got a problem with your weight, have you?"

"I don't think so. I drink a lot of water, that's because I'm always thirsty."

"You could be diabetic. They say you get thirsty all the time."

"I'm not diabetic and I haven't got a problem with my weight. I don't eat meat because I didn't like the idea of the animals getting slaughtered on that farm at Thorpe Park."

"You're not seven anymore—, Thorpe Park has a farm?"

"Yeah, I think it's still open. Anyway, I'll try a burger and take you to the secret farm at Thorpe Park."

"I think you're lying—,"

"Nah, you catch the train from the rapids and it takes you to this zoo."

"Whatever, it's a date." Said Laura, nodding.

They both laid silent. There was a clunk, then a whirling sound from the cupboard.

"What was that?"

"No idea." He said, as the spinning hum got faster.

Laura squeezed his nipples and rolled over on top of him, folding the duvet over both their heads.

"Masugar. Crusha Crusha." She said, tickling his neck, giggling.

11

pInT gLaSs sTrIpPerS

The living room was brisk. Despite the chill, Bass slouched topless on the sunken brown sofa. Curtains drawn, shafts of blinding sunlight cut through the misty cigarette smoke filling the air. Legs wide open, his black cords cut with scissors by hand, severed off below the knees, thread fraying like spiderwebs. Trainers kicked off. His acoustic bass guitar laid flat on the floor, a pint glass of orange cordial sat atop it. A soiled, chipped dinner plate with red sauce smudges and three green beans left uneaten at his feet. Sleepy eyes pierced the TV screen, playing Grand Theft Auto II, moving his head as if it helped with control of the two-dimensional vehicles. The living room door creaked open behind him.

"Hey dude." Said Bass, eyes fixed forward.

"How's it going?" said Dylan, edging sideways into the room. "Is it as good as the first?" He flapped his arms, dispersing stale air from his face.

"Yeah man, gotta get this car to the bomb shop." He paused,

clicking buttons. "Rig it and blow these loons up or some shit." His fingers tapped heavy on the controller.

"You working today?"

"Nah, mate." Bass banged pause on the controller and leaned forward on his knees, giving Dylan his full attention. "We should go down The Pot," he said.

"Tomorrow night?" said Dylan. He sat next to Bass. "Laura's bringing that Sofia, so you two can meet." He opened a new packet of sealed cigarettes, unravelling a plastic wrapper, flicking it free from his fingers, leaving the waste in a pile on the arm of the chair. He offered the fresh opened packet to Bass.

"Cool, cool." He said, sliding a cigarette free. "I mean, we should go today, at lunch."

"Lunchtime?" Said Dylan, leaning forward, sparking his lighter as Bass leaned in for him to ignite the tip. "It's not open."

Bass took a deep drag, holding smoke in his lungs. "On a Wednesday it is," he exhaled. "They turn it into a strip club. Pole dancers and that."

Dylan lit his own cigarette, his face aglow. "I'll give that a miss." He dropped the disposable magenta lighter to his lap.

"It'll be funny, something different. You ever seen strippers?"

"Life's moving so fast, I can't keep up." Dylan stretched, collecting the novelty ash tray from the floor. "No, I haven't, but I don't know if Laura would find that funny, to hear me ogling naked women."

"Chill, you don't touch 'em or anything. And ogling, how old are you?" Bass shook his head. "Who knows what happens in the private rooms? That's between you and her. Nobody else need know, mate. Think of it as practice."

"Private rooms?" Dylan wiped the corner of his mouth. "I don't know. Sounds too serious for me."

"You don't have to have a private dance. You can just watch 'em on the pole. Fiver to get in. I'll front this one. I owe you a drink as it is."

"I don't know, mate." Dylan fidgeted with the lighter in his fingers.

"You've got no lectures today, no excuse." Bass smiled with encouragement. "Come on." He grabbed Dylan's knee, squeezing. "Come on," he said.

"Sometimes, I'm far too impressionable." Said Dylan, circling his cigarette around the rim of the ashtray.

"That's why I love ya, dude." Bass patted Dylan on the thigh, excitement thundered from his wrist.

"Don't you dare mention this to Laura."

"Like I'd do a thing like that."

"You gotta promise."

"Pinky swear." Said Bass and held out a fish hook finger.

Dylan locked his little finger around his. "She ain't hearing shit from me, mate. We've all got our secrets." Bass jumped up excited, cigarette pressed between his lips, squinting to stop the smoke billowing into his eyes. "Let me get a top on and we'll bounce." He healed the power button for the PlayStation off and vaulted over the back of the sofa, hustling up the stairs.

The pair were out of breath as they descended the dusty concrete steps into the basement entrance of The Rancid Copper Pot. Bass leading the way. Dylan took a submissive deep breath as the door lurched open. A wall of sound, Turbo Lover by Judas Priest, crashed through the silence. On the stage, a long, pale legged brunette, with thigh length black leather boots, kicked her left leg up like scissors, toes pointed, arching her spine, black lacy thong cutting between her bare buttocks. Her nipples were stiff as she crumpled down, grinding her crotch into the stage. Dylan's eyes darting, uncertain he should make eye contact. Instead examined the dance floor, now used for leather bucket seat strip club audiences. Bass navigated around the tables, nodding his head along with the music. A server wearing a tiny pit lane inspired black and white checked hot pants and matching balcony bra, hair tied back in two pigtails, smiled at Dylan and turned on the spot, a round drinks tray resting on one hand. Two bottles of beer stood proud, appearing glued to the spot in the centre of the tray. Bass tapped Dylan on the arm, pointing to two empty chairs off to one side of the stage. They took their seats up close, mouths wide open. Dylan studied the club, mesmerised by how it had been transformed from a band venue to this, something he couldn't take his eyes off. A carnival of stripped women. The lanky girl on stage flapped her knees like butterfly wings. The music changed tempo, Open Up by Leftfield featuring John Lydon kicked out. She peeled off her underwear, leaving her boots laced up. She flicked her thong free into the lunchtime crowd. A man with a yellow stained beard and gold capped front tooth caught the underwear, shoving them over his nostrils like he was sniffing chloroform, his eyes churned as he flopped back in his seat.

Dylan leaned into Bass, shouting into his ear. "I didn't know they got completely naked. I can see everything."

Bass laughed and said. "Now you've looked her in the eye. She'll shake her pint glass for a pound."

"I thought we could just sit here."

"How can you not tip her with a delicate fanny like that? It's only polite, mate."

"I don't know the rules."

"Just go with it. Learn to love it."

As Lydon's vocals faded, the glistening naked woman strutted toward them, thigh muscles clenching, breasts firm. She gripped an empty pint glass. Bass held up two shiny pound coins, grinning, clanking them into the bottom of the glass. He winked. She returned a fake, forced grimace, cupping her own breast, plucking her left nipple.

"You know where to find me, if you want part deux." She said, swaggering around the stage, holding out the glass, accepting pound coin shrapnel as tokens of appreciation. She worked the crowd. Kisses on stumbled cheeks, compliments, flirting and her sweeping palm on forearms for all those that folded paper notes, stuffing them in her glass. She sauntered to the centre of the stage, scooped up her leather bra, and waved to the crowd. They threw her G string back to the stage. As she bent down to retrieve it, the crowd enjoyed another loose lipped eyeful, clapping and cheering. She bowed, jogging off the stage, her jelly bottom jiggling, breasts solid like wood.

"How often you been here for this?" said Dylan.

"I can't resist it, mate. They put on a good buffet." Said Bass, waggling his outstretched fingers. "Delicious finger sandwiches." He nodded off into the distance, as if trying to attract someone's attention. Dylan tried to see what he was seeing. The pit lane girl glided into his eye line as she approached their table, tray tucked under her toned arm. Dylan got lost in her slow motion approach. Hazel eyes sucking him in.

"What can I get you both?" She said, her lips shimmering with rose pink lip gloss. Dylan side eyed her body as she knelt beside him, her slight hand gripping the arm of his seat.

"Zoe." Said Bass with a smarmy smile, not taking his eyes off her enhanced round breasts. He kissed her on the back of her hand. "This is Dylan."

She flashed him a smiling glance. "Hi Dylan," she dragged her hand from Bass's. "I'm Zoe." She stroked his arm. Dylan nodded, his foot tapping like a telegram arm. He noticed the tiny nose piercing in her left nostril, sparkling in the light.

"Zoe, babe, can we have two double whisky and Cokes?" said Bass.

"Doubles?" Said Dylan with wide-eyed shock, his hands clasped tight.

"Relax. And get yourself a pussy juice."

"Pussy juice? What the hell is that?" Said Dylan, shaking his head.

"It's what us girls drink, sweetness."

"He's new to this. It makes them ready for anything. Isn't that right, babe?"

"That's right." She said, nodding with impatience. "You can relax, sweetie. Don't be nervous."

"You know what you're doing, though. Get us drunk and stupid, so we part with our pin numbers."

Zoe chuckled, leaned in, and whispered into Dylan's ear. "It's not all about the money, babe. Some of us enjoy it." She said and poked her stiff tongue into his ear. "It depends if they're cuties like you." Her lips pressed against his cheek.

Dylan smiled, trying to conceal his bashful eyes behind red-cheeked embarrassment as Zoe sauntered away, resting her hand over her shoulders. The tray flopped down on her defined back. She peered back, timid. Dylan was enchanted. Dry mouthed, he studied her hips, the material of her shorts riding up, exposing the slightest crease of her tight buttocks.

"Zoe's amazing, mate." Said Bass. "She has that gap between her legs, right up to her arse. I told ya, this place is fucking great."

"She seems nice."

"Trust me. They're all nice, if you make it rain," said Bass. "It's time to relax, kick off your shoes." The lights dimmed as the club simmered silent. "Here comes Lee with her tight little pussy. Bouncing her tat- tat-tatties."

Dylan looked up to see a petite, milk white, Asian girl, no obvious hips, sat atop a rainbow coloured space hopper, sucking her thumb. Wearing a tiny novelty school uniform. The blue checked short tie covered her surgically enhanced cleavage, breasts too large for her tiny frame. Spindly legs covered with white, thigh high tights, pulled over her knees.

"Tatties?" Dylan shook his head, his voice getting lost in the piano introduction of REO Speedwagon, Can't Fight this Feeling. Passion red strobe lights blinked on and off. Lee bounced up, launching the space hopper off to the side of the stage. She floated in stiletto heals, tugging at the tie, sweeping it around her neck like a noose before dropping it to the floor. She wrapped her stick legs around the silver pole, sliding and dry humping the floor. Her skirt riding up, exposing her matching thong. Black heals kicked off as she rolled onto her back, placing two fingers in the air, dropping them into her crotch, tapping her pubic bone twice, along with the beat, teasing the onlooking crowd with a waggle of her stiff finger, adding to the tension she built from bouncing. She bent over, arching her back, crawling across the stage like a stalking tiger. She looked back over her shoulder and stood, stiff legged to her feet, bending forward, spreading her cheeks, kicked her legs out wide and circled on the spot. She, in time with the music ripped free the school shirt, two silicon breasts stayed stuck in place on her chest. The room erupted in loud grunting cheers as she pinched at her cocoa bean nipples.

"They're great, aren't they?" Said Bass, smacking Dylan's hand, as he emulated the size of her breasts on his own chest, gyrating his hips into the leather chair, copying her moves.

"You can see the incision," said Dylan.

Bass ignored him, biting his bottom lip, shoulders swaying to the music. He refused to take his eyes off her.

"You're welcome upstairs," said Zoe. Her warm breath on Dylan's ear. He was shocked to see who spoke. She bent down at his side, stroking his hand. "It's quieter upstairs. You can bring your drink." She dipped two fingers into the glass and sucked them dry. "We can carry on talking up there."

Dylan looked over at Bass, still staring at the performance on the stage, his face cast in deep blue disco lights. Zoe smiled again, tilting her head, beckoning Dylan to go with her. She took him by the hand. His heart thumped in his chest. He swallowed. Saw her little finger flick like a concentrating snooker player. Zoe grabbed his glass, locking her fingers between his, not letting go. She pushed her way through the crowd. Some guys patted Dylan on the shoulders as he trailed behind. Others shook his shoulders as if it was some form of public encouragement. Zoe marched across the dance floor, past the long bar. To the other side of the club. Dylan noticed the familiar wall of Polaroids. The mysterious small green door was before him. Now, considering he would see behind it, he attempted to imagine.

Zoe knocked once, waited. Knocked again. Nothing.

"Don't look so scared," she said.

She knocked again. The door popped open toward her. She hopped back into Dylan. Smiled up at him, pressing her hot pant covered cheeks into his groin. She forced a fake breathy orgasm from her open mouth. The high-pitched whine repeated over and over in his mind. The landlord looked Dylan up and down.

"O room is vacant," said the landlord. He gulped a tumbler of dark rum.

Dylan looked around. Landlord stood in a velvet curtained cloakroom. Ahead of them was a narrow, steep, black painted, wooden staircase. Landlord passed Zoe a large key with a red letter 'O' attached as a keyring.

"And now for my O face," She said. "Can't say I'm predictable." She took Dylan by the hand, smiling.

"Get on with it." Said the landlord as he raised his glass to Dylan, nodding.

Zoe ascended the cold staircase, taking her time to climb, squeezing Dylan's warm hand. He concentrated on every step he took, his trainers pressing down, toes clenching. He considered his breathing. Zoe's back twitched. Reaching the top of the stairs, a red lit, narrow hallway with deep red, patchy plush carpet stretched out before them. Doors mirrored one another on each side of the hallway. No window at the bottom or fire exit, just a black iron radiator affixed to a bare brick wall. Zoe continued along to the last door on the left. The letter 'O' screwed to the flaky paint at eye level.

"Relax. You look so tense." She said, unlocking the door. "Kick off your shoes."

Dylan took a deep breath, stood on the back of his heals without unlacing his trainers. Zoe cracked the door open, stepping inside. The room was plum coloured, with a soft cushioned floor. Dylan bounced, waggling his toes in his socks.

"This place is like the Tardis," he said.

"I know right, it's deceiving from the outside." Said Zoe, clicking the door locked behind them. "I'm gonna freshen up, babe. You get undressed, lay over there on the massage bed." She pointed at the black leather, professional looking massage table. A purple towel laid flat over it. "Cover yourself with a towel. I'll be back in a minute."

"Zoe," said Dylan after her. "I'm not sure how this works. I can't pay for this."

"Don't worry, honey, all taken care of. You get yourself relaxed." She snapped on the light of a small bathroom, checking her brown eyes in the mirror as she smiled back from the reflection.

Dylan's eyes examined every corner of the simple room. The massage table left dents in the soft floor. A raised bed, purple silk sheets ironed flat. Single pole fixed from the floor to the ceiling. No windows. Slow, relaxing spa sounding music played from speakers, somewhere. He couldn't find them. He sniffed a damp lavender and sandalwood smell in the air. Flames flickered from lit candles on a stainless steel, corner shelving unit. Folded towels, oils and an intricately designed wooden box.

He caught his own reflection in the round mirror above the bed, shaking his head. He unzipped his jeans. Picturing Laura sat stony faced, legs crossed on the edge of the bed. His jeans concertinaed to the floor. He removed his hoodie, pressed two fingers to his neck, checking his pulse. He peeled off his socks, clambered up onto the massage bed, and laid down. The exposed leather was cold against his skin. He looked again at the space on the bed he had imagined Laura. She had since disappeared. He pressed his hot face into the cutout hole in the headrest. Pulled a towel up over his legs and covered his back. The light from the bathroom shone in, Zoe's shadow figure closed in on him. Her brunette hair free from pigtails, dangling to her naked buttocks.

"You should have removed your boxers, sweetie."

"Oh, sorry."

"Bless you. Do you have any preference on the oil?"

"Mazola." He said, giggling to himself.

Zoe slapped his exposed thighs. She read the labels of small glass bottles. "I have Hot Mist, Love Shine or Glistening Passion. Ya know what, I'll pick." She rubbed her squelching hands together. Pressed them on his goose pimpled back and walked around in front of him. He could see through the headrest hole, she was wearing a white gold ankle bracelet. He read the tattoo inscription around the middle of her right thigh. 'Love Life' in a Latino sweeping font, like gangland graffiti.

"Do you?" he said.

Zoe stopped rubbing her hands together. "Do I what, baby?"

"Love life?"

"Oh." She looked down, smiling at her own thigh. "What other choice is there, flower?"

"Do you work here full time?"

"You ask a lot of questions. No, I don't. I work for Bupa during the day. Now, stop talking."

Dylan expanded his chest, breathing deep as Zoe's hands pushed air from his lungs. Cracking his back along the spine, she worked her knuckles into knots in his shoulder blades. Rubbed her stiff fingers over his lats and pushed her thumbs into pressure points in his neck. Her thumbs kneaded his lower back. She wrenched at his boxer shorts, over his hips, peeled them down his legs, over his ankles, dropping them to the floor. Warm hands applied oil to his naked buttocks, slapping his cheeks like full stop punctuation.

"Roll over," she said.

Red faced, and breathing heavy. "I'm not sure I can," he said.

"Don't worry sweetie, for this to end happily. You need to be hard. Now, roll over."

Dylan shuffled around, laying flat on his back, cool air enveloping his throbbing groin. Zoe made no attempt to hide her eyeful examination. She smirked, then clicked a remote control. Guns and Roses, Night Train began playing out from the discreet speakers. Her soft voice singing along with the lyrics, her hips rolling with seduction to the beat. He caught sight of her swollen, naked breasts. A white feather tattoo drew his eyes to her dark-haired landing strip of pubic hair. He compared her wiry hair to the etched mental image of Laura's blonde strip. Zoe's teeth ripped at a sealed foil condom, the latex held between her lips, resembling a blow-up doll. He convulsed and flinched as she disappeared between his legs. The music echoed to distorted tinnitus.

* * *

Bass tucked a wad of money into the awaiting sweaty palm of the Landlord. He thumbed the loose notes, dropping them in a red lock box.

"Your boy is dirty." Said Landlord to Bass. "She had him eating her arse." Landlord poked at the eject button on one of eight video recorders, beneath a network of black and white television monitors hidden behind the velvet curtains. A VHS tape rumbled from the machine. Landlord slipped it inside a plain white cardboard sleeve, passing it to Bass.

"Not sure I'll bring myself to watch this one." Said Bass, shoving it in the front pocket of his hoodie, tapping it in place.

"Zoe lived up to the job, as she always does," said Landlord. "Check this guy out." He pointed at a monitor marked 'Room E'."Annabelle convinced him to shove a bull whip up his arse. I'm telling ya, primary school teachers are the shady ones. Pure filth and they're teaching our bloody kids."

"Are they done yet?" said Bass.
Landlord looked up from a sudoku puzzle, studied the 'O' room monitor. "Nah. All very romantic. They're taking a shower."

Bass smiled to himself and watched the Landlord scratch the number seven in a blank sudoku box.

12

tErRiBle liE

Florence scratched crusty, dry sleep from the corner of her eye.
Wearing tracksuit bottoms, white baggy t-shirt and flip-flops. She
shuffled into the shared kitchen, clutching a plain hessian bag in her
arms like a baby. She shoved a tub of Horlicks behind a crumb laden
toaster. Unlocked a small padlock on a cracked cupboard door,
removed a bag of basmati rice, an almost empty bottle of mirin, ginger
paste and garlic. Removing one item at a time, and laid it out on the
counter like an episode of Ready Steady Cook, turning each to read
the label. She examined a packet of garam masala, holding it up to the
florescent tube light. Her attention drawn to an open bag of four
hotdog buns, gnawed and jammed in the gap under the gas cooker.
Tutting and shaking her head, she glared toward Dylan's closed
bedroom door with squint-eyed accusation and retrieved the buns
with an impatient swipe. She turned the bag over, noticing chunks of
bread missing. Her clenched fist was close to rapping at Dylan's door
for an interrogation. Well timed coincidence had Dylan poke his blurry

eyes from inside his bedroom, wearing only his boxers.

"Ayubowan, Dylan," said Florence. "I almost woke you up, anyway."

"Morning Shreen." Said Dylan, yawning. His eyes adjusting to the bright light of the kitchen.

Florence winced and pulled her head back. "Morning breath," she said.

"Is it morning still?" He asked, scratching his left nipple.

Florence huffed. "Only just." She waved the bag of buns in front of his face. "You eat my buns?"

He looked at the buns. "No," he said, stepped forward and examined more closely. "Where did you find that? It's got rat shit in it."

"Rat shit?" She said, holding the bag with a pinch between her fingers.

"Yeah, looks like droppings." Said Dylan, pointing with his little finger.

"Shit."

"Literally," he said.

"I'll get Mitra here, put poison down again. Damn rat, eating my buns." She stamped the bin lid open with her foot like a kick drum and slam dunked the hotdog buns. "You look rough as the balls." Florence poked him in the stomach. "I can't see your rib cage anymore."

Dylan looked down, pinching his skin, and shrugged.

"You want coffee?" she said.

"Black please. You on the green tea?"

Florence looked over the top of her glasses. "You need to ask?" She clanked two mugs down. "Was it good night?" The power button on the kettle glowed orange.

Dylan stretched up, using the door frame to arch his back. "From what I remember, it was."

"Were you out with." She paused and spooned coffee into a cup.

"That new lady of yours, the Laura?"

"No, that's tonight." He said, searching his mind. "I hope."

Florence crossed her arms, staring at the rumbling kettle. "What you mean, you hope?" The kettle popped. She jolted forward, filling the mugs.

"I did something that she wouldn't be happy with."

She held the mug by the rim. "Here go. Drink that." She said, blowing cool air over the surface of her green tea.

"Is Bass here?" he said.

"I not seen him." She blew again. "Why?"

"I'm pretty sure he can explain a lot of this." He placed the mug down. "Too hot. So many things made the whole thing unrealistic."

"No, really?" She sipped her tea. "You have the sex—, You had the sex didn't you?"

"Don't act so surprised."

"I am surprised." She pinched Dylan's nipple. "You're really getting it some now."

"The expression is getting some and why," he batted her hand away. "You jealous?"

"Shreenika, don't do jealous, babes."

"You mean Florence."

"With you," she said. "I revert. When I arrive in the halls with you guys. It was only you who wanted to know where I was from." She stabbed her finger on the counter. "Like point pin. Everyone thought it was Colombo. You wanted to know exactly." She said with a wide-eyed smile.

He sipped his coffee, breathing hot air. "Wow, still too hot. I was interested."

"I know." She said, clanking a saucepan, filling it with water. "I think it sweet." She looked back over her shoulder. "Then you did that inspector thing."

"My perfect impression of Columbo, you mean." He scratched his hairline and flicked an imaginary cigar. "You should use

Shreenika," he said. "Lotus in the heart of Lord Vishnu."

Florence giggled. "That's it." She used a blue lighter to ignite the gas stove. "You remember."

"Of course, I remember." Dylan watched on as she steadied the saucepan.

"You seemed to care." She flicked a generous pinch of rock salt in the water. "Florence is nice, too. I just like name. It means I'm free and need not worry about war." She flopped on her elbows, leaning on the kitchen counter.

"I thought you were Chinese."

"Bastard." She chuckled and slapped him on the shoulder. "Everyone says this. Although you actually say, Taipei."

"You just don't look, Sri Lankan." Dylan swallowed more coffee. "It's your eyes. I still get lost in them."

"Come on now." Florence looked soft eyed over her glasses again. "None of the charm," she said.

"I can't help it. You're just pint-sized cuteness."

Florence examined the water in the saucepan, tiny bubbles zig zagging to the surface. "You must still be juiced." She stirred the water with a metal spoon. "We've had that chat."

"I know, I know, we're not meant to be. Your with Yest. I'm with Laura. So, what's your advice, what am I gonna tell her?"

Florence opened a small square packet of crackers. "Tell her truth." She nibbled on a corner. "It's an important thing to keep." She put a cracker in Dylan's waiting open mouth. "Since I left, it's all I have," she said.

He crunched. "The truth—?" He said, his dry mouth swallowing. "I don't know how to. I slept with a stripper."

Florence's mouth dropped. "You can't."

"Did you just call me a cunt?"

Florence shook her head. "No." She pushed her glasses up her nose. "You can't tell her that. She'll kill you dead, as you sleep, walking. I never thought you, Dylan, was a cheater."

"I'm not, really I'm not—,"

"It's probably a good thing we're not together. If you did that to me. I'd stab you with this spoon."

"That's what I mean. It was almost too perfect. I didn't think about her once. Well, I kind of did a bit. Not during. I was expecting to think about her."

"Sometimes the lust outweighs the mind. If you had the alcohol. Nothing matters. Check you out though, sex with strippers. There's no stopping you now, dirty boy."

"Once you pop."

"Pop what?"

"Nevermind." Dylan rubbed his palm across the back of his neck. "It feels like I want to sweat," he said.

"You're probably dehy-dra-nated."

"Dehydrated." He said, correcting her.

Florence giggled and planted her eyes on his belly button. He looked down and covered himself with his forearm, embarrassed. It was enough to break Florence free of her distraction.

"I've got this new sense of responsibility. I feel like I need to tell her. I care about her," he said.

Florence pushed herself up off the counter, peered over the rim of the now bubbling water. She looked back at Dylan, swung open the cupboard door under the sink, bent over at the waist. Her grey track suit bottoms, riding up, biting between the crevice of her bottom. Dylan exhaled as he stared, realising she was wearing no underwear, naked underneath. Florence held the position, looked back, catching him looking and raised up slow and considered. For Dylan, it reminded him of the strippers, teasing. She left the cupboard door open. Clattered a plastic, stained chopping board down on the surface, not taking her eyes off of Dylan's.

"Who knew being in a relationship was such hard work," he said.

"The chase is often more exciting." She said, raising her slight, plucked eyebrows.

Dylan rolled his tongue over his bottom lip. "It can cause some serious movement."

Florence looked at his loose, black boxer shorts as she chopped a carrot in half. Dylan gulped coffee.

"It's too early," she said. "You not survive." She held the knife up, pointing it at him. "I would let gone. If Yest told me that. That would be it, over." She sliced through the air with the blade, as if she was slashing a throat.

"Goes without saying. That's what worries me. I don't know what happened. Maybe I can text her?"

"If you have to, tell her eyes." She pointed with stiff fingers at her own eyes. "Don't text her. How would you feel?"

"Are you happy with Yestin?"

"Of course. Why you ask—, I mean, we have our problems."

"We used to get on, him and me. Now, I'm not so sure."

"Not so sure. Be better at hiding the way you look at me. He's not silly one. We had talks about moving out because he doesn't trust you. 'No more hugging', he said. 'He holds you too long. You don't hug Bass like that', he says."

"We're friends. I can't help it if Yest is jealous."

"We are the friends, but you are cheeky one. Trying to stroke my ankles that night I was telling you about Tamils."

"I hadn't heard anything like that before. I only wanted to comfort you."

Florence looked out toward the front door, checking no one was listening, whispering. "It was a lovely moment. Bad time that he walked in on us. Like you always say, it's easy for us talking. We have that." She clicked her fingers, searching for words. "What's that thing you say?"

"Cosmic synergy," he said.

"Cosmic synergy. We have that. For now though—,"

A crash and a rattle came from under the kitchen sink. Their hearts pounded in their chests, looking round at a saucepan circling to a stop on the floor. A squeak, as a greasy-haired fat rat stood up on its back feet, its grey nose twitching, sniffing the air. Florence screamed. Tossed the knife in its direction. The rat darted back inside the cupboard, kicking a cheese grater with its hind legs. Dylan smacked the door closed with bare feet, slamming it shut. He could feel Florence's soft, loose, moving breasts pressing against his naked chest. She wrapped her arms around him and squeezed tight. Out of breath, they giggled. Florence shifted her body, her hips aligned with his. She looked up at his avocado green eyes. He studied her oval face, looking down and losing himself in her chocolate allure. They held each other. Dylan swept her hair behind her ears. The front door clicked shut.

Yestin stared into the kitchen.

Dylan and Florence looked pale faced, mouths open. Yestin clenched his teeth, dropping his Tesco shopping bag. A thick vein throbbed in his temple.

Florence pushed herself off of Dylan and said. "It was rat. We've got a rat in the kitchen."

Yestin shifted forward, fists clenched. "And, his name's Dylan."

13

b AlLrOoM cAnCeR

Bass stubbed out a half-smoked cigarette in the novelty Rasta ashtray, brimming with spent dog ends. Holding smoke in his lungs, his foot tapped the carpet.

"Relax. She'll be here. Cool yer foot." Said Laura, rolling her eyes.

In realisation of her annoyance, his foot became steel heavy. Then, a jaws harp twang sprang out as he flicked the ring pull of his lager can. The dowdy living room was quiet, other than the fuzzy, crackling signal from the TV in the corner.

"I still can't believe you chose him over me." He said, shaking his head.

Laura shrugged. "The heart wants what the heart wants. Get over it."

"He hasn't told you then?" Said Bass, placing the ashtray at his feet, a dog-end escaping to the carpet.

"Told me what?"

Bass held a toothy, self-righteous smile. Powerful and dangerous, yearning to blurt the truth.

Dylan drifted into the light of the living room, standing in the doorway and said. "Everything good?"

Laura kept her eyes on Bass, shifted to Dylan's and smiled. "All gravy, baby."

The front doorbell chimed, followed by a heavy, clenched fist knock on wood. Dylan held his gaze on Laura. Then opened the latch on the front door.

"This is a raid." Said a gravelly female voice, exhaling a cloud of white smoke from a hand-rolled cigarette, stepping inside the house.

"Here she is, look." Said Laura, smiling toward the doorway.

"Here she is indeed," said Sofia. "Hey babe," she nodded at Laura, clearing her throat. "Right, where's this guy, Bass?"

Bass turned in his seat. Unable to control his bulging saucer white eyes. He looked Sofia up and down, noticing his reflection in her thick soled, high heeled black boots, with noodle thick white laces, laced up over her ankles. Black woollen socks cascading over her cauldron footwear, seven denier, black tights exposed the contour of her delicate knees, thin legs disappeared under black leather hot pants, with a silver studded anarchist symbol over one hip. She removed her brown suede jacket, that looked secondhand, worn tan coloured patches on the elbows, flicking it over the back of the sofa. Her Golden Virginia tobacco poach slipped out onto the cushion. Hex Enduction Four printed on her black t-shirt. Red hair spilled out from a faded black beanie, like flames over her shoulders. She snatched hold of the lager can Bass held in his hand and put it to her lips, swallowing the contents in one proud, magnanimous effort. She grabbed Laura and planted her lips on her forehead before slouching on the sofa next to Bass, her feet kicking up into the air. He scoped her long legs from laces to gusset, nodding in appreciation. She smiled, tossed the empty can in his lap, looked him up and down, shifting in her seat toward him.

"Look." She grabbed her bottom lip between her thumb and

forefinger, peeling it down, opening her mouth. "I got 'cunt' tattooed on the inside of my lip."

Bass read the scrawling faded ink. "Yes, you do, why?"

"Why the fuck not?" she said. She ruffled her red painted fingernails through her danger bright hair. "Today my hair is red. Tomorrow it'll be green. I might wear hotpants with a unicorn on 'em. I may even wear bleached jeans. Then I'll fucking rip 'em apart with my teeth. Just because I can. Who the hell are you to tell me otherwise?"

"I'm not telling you anything." Said Bass, his hands submissive.

"That wasn't a question," she said.

"Introductions aside," said Laura. "You know that new band is playing tonight?"

"You like punk music?" said Bass.

Sofia huffed and said. "Is that a real question? You seen how I'm dressed—, Rites of Spring have to be my favourite band."

"Rites of what? Who are they?" Said Bass, looking at Dylan for support, shaking his head.

"You mean to say there's a band that you, Bass. The maven of punk music hasn't heard of. That can't be right, can it?" Said Laura, with a beaming smile.

Dylan guffawed.

"Fugazi. You must have heard of Fugazi. Birthday Pony, back to base. You look a bit like Guy Picciotto," said Sofia. "Their first album was fucking lush. Depending how this works out and I don't mean marriage. You can borrow it. Laura told me you're in a band."

"I play bass. Hence my name."

"Oh, I assumed you were into smoking crack." Said Sofia and rolled a cigarette without looking at her fingers. "I can settle for a bass player. I was with the lead singer of Howard's Alias for a bit."

"Howard's Alias?"

"Yeah, I'm a bit of a groupie for Household Name. Capdown know me very well."

"I've got Civil Disobedience," said Bass.

"Fuck me. Everyone needs it in their life. I used to use my brother's Rocksteady figure to get off on, rocking to that album."

"What about poor Bebop?" Said Dylan in a whisper, as he sat next to Laura, placing his hand on her knee.

"See, told ya, you two would get on." Said Laura, offering out her soft hand for Dylan to take hold. As he shuffled on the sofa, she curled her feet behind her, leaning into him, lifting his arm around her shoulder.

Sofia sparked her lighter to ignite the rollie between her lips. It failed. Bass, with pride, held his flaming lighter out. She moved the white scrunched paper tip to the orange flame and inhaled. The flame snapping off as Bass released his finger.

With brief contemplation to phone for a taxi. Sofia, adamant and argumentative that they walk. She stood at the front door with her palm out, feeling for rain. When there was none, they walked the winding roadway around the side of the gold mosque at the end of the road. She dropped to her knees in the middle of the asphalt, bowing in time to the wailing filling the setting sky from the speakers inside. There was an agreement. It was just after 6PM. Laura checked her wristwatch: 6.11PM. Too early to venture to the Pot. Sofia shook her head, insisting they were not to be the first to arrive. They played three rounds of pool at a quiet, smokey pub on route. Laura compared it to 'smelling like a platypus arse', drawing much debate between the four of them, that no one was confident about what that might even smell like. Sofia hid her pint glass under her arm inside her suede jacket. She offered Laura a sip as they darted between cars. With the pint glass back in her clutch, she stopped dead centre, boots resting on the middle white line. Cars beeped horns as they passed. Undeterred, her neck tilted to the blue hour, the brown liquid contents disappeared down her throat. Bass whispered to Dylan that he approved of Sofia. Pointing out the length of her legs, as she joined them on the safety of the pavement. Car headlights shimmered off her dark tights. Bass studied them again, up to her black hot pants. There were proud positive descriptions passed between them in hushed tones as the girls walked ahead. Bass biting his index finger, he was hungry to devour Sofia. As they walked through the town centre, darkness now had fallen. Sofia stopped with the scuff of her boots on gritty, cobbled stone. She inspected her empty pint glass and launched it at the front window of Woolworth's. It exploded into light, reflecting pieces like a disco ball, encouraging loud shouts of disapproval from further along the high street. Bass, Dylan, and Laura bolted to a side alley. Sofia refused to run, instead sauntered behind with her head wagging from side to side, as if she didn't have a care in the world. To her, it was a Sunday afternoon country stroll. She placed yet another rolled up cigarette between her lips and inhaled.

The quartet reached The Pot, a long line of people queuing down the basement steps to enter. Sofia bowled over, pushing herself past punks, goths, and casual townies.

"What is this shit?" Shouted a skinhead from the back of the line.

"Leave the gal alone, brudda." Said a black guy with a scar above his eyebrow. He whispered in the skinhead's ear. "Move from me."

"I'm not here on my own, you know," the skinhead grimaced.

"As you can see, me 'ave me boys too, man."

The skinhead's eyes darted, spotting two hench guys behind, in the shadows. Stepping forward.

"Me 'ave one piece of advice, grow yer hair. Trouble man, be asking."

The skinhead turned on the spot, chains rattling against his hip, as he stepped forward, closing the gap in front.

A bald bouncer recognised Sofia, emerging through her usual white smoke, and beckoned her forward with an upward nod. Impatient tuts rang out from the queue as she cat walked to the bottom of the steps. Murmurs of odium from other girls, still waiting in line. The bouncer winked and let them enter without paying. Sofia clasped his tight bicep. Bass looked on, noticing the twitching vein in the hefty man's arm. Sofia kissed the bouncer on the cheek, creating a loud puckering noise. He squeezed her right butt cheek, tapping it twice to encourage her to step over the threshold of the Pot. She stroked her nails over the dagger tattoo on his neck. Bass was impressed, then jealous that his beloved local music venue welcomed Sofia first, over him. He felt anonymous for the first time.

Bass and Sofia looked at each other as the thunderous opening of Hook, Line and Sinker by Refused roared around the club. They head banged along with the lyrics. The dance floor filled with other appreciators of the hardcore music. High kicking boots and elbows being thrown.

Laura's warm breath on Dylan's ear. They shared drinks, cigarettes, and eye contact. Finding a table in the back of the Pot. She draped herself over his shoulder, still whispering in his ear. Dylan flinched with ticklish excitement. He studied the now familiar wall of Polaroids from the table. He noticed a shaft of white light coming from the gap under the small green door in the corner. Glanced at Laura, ensuring she had not seen his mischievous distraction. He pictured Zoe backing her arse into his crotch. That sugary, energy drink smell of Pussy Juice on her breath. He smiled, remembering walking behind her, indulging in the sight of her tight bottom ascending the stairs to the massage room of happy endings.

"What you thinking about?" said Laura.

Dylan inhaled, bringing him back to his nightclub reality. "Nothing. Just happy to be here with you."

"That's sweet, Masugar," she said. She pressed her lips on his, eyes closed tight. "Crusher, crusher."

Sofia cracked her glass down on the table and slumped in a seat opposite. Bass joined like a lapdog, almost in awe of her confidence.

He couldn't take his eyes off her.

"If you two kiss." Said Sofia, flicking her finger like a pendulum between Bass and Dylan. "Laura and I'll get off with each other."

"I hate that expression," said Laura.

"You'll love my tongue though, bitch." Said Sofia, winking.

Dylan scowled, looking over at Bass, his head recoiling in confusion.

"For that sight. I'm happy to take one for the team, bro." Bass said, standing up from his seat, jogged around the table, slapped his hands on Dylan's cheeks, pulled him forward and put his mouth on his, forcing his slithering tongue in his mouth. As they separated, Dylan took a wide-eyed intake of breath, having been caught by surprise.

"A deals a deal." Said Bass, sitting in his seat, dabbing at the corner of his mouth with his little finger. "Wait. Wait. Wait. I need a cigarette." He clicked his fingers twice at Dylan. Laura cut her eye at him, trying to catch Dylan's attention. He removed his packet of Marlboro's from his pocket and presented them for Bass to retrieve one. Laura shook her head, disappointed he didn't stand up for himself. Bass jabbed his fingers inside, shifting in his seat, exaggerating his excitement to watch the two girls kiss.

Laura took a swig from her drink and smiled at Dylan. Sofia removed her chewing gum from her mouth, still holding a rollie between her other fingers, flicking it into the full ashtray, leaned forward in her seat. Bass tilted his head back to gain a better side eye vantage of Sofia's hotpants riding between her butt cheeks. He smirked and flashed his eyebrows at Dylan. Some eyes of the pub turned as the two girls inched closer, with eyes closed over the table. Bass moved pint glasses out of the way of their drooping clothes.

"You wish." Said Sofia, laughing. She stopped and sat back.

"Psyche." Said Laura, sitting back in her seat. "More fool you, sweet cheeks." She looked at Dylan. "Don't be so impressionable. These lips are yours and not just these lips." She said, pushing her fingertip against her mouth.

"I didn't suggest anything," said Dylan. "His face was rough. My lips are only meant for you, too."

"Don't deny me, sugar. Plant them here," she said.

Bright beaming spotlights shone distraction, cutting into eyes, from the other end of the club. Loud crocodile hand claps erupted. Heads turned to the commotion. Three guys strutted onto the stage, one picking up a bass guitar, ankle socks tucked deep into his skater trainers, another inserted a guitar cable, nodding at the crowd, a Union Jack plectrum between his teeth. One topless with pierced nipples sat at the drum kit. His pristine hair alone encouraged high pitched appreciation from females in the crowd. Then, a thick hip, blonde girl leapt up onto the stage from the front row of the jostling crowd, wearing baggy flared khaki trousers, revealing her skull covered underwear. Her braided hair with pink dyed tips spilled over a green visor. She yanked the microphone from its stand, wrapping the cable around her wrist, plonked the stand down, pulled a cigarette from her cleavage. A narrow lighter flame sparked from the front row. The confident lead singer bent over, suckling the burning tip. Male heads shifted, glancing down her top.

"Hi. Buna. Ahoj." She said, one hand twiddling her hair. "We're Ballroom Cancer."

The crowd cheered. A glass smashed from behind the bar. No one paid attention.

"I'm Tiff," she said. "Radish on Bass," she pointed. Radish nodded, tuning his E string. "The guy with his milkers out is Pete," she coughed. Pete poked his tongue between narrow lips, squeezing his left nipple. The crowd hollered. "Shooter on guitar." Shooter, with a mechanic's style shirt, saluted. "We're gonna play a few songs, whether you like it or not. They won't be anything like that fucking D:Ream. You'll realise in life, nothing'll get better. Blair has raped this country. Trust me children. We ain't seen the worst of it yet. This first song is called Egg the Elite. That Prescott jab still sickens me. Next election, vote them mother fuckers out." The crowd roared as the lights dimmed.

Drum sticks clicked together. "One, two, three, four." Said Pete, his eyes squeezed shut. His shoulders clenched as he smacked on drum skin. Three power chords kicked out. Tiff tapped her foot, flicked ash from her cigarette, and poked her naked belly button with her free little finger.

Bass and Sofia hopped up from the table, squeezing their way through the crowd. They stood in the front row, Sofia laced with alcohol, took hold of Bass's arms and wrapped them round her waist. He moulded his groin into her bottom, jeans scrapping leather. She took hold of his hand, slid it down the front of her hotpants. Pete, the drummer, looked on, smirking, and flapped his serpent tongue. The song slowed, bass pedal cracked like a heartbeat, snare drum sizzled as the hi-hats whispered together.

"Thank you, thank you." Said Tiff, sipping from a pint glass. "This next one is called Census."

14

fIgHtIng mAN

The Pot breathed with a dissident life of its own. Sweat dripped from Bass's forehead. The waxy peaks of his hair were no longer magazine page perfection. Sofia swayed, crystal eyes closed tight, her ears popped. She threw her arms out like a puppet, kicking her knees in time to Clit 45's, Bullshit fucking waste of time. Drums thrashed from the sound system. Spiky mohawks cut through smoke. Personalities faded as exhaustion crashed into a comedown. Raucous cheers pulsated into murmurs. Shoulders dipped, sweat stained arm pits, squeezed tight into bodies. The DJ mixed tracks without silence, shot glasses stacked on the decks. AFI, The Boy who Destroyed the World, thumped out as two girls, one in a bright pink flowing pom pom skirt, the other luminous yellow, both wearing backpacks, invaded the stage and danced to heedless whistles from the crowd. Their pig tails flapped to the chorus, light caught their reflective backpacks, one a Pound Puppies bag, too small to contain anything. The other had a cartoon image of Janine Melnitz and Slimer from The Real Ghostbusters emblazoned on the back. Their white furry tongues probed each other's as glazed eyes looked on, distracting themselves from paranoia.

Laura squeezed a pint glass in one hand and pulled Dylan into her pillow lips.

"We have to talk about you going away." She said, her tone laced with sour reluctance.

Dylan sat up straight, scrambled for the cigarette packet amongst puddles of spilled alcohol on the table in front of them, stuffing his nicotine pacifier between his lips.

"It's only for nine weeks," he said.

"Nine weeks is three months."

"Yeah, but weeks sounds better than months."

"I don't want spin or semantics, you bellend. I want you to tell me." She pulled him in close, snatching the cigarette from his lips, resting her forehead against his. "Promise me, we're gonna be OK."

"Little lady, of course we are."

"Promise me."

"I promise."

"I know this'll be so hard for me."

"It's gonna be hard for me too—,"

"Yeah sure, a camp full of camel toe counsellors, all very Porky's."

"Porky's wasn't set on a camp."

"Whatever, you know what I mean."

"You have never used *camel toe* before."

"It's the Sambuca. Can't handle the liquorice, bitch."

"Can't control your dutty mouth either,"

"Dutty? Sean Paul will ruin you, white boy."

"You're fun when you're drunk," he said.

The small green door in the corner cracked open. For Dylan, it may as well have been in creeping slow motion. A smooth, tattooed, tanned leg poked through. Skin hugging tight shorts, a naked, pierced navel. All too familiar. Then her breasts. He exhaled, loud enough to make Laura skim her head to where he was staring. Zoe locked eyes on him and smirked, the slightest of cute smiles. Her brunette hair flowing down her back. Music video seduction as she strutted toward the table. Dylan shifting in his seat, clearing his throat, looking around to be saved, embodying his attempt at normality and cool.

"Hey Dylan." Said Zoe, her hands on her hips.

"Hi, hello, how are you? Yeah, good good." Said Dylan, a tremble rolling through his voice.

Zoe nodded at Laura, cracked a minute smile and swept her fingertips from his elbow to wrist. His eyes tracked her smooth fingers as goosebumps emerged. Laura's eyes transfixed, as if Zoe's fingertips were made of dynamite and gold. She sat up, scoping Zoe from head to toe as she walked away.

"Who the fuck was that?"

Dylan swallowed and said. "I think her name's Chloe, or Zoe or something. We're regulars here, you know that."

"She looked at you like she knew you really well. Too well for my liking."

Zoe leaned against the end of the bar, shaking her hair. Dylan maintained his fixed stare on the table, then back on Laura as she continued to side eye her from her seat, scowling.

"I'm telling ya, if that Zoe, Chloe bitch, keeps looking over here with her vulva—,"

"Jesus, her vulva?"

"Scoff all ya like. If she doesn't stop staring, well, who knows what I'll do."

"Relax. Coming here, rockin' the suburbs. You've got nothing to worry about. Leave her and her vulva alone."

"Why are you defending her?"

"Laura, I'm not defending her—,"

"When do you ever use my name? You're guilty."

"I'm not guilty. I don't know her. Seriously, not here, not when I'm in the States. Never. Like you said, it'll be just as hard for me. I'm gonna miss you so much. Like with anything, it'll be over and I'll be back. We'll be together."

"You better be right. What if I meet someone?"

"Well, you could meet someone now, whilst I'm here. When you go off to uni in Cambridge—,"

"Canterbury,"

"Whatever. When you go off, I'll be here. I'll be a part of it. It's the same thing. I don't go through life hoping for someone better. I've found you."

"Monogamy is tough,"

"Says you, worried about Zoe's vulva. Polygamy is tougher. It's just more people to lie to as well as yourself."

"You wouldn't be lying. Everyone knows the rules."

"This conversation is becoming surreal—,"

"You're telling me, you only know that girl from down here?"

"What girl?"

"Playing dumb won't save you. She's working the room like a whore."

Dylan looked over his shoulder. Male hands with calluses on knuckles squeezed Zoe's lower back. She spun in a circle on her tiptoes. Eyes of the lecherous examining her mammary offerings.

"We can still email," said Dylan. "I'll call you. I'm getting one of those prepaid phone card things."

"That was a seamless change of subject. I congratulate you." Said Laura, holding high noon eyes on Zoe. She stared at her from heel to the tip of her forty inch extensions. "I'm not looking forward to this. I can't believe you want to leave me."

"Hey," he moved her face to look at him with his finger. "I don't wanna leave you. All this was progressing before we got together. I didn't know I was gonna fall in love with you."

"You're in love with me?"

Dylan searched himself for emotion. "Well, yeah, you make me weak. I haven't felt whatever this is before. You give me this strength and Laura Nemerov has a nice ring to it."

"Alright, that'll do. I get it. You love me, don't ruin it. I'm still shooting daggers at that Zoe bitch."

Dylan laughed, his eyes attracted beyond Zoe, to the other end of the club, lights becoming brighter as The Pot prepared for closure.

Landlord bowled through the crowd on the dance floor, shoving bewildered twenty-four-hour party people in the back, moving them out of the way. He gripped Bass around the back of his arm, pulling him from the dance floor. Sofia stopped for a moment, then shook off the forceful interruption. She watched Bass's panicked face lurch away. Landlord plucked him behind the bar, into the yellow light of the kitchen. Stainless steel surfaces, microwaves with the doors removed, and empty metal beer barrels stacked near the fire exit. The music from the club drowned quieter, echoing off the stained white tiles.

"Have you shifted them?" Said Landlord, still holding Bass by the arm, squeezing harder.

"I've been trying." He said, squirming free from his grip. "It's slow at the moment." Red patchy welts fading.

"I've got an audience for those tapes. This is a student town, if you can't make it work. I'll find some other motherfucker to get my money."

"Trust me—,"

"I don't trust anyone who starts a sentence with *trust me*." Said Landlord, circling his head, his neck clicking.

"I'll get it done. I need my cut too. I've gotta pay rent."

"Get it done faster. You don't want me to assert myself with you, boy."

"Your daughter's who they want to see."

Landlord pushed Bass into a silver pull down dishwasher, denting the flimsy surface with the back of his head. His stiff fist bounced off his cheekbone with a lightning jab. Bass's left eye swelled, red and puffy. He shook his head to clear his blurry vision, sitting crumpled and contorted on the floor, looking up, seeing three Landlord figures merge to one, fist clenched, stiff, fat finger poking in his face.

"Everything all right, Daddy?"

Landlord, held his stare on Bass. Bass's head flopped to the side, looking at the doorway. Ruby, Landlord's daughter, filled the doorway.

"Business as usual, sweetheart. BAU. More flesh, darling."

Ruby looked at Bass for a beat longer, pulling her low cut top down with her hooked finger to expose more of her fleshy, pale, jiggling bosom.

"You can go now. Last round," said Landlord.

She backed out into the bar, jerked on an inch thick rope, dangling from a brass bell. "Last orders." She nodded at patient customers leaning forward on the bar.

"Don't make me crack you in the other eye." Said Landlord. "We have an agreement. Shift 'em."

He jerked Bass to his feet, brushing down his dishevelled t-shirt.

Bass, shaken, held his palm flat against his cheekbone, wincing.

"I don't want my phone ringing off anymore. You understand me?"

Bass nodded, squeezing one eye shut. "I can move 'em," he said.

"Now, tell me. Who are these people wanting to see my daughter and how much they willin' to pay?"

15

fLuFfy bLaCk eyE

Sofia suckled on her saliva soaked rollie.

"You're proper into this one, I can feel it. What happened with Charlie?"

Laura rolled her shoulders, shuffling forward on the sunken sofa in the living room, listening for movement from the kitchen.

"He still sniffs around. It's hard. He'll always be my first. The thing is, he knows that and he uses it against me," she said.

"Be careful. We all know what plum Charlie's after."

"He's a different person with me—,"

"Don't defend him. I've never liked him. I don't see what it is about that posh twat you like."

"We've got history,"

"Pol fucking Pot had history. You don't see me wanting to sit on his face." Said Sofia, untying her laces.

"Always with the eloquence," said Laura.

"I say it how it is. Charlie's a manipulator. A master manipulator at that. All I'm saying is, don't let him weasel his way back in your head, not if you like this Dylan, dude. He seems like a good guy."

"He is —, It makes me so uncomfortable when you're sincere."

"Gobble gobble, I'm gonna nosh that Bass off." Said Sofia, poking her tongue in her cheek.

"That's more like it. Welcome back."

Sofia flopped her head on Laura's shoulder as they giggled.

Dylan nudged the freezer door with his elbow. It sucked closed. Bass leaned against the kitchen counter, left eye squeezed shut, looking around the bright kitchen like a drunken periscope.

"We only have your green beans," said Dylan, shaking the frozen contents of a bag.

"I don't need anything, mate. The pints have helped."

"Seriously, you need ice on it. You're gonna have one hell of a shiner."

"I'm good." Said Bass, wincing as Dylan pressed the cold bag against his cheek.

"What was it even about?"

"I have no idea. You know what he's like. Sometimes he just wants a ruck. Nice nice fighter."

"You must have pissed him off. You should keep your eyes off Ruby."

"Ruby Soho. This time she had nothing to do with it. There's so much you don't know."

"I'm all ears." Dylan held the bag in place. "How does it feel now?"

Bass cupped his hand over Dylan's. "It's sore, but that girl in there has got me horny as balls, man. Sniff my fingers." He said, shoving two fingers under Dylan's nostrils.

"Sick." He said, jerking his head away, face screwed up like a pickled egg. "You're disgusting. Why you insist on doing that. Hold this bag, will ya?"

Titters trembled from the living room. Dylan looked from the kitchen, seeing Laura and Sofia giggling into their hands on the sofa.

"I only smoke when I drink," said Laura. "If anything, I blame Dylan."

"Here you go then, two-twos." Sofia held out her squashed rollie between her fingers.

"I don't smoke rollies, so uncivilised." Said Laura, in a forced accent, reaching for Dylan's packet of cigarettes on the arm of the sofa, taking one out and sparking it. She inhaled, letting the smoke escape her mouth like a seductive genie.

"You gotta hold it longer. You won't get any nicotine that way."

Laura concentrated and inhaled again, holding the smoke longer in her lungs. Coughing as she exhaled.

"Hey," said Sofia. "You guys got any weed up in here?" She directed her loud question toward the kitchen.

"I've never tried it." Said Laura, walking into the kitchen, holding Sofia's hand, trailing behind her.

"You're shitting me?" said Sofia.

"You know where I live. We don't do that in the country."

"Dildo." Said Sofia, slamming her hands down on Dylan's shoulders. "Your girlfriend wants you to buy her some weed. She needs to get mash up."

"Are you joking? It's too late now," said Dylan.

"Let's see." Said Sofia, peeling the frozen green beans from Bass's eye. "Proper war wound makes you look sexy—, No dealer'll be in bed now, ya little bitch." Said Sofia. She turned her attention back to Dylan.

"Keep that on your eye," said Dylan. He snatched the bag of beans from Sofia and pressed it in place on Bass's squinting eye. "Hold it on."

Bass steadied himself, leaning and sliding along the counter.

A dull scratching sound scraped from under the sink.

"What the hell was that?" said Laura.

"It'll be that rat." Said Dylan, passing a half pint glass of tap water to Bass.

"Rat. You've got a rat in your kitchen? That's disgusting." Said Laura. A vibration of disgust, rattled from her head to her feet.

"I used to have rats," said Sofia. "Ginger Fish and Twiggy Ramirez. Twiggy ate a hole in Ginger. It was a bloodbath."

"You told your landlord?" Said Laura, finding it difficult to hide her revulsion. "He needs to get rid of it."

"Florence called him, I think. It ate her buns. Hotdog buns, I mean." Said Dylan, brushing his fingertips in Laura's palm, attempting to settle her.

A scratching noise. The flashing grey blur of the greasy rat. Laura screamed, lifting one leg up. They all stood watching a fat rat scuttle from under the oven. It stood on its back legs. Whiskers twitched, sniffing the air, looking at each one of them. Laura made eye contact with it. More high-pitched screams. It darted and clawed its way up a rusty central heating pipe, squeezing itself into a black hole in the kitchen ceiling. Bass flung the bag of frozen beans into Dylan's chest.

"Get me something to spray in there," he said.

"Like what?"

"I don't know. Anything will do. Find something."

Dylan bolted into his bedroom, returning with Lynx Africa. "This is all I have." He said, shaking the can.

"That'll do." Said Bass, snatching it from his hand. He grabbed an empty lager can from the kitchen sink, crushed it, took hold of the antiperspirant, hopped up, sprayed until it emptied into the hole and shoved the crushed lager can, moulding it tight into the ceiling.

"That's a great idea." Said Laura, tutting, offering a slow hand clap. "Bad enough there's a rat in here. Now you're gonna have one that smells like a prepubescent drunk."

"Sorted." Said Bass, clapping his hands together, using the back of his hand to cool his eye.

"Well, if it wasn't decided before, high times is it?" said Sofia.

"Seriously, you want me to sort it?" Said Dylan, looking at Laura. "I can try Big D, he might spare an eighth."

"Yeah, come on Tony Montana." Said Sofia, pinching Dylan's cheek. "Ring off Big D's phone for a Henry."

"Little lady, you sure?" Said Dylan.

"I wouldn't mind trying it. I mean, it won't lead to harder stuff?"

"Who are you, Mary Whitehouse?" Said Bass as he followed the others into the living room, frozen beans pressed against his eye socket again. "It's a bit of puff the magic dragon."

"I love that song," said Laura. "It's not about weed, is it?"

"Dildo, can you sort it?" Said Sofia.

"A room full of master manipulators." Said Dylan, huffing with playful impatience.

Laura stared at Sofia, concerned he may have overheard them talking earlier.

"You know it, bread bin." Said Sofia, changing the subject. "Big D. What kind of name is that?"

Dylan grabbed for his mobile phone from the mantelpiece, atop the stack of empty beer cans.

"I don't know his real name. Not sure anyone does. He's just Big D, but kind of a midget. I'll try from the kitchen," he said.

"Feeling better?" Said Laura of Bass.

"You should have seen the other guy." Fe said, forcing a smile.

"Whatever ya pussy." Said Sofia, as Bass sat down next to her, resting his head on the back of the sofa, holding the frozen beans in place. Sofia lifted her feet up and rested her legs on his lap, cupping his testicles in her hand. "You better recover. I want you to do me Johnny Rotten later."

"You're so crass sometimes," said Laura.

Sofia stuck her tongue out and said. "Learn to love it."

"Right." Said Dylan, stomping into the living room, clicking his phone off. "He's got some he can spare."

"Is he coming here?"

"It's not a delivery service."

"Bit shit," said Sofia. "My dealer would be here in no time."

"You should've called him then. Anyway, if Big D comes here, he'll wanna stay. We won't get rid of him and he'll end up smoking half of it. If I go to him. I can be in and out."

"Nothing wrong with a bit of the old in out, in out," said Sofia.

"Righty, if I go now, I'll be back in, like, forty minutes."

"You want me to come with you, Masugar?" said Laura. She stretched out to touch Dylan's hand.

"No, you're good. Stay here. I'll grab and go."

Laura leaned up, waiting for him to plant his lips on hers.

"Be safe. See you in a New York minute," she said.

"Everything can change." They all sang aloud.

"Make sure he keeps that ice on his eye." Said Dylan, pointing at Bass.

"Get on with it, man," said Sofia.

"You've got such a sunny disposition, Sofia. Make sure you don't go anywhere. I'd love to hear your opinion on Harold Shipman."

Sofia shrugged.

"In a bit." Said Dylan, clicking the front door closed behind him.

16

bIG d

Double trouble stepping along the lonely pavement. Converse laces threatening to come undone like his dissolving loyalty. Dylan dodged car headlights, his head spinning, speed walking, ensuring he wasn't being followed. A drugs bust for an eighth. He shook off silent paranoia, realising he was never important enough to be stopped by the filth. The 'filth', he chuckled at the thought.

Making his way from one side of town to the other. A distance travelled, blinded by time. Daydreams his only company, the blinkered encouragement. Motivated by the mission. Guilt rocked up through him as he imagined Zoe's hands gripping at his convulsing naked body, disguising his come face. Laura's smile flashed into his mind. How would smoking affect her? The answer being a reality as soon as he returned. At least they would experience it together. She could leap from the bedroom window, raging to fly or smear mayonnaise in the crease under her breasts. More likely, it'll end with low blood pressure, shaking, sliding down a wall. Holding her hair from the toilet bowl as she vomits away a night's worth of social anxiety. Practical joker giggling amongst friends, scrawling sharpie genitalia on foreheads. That midnight cupboard rummaging for savoury snacks. He refused the emerging stereotype.

Dylan's eyes peaked. The Pot on the horizon. Zoe grinding on his lap, whipping her hair like a rotor blade. Her soft tone compliments, the way she squeezed his bicep. 'Not the biggest muscles in the world, the perfect size'. She said into his ear. He heard it as a whisper. Fingernails tickling over his tight ribs. 'Let me see your love muscle.' Just as he did then, he chuckled to himself. Only Zoe didn't press his head with hers and giggle as he hoped she might. Devoid of perceived intimacy.

Was it a farce? An elaborate pantomime? Or, was she feeling his soul? Disappointed, still tantalised, the service paid for. An obsession easy to subscribe. A hip-hop video. The girls flashing cash. Oiled hands on muscle groups. Stiff fingers clutched credit cards. The ladies became sexual drug dealers. You'll catch your breath, slap your face awake, knowing they're not your property. Accelerated education means patrons can't bowl over to another flesh obsessed subscriber and box him in his head. They, too, only exist for a good, hard time. You may share a happy ending. Infatuation is just the beginning.

As he caught his breath, hopping up on the curb. He knew he was a victim of a masquerade, lulled into a false sense of security, to make him return in the future, spend his student loan on Zoe's naked, shaking flesh. Become one of the regular flummoxed customers that the girls of the club go home and tell their mothers about. Bringing personality to titillation, project a grace of seduction to the act of making it rain. Selling the promise of individuality by singing songs by Billie Davis, pawning them as their own. She was only ever working the room. Restraining orders and doorman rejection. 'She isn't here. She doesn't wanna see you. You know it's only a job, right? No. Are you crazy? I won't go to dinner with you. It's a hustle.'

Dylan approached a semi-detached house, like all the others on the dark street. Street lamps dented at the base, taking the brunt force of student drop kicks to disable the bright brilliance. Number forty-five. An orange traffic cone, lifeless and toppled in the front garden. A student ornament, souvenir from a Friday night. He entered through a rusty, squeaking gate, stepping over a toppled triangle road sign. He ascended three concrete, moss-covered steps and pushed the front door open, entering without announcement. The kitchen light was yellow. A girl with her hair tied up, counterfeit Aviators covered her eyes, wearing nothing but a thong and grey hoodie. She sat at a picnic bench used as a table, slurping on cheap packet noodles, surrounded by piles of dirty washing. She looked up, stringy chow mein tentacles dangled from her lips, her eyes piercing.

"D'you not knock?" She said, almost unintelligible, spitting hoisin sauce.

"Big D said I was always welcome to walk in."

"I'm not sure he expected anyone to do that. I'm in my pants, man."

"I can see that," said Dylan. "Apologies." His eyes studied the chipped green nail polish on her big toe. "I'm confused by the whole convention. Is he in?"

"His usual spot." She said, pointing toward the living room with her fork, clapping on noodles.

No door on the hinges. Dylan held his eyes on her naked legs, under the table. A coffee stain coloured mole, in the shape of Gambia, above her left ankle.

"And eyes up." She said, squeezing her knees together.

Dylan shook himself from distraction, stumbling into the smoky living room. A pungent smell of sweet marijuana. The room lit by a dangling red light bulb, no lamp shade. TV on, he recognised a floppy haired face, covered in blood. American Psycho. The name of the lead actor escaped him as he danced in a plastic raincoat. The film on mute. Jungle music skipped from a portable stereo on the coffee table. The bass shook mugs of cold tea and stolen pint glasses, three quarters full of flat cola. Makeshift ashtrays made from sliced beer cans and plates of half eaten food with smears of sauce mixed with ashy dog ends strewn around the room. A collection of multi-coloured bongs, with stagnant water, a layer of green algae forming.

"Hey Dustin." Said Big D, as he laid outstretched on the sofa, looking back, red eyed, one hand down his shorts.

"It's Dylan."

"My bad, blood. I haven't bagged it yet. Let me weigh it out. I hear you've met Zara."

"Yeah I guess. Thanks for this, D. Not seen you at uni in a while."

"Nah, fuck that shit, bruv. I'm thinking 'bout dropping out. Feels like a waste of time."

Dylan took a seat on a sun chair pushed up against one wall. Rachel Stevens, wearing a silver bikini above his head. The page ripped from FHM, stuck to the wall.

Big D sat up from his slouched horizontal position, clicking his neck to the left, then right. He took a gulp from one of the pint glasses. Sparked a flaccid joint between his black lips, plucking at large green buds of compact marijuana from sealed plastic containers. They popped open as he used his stubby forearm to sweep space free on the coffee table, placing the buds on electronic scales. Jabbing his finger on the reset button, waiting for a zero to be displayed.

"I've been offered a job on that Big Breakfast as a runner," said Big D.

"You serious? You hate video production."

"I do," he said. "But, it's good money. Means I can carry on dealing, hide behind a proper job. Good cover, ya know. Plus, that Donna Hair is on it."

"Donna Air, you mean."

Big D shrugged, sniffing a bud.

Zara shuffled, barefoot into the living room, now wearing a pair of loose track suit bottoms with a leopard print pattern, tying the waist string into a bow. She slumped back next to Big D, pulled his head close to hers and kissed him on the mouth. He tutted, pulling away.

"Do we know each other?" said Dylan to Zara.

"If you're asking that question, then we don't." She said, not taking her eyes off the TV, forcing her sunglasses up her nose.

"I think I've seen you around."

"It's a small town and if you go around barging into houses without knocking, means you must see a lot more of people than intended." She said, smacking Big D on his spindly arms. "Start locking that pissing door or stop telling people to rock up, D."

"OK, Babe." He said, rubbing his eyes.

"If he had been five minutes earlier," she said. "That could have been embarrassing."

"How do you know I don't leave the door open so they can join in?" he said.

Zara rummaged for a dog end. "Fuck off," she said. "Weigh this shit out so he can do one." Her fingers rifled through the ash of extinguished cigarettes. She found one, blew her fingers clean and pressed it between her lips.

Big D shook his head, rolling his bloodshot eyes. "See what I have to deal with, bruv."

"Tough life," said Dylan.

The front door banged shut. A girl with blue hair caught Dylan's peripherals. He cast a double take. Holding a folded book, she pressed it in half along the spine. Her blue framed glasses steamed up.

"Hi," she said.

"Moira?"

"Hey, Dylan. What you doing here?" she said. "I missed you the other week. Ended up downing your snakebite. How was the Bragg gig?"

"Amazing. I mean, it was a good gig, yeah." He tried to hide his beaming smile. "Sorry about not coming down the union. I didn't know you lived with D."

"You do now," said Zara.

"What book you reading?" He said, not taking his eyes off her.

Moira put her hands inside her denim jacket pocket and powered off a personal CD player.

"You're listening to music too, what is it?" he said. Dylan studied the Toy Machine devil patch stitched to her jacket.

Moira giggled. "I wasn't reading whilst walking, but it's a Confederacy of Dunces. You inspired me to pick it back up. Question two; I'm listening to Knifehandchop."

"I'm impressed," he said. "Never heard of Knife--" He gave a look, inviting her to finish his sentence.

"Handchop," she said. "Knifehandchop. He's Canadian. I discovered him on the web. You wanna listen?"

"I really should be going."

"Yup, you should." Said Zara, coughing into her fist.

"It's ready when you are." Said Big D, running his fingers along the baggy seal, a cartoon marijuana leaf on both sides.

"I see," said Moira. "That's what you're here for. In that case, no worries." She turned in the doorway.

"No," said Dylan. "Wait. I've got time. Seriously. I wanna hear it."

"You're not listening to it down here." Said Big D, flopping back on the sofa, tossing the baggy on the table.

"You're welcome to come up to my room," said Moira.

Dylan smiled, apprehension bubbling. His cheeks stiff.

"Behave yourself," said Zara. "She's got a boyfriend." She stared at him over her shades.

"I've got a girlfriend," he said.

"Ask yourself what you're doing going upstairs with her then."

"You a fan of the film?" Said Dylan, pointing at Zara's hoodie. "What film?"

"Super Fly." He nodded in her direction at the writing on her top. "I just like the hoodie. Is it a film?"

Moira gestured for Dylan to follow her. He pinged up from the chair.

"She's ignorant of the film," she said. "I've told her to watch it. Not interested." Moira passed Dylan the CD case. He turned it over in his hand, skimming the track listing on the back.

"Sounds interesting." He said, grabbing for the baggy from the table. "Thanks for this, D." He slapped his palm on D's, money folded within. A shake of gratitude.

Big D saluted, pressing a joint back between his lips. Zara snatched it and toked.

"Hey, did you know," said Moira. "I didn't, but John Kennedy Toole." She planted her hands on the bottom of the stairs, climbing to the top with a crawl. Dylan studied her ebony tight calves, clenching.

"He wrote Confederacy, couldn't get it published," she said. "So, ended up killing himself. His mother then worked to get it published." She reached the top of the stairs, taking a deep breath.

"I didn't know that," he said. "I'm thankful she did though."

With him trailing behind, Moira used a large silver key to unlock her bedroom door. She snapped on the light. The sight of quality white, floor to ceiling wooden bookshelves struck his eyes. Book after book, top to bottom. Organised by size. The opposite wall, CDs packed in with no gaps, the cases shimmering. No posters on the walls.

"Wow," said Dylan.

Moira laughed, nodding her head. "I don't have a TV. This is how I entertain myself. Books and music."

"You could open a shop. Moira's books and music. Come for the books, stay for the company."

"That's what everyone says—, Well, except for the last part."

"You can't have read all these?"

"I've worked my way through most of 'em. Still some Penguin classics over there I haven't got to yet."

"That's so cool."

"I've never been described as cool, but thanks, I guess. Books are my thing," she said.

On a desk, next to a personal computer, she opened the lid of a large CD player, removed the plain black CD by the edges, avoiding touching the surface.

"Prepare yourself." She said and clicked the lid shut. "This is Knifehandchop."

"Such a weird name, but it works. You want to have a smoke whilst we listen?"

"It might surprise you, I don't smoke weed. Goes against every stereotype, but I have an addictive personality. I know if I started, I'd keep it up. So, not for me, but thanks. Get yourself ready. This is the album, Rockstopper."

The stereo spun into action, a crackle and hiss from the speakers. Dylan's eyes popped as the first clicks of the opening track, sounding like a gun being cocked. Then the beat kicked in, backed by repetitive vocals until the riotous track finished.

"What kind of music is this?" He said, competing with the noise.

"It's described as a blender, mashing together techno with breakcore and a mess of other stuff. You like it?"

"I love it. I haven't heard anything like it."

"It's just him on his own, apparently," she said. "Tigerbeat puts it out. I think he uses a Roland JP-8080. It's so good, proper banging."

"How do you know all this?"

"As you can see," she said. "I read a lot." She removed her septum piercing.

"Impressive. You use your computer?"

"All the time. I'm writing my third novel."

"You too?"

"What d'ya mean, you doing the same?"

"I can't say I'm on my third. But, I've been writing my first for a couple of years. One day I'll get it finished." He said, as track two blurted out.

"Two more have gone to my agent," she said. Grabbing for two paperbacks from a shelf. "These are mine."

Dylan snatched for the books, not able to hide his intrigue. He flipped the paperbacks over."Holy shit." He scanned the blurbs. "I can't believe you've got an agent. I can't believe you're published."

"It was hard work for sure. I won a short story competition a couple of years back, with a story called The House that fell to Earth. Everything snowballed after that. Got an agent, which these days, you can't do much in the industry without."

"I never had a clue. This one though." Dylan held up one of the books. "Murmuration, sounds good."

"Thanks. It's not my favourite but it links to, the first one I guess. Alarm Dog Prince." She tapped her finger on the front cover of the other book he held.

"Interesting title."

"Yeah, I'm proud of that one," she said. "Just keep writing. That's my only advice. Not that you asked for it, but no one else will finish it for you."

"You find it lonely?"

"What, writing? No. I can't get enough of it. Rescues me from my demons."

"You got a lot of 'em?"

Moira laughed, turning up the volume on the stereo.

As the album played out, Moira cut her hands through the air as if holding lasers at a rave. In between tracks, they conversed in a way Dylan had longed for. Chat that didn't just end with music.

"It's like we're kindred spirits or something. Your passions are my passions," he said.

"You ever been to a free party?" said Moira.

"Free party. What's that?"

"Kind of how it sounds. A rave in a field. You phone a party number, you're given directions, kind of, you find your way there. Sometimes on farmland in the middle of nowhere, in a forest or something. Guys set up speaker stacks and you party all night long. I like the threat of it getting shutdown. That's one of my passions. You wanna come? The next one I hear about, I'll let you know?"

"I'd bloody love that," he said. "I'm away for the summer though."

"The entire summer, what you up to?"

"I'm working in the States on that Sleepaway America programme."

"The thing with the kids?" she said. "Jesus, that's my worst nightmare. I couldn't cope with that. A few of my friends have done it. Some loved it, others hated it. It doesn't sound like it's for me. I'd need my space. You're coming back though, right?"

"I'll be back for the third year."

"There I was, thinking we might have a whirlwind romance." She said, hiding a smile.

"You've got a boyfriend, apparently," he said. His eyes dazzled again by the gap in her teeth.

"Doesn't mean I can't indulge my attractions. You'll be grateful you met me, Dylan. I promise."

"I already am. I've never heard anything like this music and you're an author."

"Here, before you go, let me burn you a copy of it. I won't give you a free book. No one appreciates 'em that way." She knelt on her desk chair, her feet waggling beneath her. She inserted the album and hit burn. It chugged, humming and spinning and popped free from the CD drive.

She wrote on the blank surface.

'To dearest Dylan, Rockstopper, Knifehandchop, listen and think of Moira X X X.'

"That's sweet, thank you," he said. "I really should get going. I kind of don't want to, but I need to get home."

Moira pulled on her bedroom door, locked it behind her. "I'm working this Friday." She said, descending the stairs. Dylan following close behind. "You should come. We've got this other DJ I like, Drop The Lime is playing." She opened the front door, crossed her arms to shield her from the cold outside. It was too late, Dylan could see her erect nipples, two tiny bars piercing both.

Clearing his throat, he said. "You know what, I think I will. Sounds sweet." He made sure he looked her in the eyes and not at her chest.

"Do you want me to walk back with you?" she said.

"To my house? I'd love that, but then you'd have to walk back alone and I'd worry about you getting home safe. But, I'll defo see you Friday."

Moira stood at the front door. "Dylan." She said after him as he stopped next to the traffic cone. "Don't say, 'sweet'."

Dylan stood confused, his frown prompted her to clarify.

"The word sweet," she said. "Don't use it as a superlative. I can't stand it. I know that won't offend you. You're as mad up as me."

"Such a sweet thing to say," he said.

She concealed a laugh behind her hand.

"Now you've covered your teeth. I can't see you," he said. "That's not racist, by the way. I didn't mean—,"

"Go home, ya lunatic," said Moira. She watched him get smaller into the distance, looking back and waving at her as she remained on the top step in the doorway. Exploring the darkness as it turned to the light of a brand new day.

17

mYAgE

Dylan strolled the streets, returning home the same way he arrived.
Down Hammer's Hill. Blue and white police tape flapped from the
bonnet of a dumped green Mazda MX5. Past the train station, where
Laughing Russell with his red Afro was rifling through bins, although
he wasn't laughing. The town centre was still. No threat of twilight
drunken collar shaking. He toe tapped loose stones along the
pavement, indulging in his own game of improvised curling. It didn't
matter to him he had to wait at traffic lights. Moira's plump lipped
smile indulged him. The roads were quiet, no cars zipping. Still, he
waited at crossings, distracted, his mind wandering faster than his feet.
He considered turning around, picking up one of the heart shape
pebbles that have accompanied him. Plant on it a soft kiss for good
luck and toss it at Moira's window. Get her complete attention, her
surprised glowing face, septum ring dazzling from her window. She'd
open the front door, hardback in hand, without consideration for the
dust cover. Let it float to the floor, fling her arms around his shoulders,
descend into their lips. All to the orchestral crescendo of Mercury

Rev's, Endlessly.

The traffic light flashed amber, his cheeks blushed as red shone out. Amusing himself with the possibilities of attraction, his hand was in and out of his inside pocket, ensuring he hadn't dropped the green bagged, night-time errand.

He took a deep breath before opening the front door, not certain how he made it back. He clicked it shut behind him. Laura hustled from the living room, frowning.

"I was so worried, you OK? You were gone ages," she said.

Dylan shook off his woolly distraction, forced a bemused smile and kissed her on the tip of her cold nose.

"Took longer than I thought. He had to weigh it out," he said.

She took him by the hand, leading him into the living room. Bill Hicks playing on the TV, the green digital counter of the VCR ticking over. All eyes were on Dylan.

"I come bearing gifts." He said, shaking the small baggy between his icy fingers.

"Don't come over me," said Sofia. Grabbing for the bag, she popped it open, shoving her nose inside, sniffing deep. "I shall call you Jesus, all hail Geee-sus. Sniff that." Sofia wafted the bag under Bass's nose, like sniffing salts. "That smell," she paused. "Almost as good as my pussy."

Bass smirked, nodding, as she winked at him.

Dylan reached into his pocket and said. "We need to listen to this." He held up the CD, pushed down in its plastic sleeve.

Laura reached out, reading the handwriting on the front. "Knifehandchop—, Who the hell is Moira? There's three kisses on this." She said.

"Big D's housemate."

"With three kisses?"

"She was being ironic."

"Funny that, Alanis Morissette explained irony pretty well." Said Laura, flapping the CD in her hand. "Never mentioned three kisses on CDs from other women. Don't cha think?"

"Pretty good dealer though, mine only ever tries to fuck me," said Sofia. "I can do us a proper cherry popper with this shit." She flicked the bottom of the baggy, as if it contained powder. "Where's your grinder? I'll get this started. Then, you can explain irony to me. Because I really care."

Bass tossed a plastic grinder at her. Sofia caught it in one hand without looking. King-size red Rizla papers between her lips. She lent on the rickety TV table, distracted for a moment by Bill Hicks, screaming, vibrating closed lips into the microphone, emulating noises made by an aroused devil. She rolled flat three papers, two connected in the middle, a third creating a large 'L', sprinkled ground marijuana along one edge, adding more to the end of the tip. She licked along the seam of a cigarette, tore a piece free and peeled it open like a banana, along the moist edge, splitting it in two, the tobacco dropped into the Rizla. She picked up loose corners of the thin, tracing paper Rizla and began rolling it between her fingers, she licked from one end to the other, along the gum glue, creating a perfect cone shaped joint, she held it up to the light with admiration.

Dylan laid the CD in the stereo, his fingers delicate, before he popped the lid shut.

"Since I rolled this, no one minds if I spark it, right?" said Sofia.

"Puff-puff pass," said Bass.

"When it comes to sharing the wealth, babe. I'm a pro. Let the party begin."

With the living room door shut closed, the idea promoted by Sofia, suggesting an airlock would contain the smoke, 'make us higher', she kept insisting.

Yestin and Florence arrived in oversized clothes that resembled pyjamas. Yestin shot a look at Dylan, with Laura's legs sprawled out across his lap. He nodded in subtle acknowledgement. Yestin ignored him with a tut.

Florence smiled. "You must be the Laura," she said.

"It's good to finally meet you." Said Laura, taking Florence by the hand. "Hopefully, I'll be seeing more of you both."

Florence bowed with a full tooth smile.

"We could smell that from upstairs," said Yestin. "Woke us up."

"Sorry, bud," said Bass.

"Don't apologise, pass that dutch and give a brother a toke." Said Yestin, with a nervous laugh.

Dylan stood up, hoisting Laura's legs free from his lap. He held a joint between his fingers. Nodded with a submissive glance. Yestin snapped his fingers around the middle like pliers, shoved it between his lips, inhaled as if he hadn't smoked for an eternity, enjoying every second of its exposure again.

"That's some good shit." He said, exhaling, followed by a lip smashing cough. "Fuck me, that's good."

Florence looked on at Yestin with disappointment.

"Babe, you wanna have a go on this?" He said in his Welsh accent, holding up the joint.

Florence scowled, shaking her head. "It nice to meet you." She said and traipsed toward the door. Her footsteps disappearing up the stairs.

"I suppose I better go after her," said Yestin. "Cheers for that. Lovely to meet you both, enjoy." Yestin ran his palm over the back of his head, shut the door behind him, and called out up the stairs in apology.

"Poor guy, sounds like he might be in trouble," said Sofia.

"They're always arguing," said Bass.

"What time is it?"

Looking at her wristwatch. "Five-fifty-seven," said Laura.

"I'm going upstairs," said Sofia. "Which one is your room?" She asked of Bass.

"The box room at the front, opposite the bathroom."

"Talking of the bathroom. Masugar, do you mind if I have a quick shower," said Laura. "I've got a really gacky mouth."

"Go for it. Mine is the purple towel," said Dylan.

"Then, you coming to bed? It's late." Said Laura, blurry eyed.

"Or early," said Bass.

Laura and Sofia both jumped up, Sofia sweeping her hand along Bass's forearm. He slapped her on the bottom as she giggled out of the room.

"Don't be long." She said, looking coy back over her shoulder.

"You having a shower too?" said Bass.

"No, I want you to taste me as I am," she said.

Dylan grimaced at the thought.

Laura and Sofia hot stepped it up the stairs, giggling all the way. Sofia hugged Laura at the top of the stairs, honked her breasts over her shirt. Laura batted her hand away with a chuckle. Sofia staggered toward the open bedroom door to Bass's room. Laura clicked the bathroom door shut behind her.

"Mate, I met this girl at Big D's," said Dylan to Bass.

"That why it took you so long? I had to sit here listening to them two flapping. You didn't fuck her, did ya?"

"No, it wasn't like that. It was so much more, deeper. I haven't met anyone like her. It was like sitting talking to myself. You know, one of those moments that comes into your life without explanation and then shakes the shit outta your world."

"Never experienced it. Sounds like bollocks to me. I only go as deep as my balls."

"I don't know what to do," said Dylan.

"What do you mean? If you wanna see her again. You do. I know you two are getting close, but you should be free to discover other people. I'm not down with this one partner shit. It makes little sense. My dad's the same. If he's away from Edinburgh. I don't know, visiting clients in Cambridge or something. He won't deny himself an experience just because mum's at home."

"Doesn't that make you think less of him, knowing he's cheating on your mum?"

"Nah mate, he's my hero. It's what you do. I refuse to go through life being restricted, resisting opportunity."

"Why is it, now I'm in a relationship, all this other shit comes flooding in? No one paid attention to me before."

"They say, if you're looking for it, you'll never find it. Women aren't attracted to desperation."

"I wasn't desperate."

"You weren't cool about it either. What 'ave I been telling ya, as soon as you get it done, that acidity leaves ya, you learn to relax. I can see you've changed."

"I do feel more confident."

"Make sure you hold on to that. It adds sex to your swagger. Dem girl can't resist."

"I'm getting another beer, want one?"

"Yeah man, I put tins in the fridge earlier. Should be just right."

Dylan jumped up from the sofa, "Hey, you paid that girl at the Pot, didn't you, that Chloe?"

"Zoe, you mean. Yeah, it was my treat."

"I knew that wasn't real."

"I bet it felt real though, when she sat on your face in that lacy number and sucked your toes. That's all that matters."

"How did you know she—," Dylan stopped himself from talking.

"I guessed. It's what she does, it's her party trick."

Dylan laughed and continued out into the kitchen. He opened the fridge door, looking for the beer placed under the ice compartment at the top, and pulled out two cans. With his chin, he pushed the door shut. He jumped, his heart pounded. Bass stood in front of him, looking at him without a smile. His jaw locked.

Dylan frowned and said. "You good?"

Bass didn't answer. He stepped forward, planting his thin lips on Dylan's. The cans dropped to the floor. Bass forced his tongue into his mouth, smacking teeth. The strong taste of cigarettes on his breath. Dylan's eyes wide open, struggling for breath. Bass's eyes shut tight, gripping at the back of Dylan's neck. His stubble grating his smooth face. Bass thrust his hips into Dylan's, putting his body weight on him, pinning him against the fridge. Dylan could feel Bass's erect penis prodding through his jeans, stabbing into his thigh. He pushed him, shoving him off.

"What are you doing?" he said. "They're both upstairs." Dylan wiped his mouth with the back of his wrist.

Bass dropped his head. "Sorry dude," he said. "When they're gone—,"

"When they're gone? Laura's staying here mate, so is Sofia. You all right?"

"I don't know what happened." Said Bass, his pupils dilated. "It must be all the smoke or lager, or both. Sofia's been a prick tease all night. I'm off my nut, mate."

"It's fine. Like I said, she's upstairs. You should go be with her."

Bass shook his head, as if coming to his sober senses. "You're right. I'm sorry," he said. Confused, he left the kitchen, exhaling deep breaths like he was holding back tears. He poked his head back round the corner of the kitchen door. Dylan, still motionless against the fridge. "Can I just ask, am I a good kisser?"

"I'm not the best place person to answer that."

"You're right." Said bass, knocking his knuckles against the door frame. "We don't need to talk about this again."

"We don't," said Dylan. "You've had too much to drink. We'll leave it at that."

Bass nodded, his feet thumped up the stairs.

Dylan heard the shower water stop. He picked up the two cans, returning them to the fridge, scratching his head, walking into his bedroom, sitting on the edge of the bed.

Laura wrapped in a towel, still dripping wet and said. "That has to be the worst shower in the world. I don't know how you guys cope. If that's what being a student is all about, I'm not looking forward to it." She stopped patting her hair dry. "You OK? You look scared shitless."

"I need to tell you something."

She took a seat next to him on the bed, crossing her damp legs. "Go on then, put me outta my misery, sweetheart." She said, in a passable impression of James Stewart.

18

tHe clASS sYsTeM

Blue sticky mohawks look improper in Henley-on-Thames. The diamond eyed elite, clicking fingers, wearing pearl necklaces and clapping platinum tie clips. They dissected Dylan with side-eyed, ostracised judgement. He caught his reflection in a mirror decorating the wall. He too, felt out of place. Obvious to strangers, clear to himself. To avoid making eye contact with those whispering behind hands, shielding mouths. He studied framed pictures adorning the walls around The Gold Leaf Indian Restaurant. A still picture of, he presumed, the owner, bowing to a turquoise vase on a gold plinth. A white-haired, wrinkle skinned presenter holding The Antiques Roadshow logo. Another picture of the 'Blue Boats', from the annual boat race. Henley Bridge, with its five arches. Watercolour narrow boats breaking through white river peaks. Black and white aerial views of the Thames again. Eastenders and Dot Cotton filled his mind. A blurred silhouette of the church spire cast in an egg yolk sunset. He attempted to block out everything around him. It remained a blur. The way he wanted it. He gazed around the restaurant, confused that there was no semblance of Indian culture, other than the warmth of cumin in his nostrils. It compounded his thoughts when four waiters, and one waitress, all dressed in pristine black and white attire, no ties, were all white English. They could have been related. Not even the owner was Indian. He sat, head down, next to Laura, projecting his best behaviour, twirling his tongue over his fresh lip ring piercing. Using his knuckle to brush away crusty discharge forming from the pink, healing hole, still sore. It wept when he rotated the ring, as he did by habit, every hour, on the hour.

"It was a flat in Hampstead." Said Tilly, flicking her blonde hair from her forehead. "What on earth are you doing? You savage."

All eyes watched Henry, with his leathery face tipping mango chutney on his plate from the silver sharing bowls.

"What's your problem?" he said. He shrugged, his blue and white rugby shirt ruffled.

"You can't do that," said Tilly.

"Sure I can, works brilliantly. Look."

"Are you all witnessing this?" she said. "Despite longstanding table etiquette. Henry is ignoring his manners. Here, he is insisting on being a greedy gosling."

"I'm the oldest." He said and cleared his throat. "I need to eat. No one was touching it." He shovelled lumpy chutney covered rice in his mouth. "Waste not want not, my dear."

"Close your mouth when you're eating." Said Tilly, turning her disgusted face away.

Henry brushed his discreet index finger along Tilly's toned thigh, doing his utmost not to disturb the table cloth.

"How uncivilised," said Laura. A forced British, deliberate articulation.

"You always did enjoy having your mouth full." Said Charlie, giggling from the head of the table.

Dylan sat forward. "Hey, dickhead." He said and jabbed his fork in Charlie's direction. "You may be her ex, but keep your regal stubble and designer glasses from chatting this disrespectful, flirty shit to my girlfriend."

"Elizabeth." Said Tilly, turning her attention to the olive skin blonde opposite Charlie. The same girl from The Potoo. "How did you and Charlie meet? I haven't heard the story."

"It's Lizzie, no one calls me Elizabeth." She Said.

"Apologies,"

"No problem. My Uncle used to call me Elizabeth, that's another story."

With impatience, Laura swigged her drink. "Spill the gossip." She said, toeing Charlie's foot.

"Where did we meet, babe?" Said Lizzie, tapping her finger on the table, to encourage Charlie's attention on her. He remained fixed on Laura's eyes.

"Oh," said Laura. "You're already at the babe stage?"

"I say we are," said Lizzie. "We met on an editing course."

"An editing course?" said Dylan.

Tilly gasped. "Sorry, other than your threat. That's only the second thing you've said tonight."

"Dylan's a thinker—," said Laura.

"You don't have to talk for me." .

"Awkward." Said Charlie, making use of the Americanised exaggeration.

"Nothing awkward. We don't need a drama. The curries are hot enough," said Dylan.

Polite giggles rumbled around the table. Charlie refused, instead concentrated on taking a mouthful of gin and tonic from his tall glass, sucking his lips through his teeth.

"Yeah, an editing course," said Lizzie.

"Like film editing?"

"Not quite," said Charlie.

Dylan cut his eye at Charlie.

"Sort of," said Lizzie. Dylan felt her soft touch on his forearm, similar to Laura's touch, drawing his eyes to hers. "It was a film course at college," she said. "We did a week's intensive DV editing, too."

"That's not where we met, though," said Charlie. "It was Series 23 of Grange Hill."

"Grange Hill?" said Laura.

"Yeah, work experience."

"At the BBC?" said Dylan. "How did you wrangle that?"

"Connections, mate. My Dad knows people."

"Convenient," said Dylan.

"Where did you do yours?" said Charlie.

"It certainly wasn't the BBC. My dad doesn't know anyone. I had to be pulled out. The guy was a convicted sex offender."

"Anyway," said Tilly.

"Grange Hill?" Said Laura, repeating herself with more incredulity still, staring at Charlie.

"We heard it the first time," said Dylan.

Laura held her eyes on Charlie, not flinching. No one dared say anything.

"What?" Said Charlie, spurring her to say something. "I'm not a mind reader."

"We were together when you did work experience," said Laura.

"Oh," said Lizzie. "I see what you mean now. Nothing happened back then. Trust me."

"It better not have." Said Laura, shifting her steely stare between Charlie and back on Lizzie. "FYI. I don't trust anyone who starts a sentence with trust me."

"Still jealous I see," said Charlie. He stabbed his dirty fork into the white linen tablecloth.

"It's not jealousy, you arse. It's more the deceit. You're all the same. All of you. Acid everywhere."

"What's the matter sweet?" said Tilly.

Dylan poked his finger on Lizzie's arm. "Anyone ever told you, you look like a blonde Nelly Furtado?"

Lizzie giggled. "Not the first time I've heard that. I'm like a bird," she said.

"Don't change the subject," said Tilly.

"Weirdly, you look like Laura, I said that the other night," said Dylan.

Laura scoffed and said. "We look nothing like each other. I said that the other night too."

"There's a striking resemblance." Said Henry, leaning forward on his elbows.

Tilly slapped him to move them from the table and said. "Yeah, I hadn't noticed at first. You could be related."

"I wouldn't go that far," said Charlie.

"What's the matter, uncomfortable? Knowing you've hooked up with a girl that doubles for your ex."

"Dylan," said Tilly. "Stop it." She turned her attention back to Laura. "Babe, I don't wish to force it out of you. We know something's up. We can all feel it."

Laura pondered. Her eyes exploring the coffered ceiling. An attempt to conceal tears building in her eyes. "I didn't want to burden you," she said.

"It's never a burden. It's us, we're your friends. No one here takes pleasure from your pain."

"You don't have to tell 'em," said Dylan.

"I think it'll help me," said Laura.

Charlie rolled his head. "Put us out of our misery already."

"If I haven't been right, it's because it's hard to hide."

"Please don't do this," said Dylan. "I'm making it right."

"Dylan cheated on me."

He heard only gasps. Then, sudden clattering of cutlery. A faint plucking of a sitar. Lips moving but he couldn't hear words. The clinking stringed instrument played out over small speakers attached to the wall, concealed by fake green pot plants. He stared into his vegetable biriyani, fork flicking and separating individual grains of basmati rice, chin resting on his chest. Tilly was gesticulating, red faced.

"I see now," she said. "The mohawk, the lip ring. That tattoo." She stared at the inside of Dylan's forearm. "I am the resurrection, yeah right. It all makes sense. Your blemished rebirth. Bit desperate, don't you think, hardly the second coming?"

Henry spoke with his mouthful of poppadom and rice. "You cut your hair to impress her?"

Dylan refused to make eye contact.

"How d'you get it to stand up like that, copious amounts of hair spray or guilt?" said Tilly, shaking her head.

"It's Dax wax, isn't it?" Said Laura, prodding Dylan. He nodded with silent, shamed interest.

"It probably looks how it is. You're right. I am desperate." He said. "I cut my hair and dyed it blue. The lip ring too. I want to make her happy." He gave Laura his attention. "Give you everything. I'm ready to do all I can to prove to you that I made a stupid mistake. I wish I could take it back. Of course I do."

"All very Blink one hundred and eighty-two," said Tilly. "Who's the girl?"

Charlie laughed. "Or guy." He said under his breath.

Dylan tutted, swigging from his lager glass, smacking it on the table. Refusing to explode with rage.

Laura stopped herself from speaking. She glanced at Charlie.

"Who was she then?" Said Tilly, leaning between her legs to the floor. "My serviette."

"You mean napkin," said Dylan.

Tilly waggled her linen cloth napkin like a flag of surrender. "This, cheater, is a serviette."

"Being as pompous as you are, sat there judging me. Counting the money in your trust fund. You'd know, serviette is French and the English royals insist on the use of napkin." He said with a smile. "What you're flapping is a napkin."

"Tell me more," said Tilly. She dropped her napkin to her lap.

"What with everything Laura's been saying about you, how lovely you are, then you do this to her. You're a fraud." Tilly turned her attention to Laura. "It's none of my business. You know what's right for you, babe. If you wanna work it out, you do that. Doesn't mean I need to like him."

"I want to work it out with you," said Laura, nudging Dylan with her shoulder. She sniffed.

"You know where I am. Anytime you want to talk." Said Tilly, squeezing Laura's hand. "You've got a lot of work to do, Dylan." She said glaring at him.

"You could pass for twenty, the way you act," said Dylan. "I forget you're only fifteen."

"Are you patronising me?" Said Tilly, leaning closer to scold him with her eyes.

"I wouldn't dream of it."

"Right, that'll do," said Laura. "Both of you, Tilly, I appreciate your support. If I need to, we'll talk. Like we always do. For the benefit of the table. I intend to make this work with him. It hurts every day. With time, it'll get easier. It's our issue and we'll figure it out."

A waiter scuttled behind their shoulders. "Can I get more poppadoms for the table?" he said.

The interruption released the tension for a moment. Charlie waved the waiter away. The waiter obliged with a nod, collected unused plates, returning them to the kitchen.

"What's the plan after we finish here, that place on the high street, The Swan?" said Laura.

"If you can plaster on a fake smile, then I'm up for that or we can have a boat party," said Tilly.

Laura laughed. "And plaster on a fake smile there instead?"

"My parents aren't using it this weekend, so we should make the most of it."

"You getting on with them better now?" said Henry.

"They're still insisting I go to Oxford." Said Tilly, dabbing her forehead. "It wouldn't be home if we didn't hate each other. Reminds me of that poem." She clicked her fingers. "What's the poem, the one about parents?"

"This be the verse," said Dylan. "Philip Larkin."

"This be the verse, that's it," said Tilly. Her words spoken in an accent worthy of the Queen's servants. "It was a ghastly way to start it." Her straight white teeth filling her mouth. "With that declaration, like an epiphany. First I heard it in school, Mrs. Dorsey recited it. She didn't censor the swearing. Once the class stopped laughing, she had our attention. I've been a fan of his since. I'm impressed you know it."

"I read," he said.

Laura jabbed Dylan's ribs again. "Be nice."

"Yes, I like Larkin. I read as much as I can."

"Dylan wants to be a writer," said Laura.

"A writer with a mohawk, you could have a niche there, mate." Said Charlie, laughing into his fist.

Dylan leaned forward in his seat to attack him with narrowed eyes. "Thanks, *mate.*"

Laura slid her hand to the end of Dylan's knee and squeezed, an attempt at private placation.

Knives and forks screeched across plates and stale poppadoms cracked in two.

"Tilly, you read A Confederacy of Dunces?" said Dylan, poking at his food, fanning his red face.

"I think I've heard of it. Never had the divine pleasure." She said, taking a sip from her large glass of white wine. "Tell me," she leaned on her wrist, not breaking eye contact. "What's it about?"

"I was reminded of it the other day," said Dylan. "The guy who wrote it killed himself, his mother honoured him and got it published."

"Out of interest, was the book review from that, Moira?"

"Wait, who's Moira?"

Charlie laughed and said. "There's another one?"

"There isn't another one," said Dylan. "Moira's just a friend."

"Funny that. The other one was just a stripper."

"Wait. The girl you cheated on her with was a stripper?" said Tilly. Her chin so far forward it almost rested on the table.

"Sorry, I thought we were dropping this."

"You'd like that wouldn't you, ya snake," said Tilly. "You've only got yourself to blame. This story just keeps giving."

Dylan stood. "I need a cigarette, can I 'ave my phone?" He said of Laura, holding out his flapping hand.

"Please." Said Charlie, spinning his wineglass in his fingers.

Dylan poked his tongue to the side of his mouth, stifling simmering anger, and forced his eyes to the ceiling. "You know what, Charlie. Say one more smug thing."

Charlie swallowed, leaned back in his chair and raised his hand to get the attention of the waitress. She shuffled forward, noticing him winking.

Laura's hand was deep inside her clutch bag, wrapped around Dylan's phone. She dropped it on the table. It bounced and rattled cutlery, shook wine glasses with the contempt she intended. Tilly steadied her glass, threatening to topple. Lizzie collected the phone up, passing it to Dylan in two hands like a duckling.

"Thank you." He said, leaving the table, not taking his eyes off the door. His escape to nicotine tranquillity metres ahead.

"Don't go after him." Said Tilly, crossing her legs and flinging her napkin on her plate. "Let him be for a minute. Unbelievable. Give him some time." She took hold of Laura's hand in hers. "Be sure about him, before you go much further."

"I could be crazy, but I am sure," said Laura.

"You always did like to be tortured," said Charlie.

Lizzie threw a white mint at him. "No one laughs at their own jokes," she said. "It's not cute."

"I should talk to him," said Laura, collecting her clutch bag from the floor again.

"At least give him five Mississippi's." Said Tilly, tugging on her hands.

In the cold, street lit night. Dylan jammed a cigarette through tight lips, fighting the urge to grit his teeth. He sparked the lighter, failing to ignite the first, second, even the third attempt. It was the two handed forth technique that breathed the glowing flame to life. He inhaled deep, perching on the narrow, low window sill of the Gold Leaf's front window. Car headlights smudged by on the busy road. He exhaled smoke, confusing himself as his hot breath turned to mist. Shuffling his feet to stimulate heat. Candle lights floated off on the river, long boats converted to restaurants. Couples sat opposite one another, toasting champagne glasses. Jealous of the romance, he longed for simple sentimentalism.

The brass bells above the entrance to the Gold Leaf rang out.

"You wanna talk?" Said Laura, swapping the bag in her hands, joining him on the pavement. Her deep-sunken eyes dug into him. "Hey, I'm talking to you," she said.

Dylan leaned on his elbows and said. "I can't stand it. You humiliated me in there." He said and coughed smokers phlegm.

"It's always about you, how you've been humiliated," said Laura. "You're not even capable of thinking how you've humiliated me. You can't grasp the concept. How much it hurts me, deep down right here." She slammed her fist over her heart, thumping three times.

"I can grasp it."

"No, you can't. You're a fucking robot. So cold. D'you think it was easy to hear what you did to me, knowing you'd been inside that whore."

"I know what I did. I'm not cold. Well, it's cold as balls out here, but, you're still punishing me. I'm sitting in there, listening to your posh, toffee nosed friends. They're all playing at life, and that twat, Charlie. Why the hell you felt the need to invite your ex-boyfriend, I'll never know. It's like you're testing me at every stage." He poked with his cigarette. "That lot in there, they're harmless, but they're just making shit up. Oh, isn't ballet the greatest? I love Dickens. What's

the name of that author? Scoff scoff. Harrods for brunch time brioche.
None of 'em know fuck all. They haven't lived. That Tilly's fifteen,
lecturing me about shit. What does she know? Every man to her is
Mr. Darcy."

"Firstly, the impression," said Laura. "Shocking. You're taking the
piss out of my friends and cussing my ex-boyfriend. We have the
same circle of friends. What d'you want me to do?"

"Get new friends," he said. "Ones that don't hold a wine glass like
they're wanking it off."

"I'll just get new friends. Easy as that."

"What am I to you? I don't get it. Am I a bit of rough?"

"Don't get self righteous with me. Let us not forget, you're the
one who fucked this up. Sat on the floor, crying me a river. That was
all an act."

"It wasn't an act. I've said I was sorry, how much longer you
gonna make me feel like this?"

"You didn't think about me when you were doing that bitch, Zoe.
When I know you're serious about us, we can move on."

"I am serious about us. I wouldn't be here, enduring all this shit, if
I wasn't."

"I want to feel it from you."

"How do I show you that? I'm playing by whatever rules you
make up. I've given you my phone, I don't look at anyone. I fucked
up, big time. I know that. If I didn't love you, or wanna be with you,
then I wouldn't of told you. It was a one night stand, I made a
mistake. That's it."

"You prolonged the lie too. I asked who she was. You said she
was nothing to worry about. A part of me wishes you didn't ever tell
me. I don't know how I can forgive you, or whether I even want to.
They all think I'm a lunatic. I was happy with ignorance. This is gonna
take time."

"I told you the truth. I didn't want this hanging over us. We've got
something special here and I know, I know it's my fault we're in this
mess, but you have to let it go. I want you, Laura."

"Using my name? You are serious. I'm not sure if you're trying to convince me or yourself?"

"Why won't you let me love you?"

"Clever, turning it around on me. As if I'm devoid some how. You know, I'm scared I'll always see it in you, deep down, reminded of it every time I look at you. Tortured that it'll always be there, that doubt. I'm not stupid, I know when you're comparing me, you try to hide it, but, you're too obvious. Sure, I do it too, not as glaring as your drooling lips. I've seen the way you look at Sofia, even that Lizzie girl."

"What? Lizzie? I wasn't drooling over Lizzie. I don't even compare you, and Sofia? She's not my cup of tea—, Wait, who are you comparing me with?"

"Charlie," said Laura.

"Oh, fa fuck sake, what is it with this guy? He sits at the end of that table, making sleazy arsed snide comments, and you're worried about me looking at Lizzie. Holy shit, the way he looks at you, you're havin' a laugh. It's bad enough thinking about you naked together. Forever the ex. The guy's a prick. D'you wanna get back with him, is that what all this about?"

"I'm not saying that, all I mean is, it's what we all do. In order to move on, we look at our past. It's not so much a comparison, it's more, maintaining standards. What I'm willing to put up with from the next one. I broke up with Charlie, knew it was over. I smashed all the mixed CDs he gave me, tore the head off Ethan—, Don't worry, he was a toy giraffe he gave me on my birthday, had him since I was nine, chucked him in the fire. Then, I burned every letter he'd written, one at a time, crying, and not just a single tear, I mean my eyes were pouring. It's always the last photo booth picture that'll have you. The one of our first real date. When Charlie asked me out, I couldn't believe it. We were supposed to see Titanic, but couldn't get in so, ended up watching Good Will Hunting. I liked it, and started putting my own spin on my favourite line; how does one like them apples. I won't forget any of that with him. The first time we went bowling, the first time we, well, you get the idea. You go through all that to cleanse yourself, to let yourself feel something else. You still can't help but compare. I broke up with Charlie, not because he cheated on me, but because it felt like it wasn't going to work. I've raised my standards of the pain I'm willing to tolerate, for you. I wouldn't have put up with it from Charlie, he'd be long gone. I must be insane to want this to work with you."

Dylan pulled Laura in close, wrapping his arms around her. She felt the protection from his squeezes, those subtle touches of warmth, holding her from fallen back into the road, as they spun on the pavement.

Laura looked up at Dylan, poked him in the chest with her jabbing index finger. "Masugar." She said, in a cartoon voice. "With every woman that you meet, gusha gusha. I can only hope you'll think of me and be Masugar loyal." She reverted, talking serious, her eyes becoming less clownish and cute. "It won't matter if they tell you belly aching thigh slappers or, introduce you to new banging music you've never heard. And, if they write coy notes with kisses on CDs. It won't mean anything and you'll feel comfortable telling me the truth. The day'll come when you won't want to run away with them instead of me. You need to get past this, your hope or wanting, whatever you wanna call it. That need for the jokes to get better and the laughter to never stop. We need to work at this, I need to work at this, on us. If we don't try, we'll never know. And, if it's meant to be, then, it'll take both of us to want it. I want you to run home and share your life with me, just to hear me giggle. It feels like so long since we've laughed together. I want to be everything you need, and I promise I'll let you love me."

"You are everything I need, you're all I want little lady. You just can't keep me a prisoner or my dick in a jar."

Laura kept her fingertips tight, clinging on to Dylan's.

"Come back inside," she said. "We're going to a toffee nosed houseboat gathering now."

"I'm sorry. I didn't mean that, they are a bit snobby though."

"Just try to be nice," she said.

"But, a house boat gathering." Said Dylan, following behind, back to the restaurant "I don't even know what that is."

Laura stopped in the doorway. "It's exactly," she said, kissing him on the lips. "What it sounds like." Their lips touched again, the smooch echoed in the foyer. "Being that you're my bit of rough. I can understand how a boat might be confusing for you."

Dylan suppressed a laugh.

Laura stopped before shoulder nudging the door open. "You can laugh," she said. "You're allowed." She poked his cheek away with her finger. "Give me some Masugar sugar."

As their lips met, car horns beeped.

"You like walking, punk?" shouted a passing voice from an open van window.

"Did you hear that?" Said Dylan, thumbing back over his shoulder. *"Do I like walking, punk?* I'm telling ya, this haircut is more trouble than it's worth."

Laura nudged the door, the noise from the restaurant faded out the rumbling traffic from the road as they re-entered, sitar strums chiming.

"I'm still pissed with you. But, just so you know; the hair, the lip ring, that tattoo. I know why you did it and it's working for you. Oh boy, is it working. I could do with a joint right now," she said.

"You're brilliant," he said. "Maybe on the houseboat?"

"I'm begging you." She laughed loud, drawing the attention from the tables near the entrance, heads turning, stopping mid-conversation. Laura mimed an apology as she pressed herself into Dylan, clutching his arm. "I'm gasping," she whispered. "Hey." She held him in place, stretching his arm like a handbrake. "I don't actually look like that Lizzie girl do I?"

19

nAmEs oF, tYpEs oF

Dylan surveyed the inside of the houseboat, more than intrigued, at the same time disappointed. Left thinking it was small, unimpressive, like a caravan on water. Nothing luxurious about it, thick, beige shag pile carpet. To him, it resembled crusty, flaked puff pastry, with an air of 1970s chic. The setting for a key exchanging swingers party. The kitchen was pokey, out dated, faded cupboards with half-sized appliances. Distracted, he examined his itchy tattoo, skin red and raised around the capitalised old English lettering. The group sat in a circle on canvas directors chairs. Knees covered with fleece blankets, on the back deck of the boat, under the lost illumination of distant stars. Tilly took up position on Dylan's left, her feet tucked behind her. She made it obvious she was holding her eyes on Henry's, a blanket wrapped around his muscular, broad back and bowling ball shoulders, long, thick thighs, legs wide open. Tilly's eyebrows danced each time he smirked and forced his legs wider, eyes whiter. Lizzie, drinking bottled beer through an orange straw, blew bubbles when she noticed the two flirting. She rested her sock covered feet on the end of Charlie's knees. He shifted and lifted her ankles up and down his legs. Laura sat between Henry and Dylan. Glancing at Dylan with peripherals, a quick shift, jealous smiling at Lizzie, still glancing at Charlie. Laura knew how much he loathed feet on his lap, unless they were hers, could have been lies too. The boat bobbed on a trembling wave. They held their drinks tight to their chests. Tilly hopped up, bending over for two bottles of wine, shifting her hips like a see-saw, long enough to catch Henry licking his lips. She bounced, filling glasses, finger gripped by the stem with white wine from a bottle in her left hand, offering the choice of red from her right. Voices and murmurs of gratitude, joined with glasses held aloft in appreciation and makeshift toasts. Dylan watched as teenager Tilly swept with grace and confidence around her grateful guests. He shook his head at the thought she was fifteen. Amazing the way she carried on.

Charlie, with his chin high, stiff rowers back. "I know a game we can play—,"

"Shush peeps. Charlie has a game." Said Tilly, interrupting the bubble of conversation.

"Oh wait," said Dylan. "Quentin wants to play a game."

"Behave." Said Laura, snapping a look of disdain, smacking his thigh.

"Thanks Til," said Charlie. "It's called 'names of, types of'. We play it at the clubhouse, right Henry." Henry nodded, not taking his hungry eyes off Tilly. "Someone will start, you say; 'names of, types of', then slap your thighs and clap your hands. We go around in a circle, until someone can't name something, then they down their drink. For example, 'names of, types of'." He slapped his thighs twice, clapping his hands to demonstrate the premise. "Leather."

"Sorry. Leather?" Said Dylan, finding it difficult to hide confusion under his frown.

"Yeah, names of, types of, leather." Charlie repeated, slapping his thighs and clapping his hands again.

"And this is a drinking game? I don't know types of leather." Dylan looked around for agreement. "Leather is leather, isn't it?" He said, chuckling to himself, attempting to conceal his nerves. Laura backhanded his knee again.

"Well, Dylan, it was an example. But, one could say—," Charlie tilted his head, seeking inspiration from the night sky. "Full grain, top grain, bonded." He met his eyes with Dylan's, smiling. "You could have aniline, nappa, nubuck, even suede."

"Chamoise," said Tilly.

"Good one." Said Charlie, clicking his fingers and pointing at her. "Well done, Tils."

"Right, hours of fun then," said Dylan.

"If you have a better suggestion, I'm all ears."

"No, no, you carry on. I need the lavatory, dear sir."

"Consider yourself excused," said Charlie.

"Not that I need your permission," said Dylan. "Who doesn't love a drinking game?" He stretched, cracking his back.

"Right, names of, types of, STDs." Said Charlie in a booming guttural voice. The group chuckled and clapped in joyous rapture at his middle class suggestion. Dylan looked back, firing stares of disappointment at Laura. The way she laughed, covering her mouth, he had seen it all before. It was her fake laugh. He hated the deliberate attempt at self-imposed hysteria, as if it made her more intuitive and obscure. He stumbled, standing, carrying his empty tumbler. The patio door was heavy to slide, it rumbled open like a freight train. The carpet was spongy underfoot. He slid his tumbler along the kitchen counter. It spun to a halt. His feet made their way, slow and steady, to the narrow toilet, elbows balanced against the walls. He poked his head into open doorways, travelling bags on beds, claimed for late night, drunken slumber. A closed door at the end of the hallway pulled him in with inquisitive attraction. The door popped. He braced it from banging open. French new wave lighting, a double bed arranged with delicate red silk sheets, folded along precise edges. Plumped pillows like a 1940s boudoir, frilled lace detail. Photographs of Tilly smiling, her parents arms wrapped around her shoulders, sepia finish, posing by an elephant in an authentic orange sari. Another had her sat atop a proud horse, wearing skin tight avocado green jodhpurs. Shaking hands with a stiff dignitary, accepting framed paper awards with a grin.

Dylan wondered how often the toilet needed to be emptied, having now flushed it. Must be chemical, he thought. He wiped his wet hands in his jeans as he manoeuvred his way through the kitchen again, grabbed for a clean glass from a cabinet of other crystal tumblers. Opened the fridge, slid packaged smoked cheese around, poked at seedless grapes in a bowl. His hands landed on a tiny jar of caviar. Sniffed it, not convinced it hadn't gone mouldy. There were lemons and limes strewn on a chopping board next to a cabinet. A half filled bottle of bourbon. He took hold of it by the neck, held it to the light, unscrewed the top, sniffed the contents, smoked oak and cigars hit him in his throat. Knowing it was good, strong, and rusty. He poured a three finger measure. He whistled as his glass filled. Sloshing it over his fingers, he gulped it, inhaling through his teeth as he swallowed, exhaling heat. He staggered outside, steadying himself on the door frame. The wall of laughter hit him harder than the bourbon, making his vision shudder.

"Pubic lice." Said Lizzie, chuckling, slapping her thigh.

"Dylan, your turn. We're still on STDs." Said Tilly, wiping tear laughter from her eye.

"Have we had AIDs?"

"We haven't," said Charlie. "But that's finished that round, then." He slapped his hands together at the conclusion of the game.

"It's treatable now." Said Dylan, stumbling forward, grabbing for his chair. Laura caught him by the arm, guiding him to the seat.

"Is this sea legs?" she said. "Or pissed up legs?"

Dylan placed a cigarette from his packet between his lips and sparked his addictive vice. Before he could inhale nicotine smoke, Laura swiped it from his mouth and inhaled a deep breath, as if she had chased the dragon. She flopped her lifeless head to the side, giggled and held the cigarette upright, stiff like a pencil.

"Can I have one for a joint?" she said.

Dylan tossed her a fresh cigarette. It landed in her lap, as she reached into her bag and removed a green filled baggy. She tapped it, held it to the light and pinched a small amount, sprinkling it into Rizla on her lap. He watched, seeing a lapping maniac in Laura, slurping her tongue along the glued edge.

"You're getting better at that," said Dylan.

"Thanks Masugar, the proof is in the smoking." She said, holding the joint with obsession in her fingers, inspecting it.

"Evening." Said a female voice from the wooden jetty.

Dylan, the last to make his way to the back of the boat, to investigate the origins of the soft tones.

"I'm Tabitha."

"Hey, I know you," said Dylan. "What are you doing here?"

"If you know her, then there's no reason to ask." Said Henry, tapping him on the back.

Dylan, confused, looked at Laura. Henry grabbed Tabitha's hand like a regal princess and helped her aboard. She straightened her skirt, smoothing it as she stepped inside the boat.

"Take a seat," said Tilly. "You want a drink?"

Tabitha nodded, her knees close together, shoulders back, swaying on high heals like a skyscraper in a noon gust of wind. She was wearing a New Found Glory t-shirt.

Tilly passed her a wine glass with a splash of white wine. Tabitha eyed the glass, lips stretching around the rim, tilted her head back. The contents disappeared down her throat.

Dylan embraced the reassuring taste of comfort from his cigarette and noticed Tilly flicking her head toward the front of the boat. Henry pursed his lips like an anus, his brown eyebrows shifted above his eyes. Tilly clutched at empty bottles, cuddling them into her chest, making her way, inch by inch, inside the boat. All the while, holding her eyes on Henry, dragging him in with underage hypnosis. Dylan squinted, waiting for Henry to follow. Intuition proved correct when Henry caught his eyes. He took Tabitha by the hand. She left the empty wine glass wobbling on the edge of the table. Dylan sat forward and steadied it in place. Henry shrugged, smirking at him, and stepped inside, Tabitha in tow. Sliding the patio door closed behind them. The blurry silhouette of Tilly, Henry and Tabitha shrank smaller as they faded behind the door of the end bedroom,

"I could be wrong." Said Dylan, leaning into Laura. "I'm pretty sure they've all gone to—,"

"It's what she does," said Laura. "It's her boat."

"Right, of course, who are we to judge, but how old's he?"

"Twenty-seven, near as damn it." Laura sipped her wine, avoiding eye contact. "He's married too," she said.

"Married, and he's in there," Dylan pointed, lowering his voice. "And he's in there, with a fifteen-year-old and some girl from The Pot?"

"Relax, you're ruining my buzz." Said Laura, flapping her hand in dismissal. "It's a service. They know what they're doing." She took hold of Dylan's cigarette. "She's a big girl." She inhaled, folding her slithering tongue over her top lip.

"I give up trying to understand," said Dylan. "This is a different world, how the other half live. There isn't enough bourbon in the world to numb my perplexity?"

"Perplexity?" Said Laura, her eyebrows stiff. "Enough to spark your vocabulary."

"A myth, my darling. Inebriation doesn't act as a conflagration of creative enunciation."

"Dick," said Laura. She slapped his thigh with the back of her hand.

Dylan's eyes cracked open. He patted his body, realising he was fully clothed. Shimmering with a thin layer of salty, cold sweat. His lower back stabbing. Eyes open, still lost within in the darkness of blinding disorientation. He felt the space in the bed. No sign of Laura, nothing but ruffled bed sheets, stripped from the mattress. He staggered to his feet. Water sloshed against the hull. Reminding him he was on a houseboat. His feet slipped on four used condoms. One sticking to his heal. He pealed it off, dropping it to the floor, flicking his fingers. He finger spilt the Venetian blinds, his eyes squinting to see the yellow dawn glow casting shadows on the jetty outside. The boat tied, using a two half hitches knot. His bloated belly, poison solid. That desperate urge to urinate. In near pitch black, his eyes readjusted from drunken slumber to stiff-necked consciousness. He ran his hand along the smooth wall, reached the corner, chaotic swipes, wax on, wax off. He palmed for a door handle, sweeping his arms around and around, praying to feel a protruding light switch. Anything that could aid his escape. The need now to rid his bladder of an evening's worth of bourbon on the rocks, two old fashioneds, a bottle and a half of Diet Coke and shared sips of Laura's creamy Advocaat. He clenched his fist on his crotch. Relief for a moment as he caught hold of the door handle, yanking it open.

The lights of the boat were off. Unsteady on his feet, he recognised the stretching route to the toilet, getting further and further away. He bounced into one wall, pulled on a polished door handle, stepped inside the narrow cubicle toilet. The 60-watt bulb burned his eyes with brightness, sparking a migraine. A high pitch buzz in his ears. His body shook. Before he lifted the toilet lid, warm wet urine ran down his legs. Unclasping his flies, he sprayed over the seat, splashing back on his sock covered toes. He sighed thankful relief, tense shoulders deflated, eyes closed and flickering. The smell of curry leaves and stale sourdough wafted from the toilet basin. The butterscotch yellow water almost bubbled with radioactivity. Incredulous that he had created such an odour, his stomach flipped and gagged. Making him hack, threatening lumpy vomit. He gasped for air. Clasped the top button of his jeans closed. Soft female laughter heckled from outside, stifled by the closed patio door. Empty bottles of alcohol turned on their side, glasses in the sink and snack packets strewn over counter services. Emulating a secret agent, Dylan tried to spy, looking beyond his grey reflection. He could make out Laura laid flat on her back, covered with a blue and white striped fleece blanket, her naked, delicate white feet poking out from the end. Charlie's firm hands rubbing her arch, an entranced smile on his face. Laura's legs raised up, resting on his lap. Dylan yanked the door, sliding it open, making the pair jump. Their faces wobbling with embarrassment. Laura sat up on her elbows, breathless.

"Morning, Masugar," she said. "How you feeling?"

"I'm great. You two look relaxed."

"I'll always be the one that got away."

"Charlie. You're trying me—,"

"You are aware you've pissed yourself?" said Laura.

Dylan peered down, noticing the dark two tone wet patch, shaped like Poland. It covered the inside of both thighs. His eyes darted to Laura's concerned eyebrows and a smirking Charlie, shaking his head, swallowing his need to laugh.

"It's only water."

"I think we all know you've pissed yourself, mate," said Charlie.

Dylan spun on his heal, slammed the patio door shut behind him and headed back to the toilet.

Charlie released a vein throbbing laugh. Covering his mouth, shielding Laura from sputtering spit as she slapped his hand and shushed him. She couldn't resist and joined in with Charlie's infectious laughter, biting on the blanket, pulling it, covering her head.

Dylan peeled his bloodshot eyes open. The expectation to see his whitewashed defeated face staring back at him. Instead, he saw through himself. The running hot tap, steaming the mirror. He cupped the water, splashing his face, droplets dribbling over his shirt. He whipped it off over his head. Explored his body, noticing the grey wet patch on his jeans. He shook his head, staring at his sagging mohawk. Tongue flipped his lip ring. Winced as he caught the inside of his forearm, scraping his tattoo on the side of his jeans. He traced his fingers over the warm, bumpy, scabbed letters on his skin. He lost himself in seeing Charlie's smug rock star cheek bones tormenting his own reflection. He saw it again. Charlie rubbing Laura's feet. That thick vein pumping in his smooth forearm. Laura's head tilting the way it did the first time he laid atop, entering her. Giggling faces in stop motion manipulation. He could only hear Laura. Her voice soft. She spoke the language of C. S. Lewis, pronounced with an afternoon tea party dialect. Explaining the size of Charlie's testicles. A vision Dylan couldn't rid from his mind.

With his nipples erect, he swiped for a disposable razor, snapped the handle, cracked the glistening blade free. Held it between his shaking fingers. Looked himself deep in the eye. His reflection taunting him with pain from within. Hearing rich kid flirtation. He gauged a heart shape into his chest; it trickled blood, splatting in the sink, diluted with running water. The blade dropped, clattered, and rattled down the plughole. Pressed his hand into his chest, blood cascaded and dripped through sticky fingers. He noticed duct tape shoved behind the toilet cistern, he ripped at a loose piece with his teeth, tore a strip, scrunched up sheets of toilet paper as gauze, pinched his skin together, pressed the tissue hard and taped over the wound. He ripped another piece and smoothed it, ripped a smaller piece and layered it diagonally. He repeated until the blood stopped, stuck between adhesive residue and skin. Putting his arm down, he jolted. The wound stinging as he pulled on his t-shirt.

Laura outstretched like Cleopatra. Charlie's hands back, rubbing her feet. Dylan wrapped his hand around the neck of an empty bottle, flung the patio door open and launched the bottle at Charlie's head. It sailed past as he ducked, glancing back, thick fear in his throat. The bottle floating on the surface, sinking to the bottom of the Thames.

"I'm living this new haircut." Said Dylan, rubbing his hand over the side of his head, wagging his fist. "Next time I won't miss. I'm not putting up with your shit anymore."

Charlie raised his submissive palms in the air. "We're good, we're good," he said.

Laura sat up, tongue dangling, her eyes twinkled. His reaction impressed her, and he knew it. Breathless, she calmed herself. Hiding her habitual attraction behind her fanning hand. Charlie knew too she was aroused. He buried his sexual memories deep with resentment. Dylan did his best to maintain his melodramatic machismo. Now he had felt the weakness in Charlie. He knew he could shake him ragged by the neck, and he wouldn't defend himself.

"We are good, little lady." Dylan nodded. "We'll be better when we're off this boat."

Laura played the role of cinematic damsel, falling short of throwing her arms around Dylan and riding sidesaddle. She smiled, her eyes submissive with arbitration.

"Names of, types of. My arse," said Dylan.

20

tHeY wAlK aMoNg uS

Bass poked at the shiny intercom to a three storey, red brick townhouse. Flat B, an engraved surname, written in a sweeping black and gold handwritten style. An eloquent and deliberate joining of letters. He used his fingers to trace.

'Kilpatrick'

He shuffled the stuffed backpack on his back, running both thumbs between the shoulder straps and his crushed chest. Impatient, he pressed the buzzer again, jamming his thumb into the button three times, force coming from his clenched cheek bones.

A crackle and a hiss spat from the modern silver speaker. The heavy door popped open with a buzz. Bass shoulder barged it, leaving it to slow close behind him. He stepped on to a black and white check linoleum floor, only standing on the white squares, stretching his legs for the next one, making his way to the bare wooden staircase, running his hand along the intricate, carved oak bannister, with ornate balustrades. Step by step, he edged closer to the landing on the first floor. Crisp white walls with plain empty black picture frames decorated around him. It encouraged a frown of confusion, reflected in a large gold trimmed frosted mirror above a small browning potted plant. He spotted the grand, solid black door at the end of the hallway. A Gold capitalised 'B' reflected light from the impressive glass chandelier hanging overhead. Walking beneath, he palmed a dangling piece. It rattled and smacked off other pieces. Bass pushed the doorbell, turned his head to listen for movement from inside, holding his breath. Nothing. He banged his fist off the door three times. Heavy footsteps thumped floorboards the other side. The door cracked open and Kilpatrick poked his flared nostrils through the crack, his white eyes staring at Bass, darting back over his shoulder, down the hallway. Without time to steady himself, Bass felt a grip on his shoulder, a jolt on his backpack. He was dragged inside. The door crunched closed behind him. Bass shuffled the bag on his shoulders, readjusting his stretched hoodie. Kilpatrick flat palmed either side of the spyhole, his dread locks rattling over his silk dressing gown. He closed one eye and peered out through the circle stretching hallway before him, swapping eyes.

"Dear boy, there was nothing discreet about that knock," said Kilpatrick. "I may have to rethink this whole arrangement. I can't have the neighbours thinking I'm being visited by the Police on a weekly basis."

Dr. Kilpatrick tied his dressing gown at the waist, not looking Bass in the face, he rushed over to a corner cabinet and poured himself a drink, reaching inside a mini fridge, pulling an ice cube tray, cracked it and clattered three ice cubes in a crystal tumbler. Splashes of whisky spitting over the rim. He thundered toward a large dark TV cabinet. A black leather armchair in front of it. He retrieved a boxed video cassette from the top of a VCR, turned and tossed it at Bass.

"When are you guys migrating to DVD? It's a pain having to maintain this old thing." Said Kilpatrick, tapping his rolling fingers off the surface of the grey VCR.

Bass shrugged, holding the cassette in his mouth, dropped his bag from his shoulder, retrieving another tape from a pile he had stacked inside, swapping them over. Kilpatrick stood with one hand on his hip, sipping from his glass of whisky.

"I'm reminded of a piece of art," said Kilpatrick. "It has no basis in reality, but what it does show is my complete contempt for all you represent. Throughout history, for hundreds of years, and you'd be foolish to judge me. Foolish. For I have the PHD. You work in retail, dropped out of Uni and I have to feed my intellect with debauchery, just to remind myself that I'm alive. Being so damn proper is exhausting."

"You should enjoy this one," said Bass.

Kilpatrick turned the case in his hand, looked over the blank cassette inside. Inserted the tape, the VCR sucked; it rumbled to life. Inner mechanisms churned and hummed. Digital numbers ticked over alongside the play symbol. He grabbed for another remote control, fumbling it with his haste. He poked at the TV power button. It illuminated the dark room with a bright blue screen. Play symbol top right corner. CCTV footage captured a room, a massage table, a single lamp shade. The door opened, a shaft of light cut into the room. Zoe leading a bewildered Dylan behind her. Bass looked on with familiarity, knowing it was The Pot. Her arms stretched, connected by interlocking fingertips. The door closed behind them. Dylan looked around the room. Bass recognised his nerves.

"Dylan Nemerov," said Kilpatrick.

"That's right. We got him for ya."

"Excellent. Every penny, dear boy," said Kilpatrick. He kept his eyes on the TV, walked over to a cabinet, opened a creaking door, retrieved a manilla envelope, and flung it in Bass's arms.

Dylan undressed, looking off at the bathroom door. He laid in his boxers, covering himself with a towel.

Kilpatrick stretched out his arms with contentment. Bass stuffed the envelope deep, zipping up his backpack, throwing it on his back.

"Pure art." Said Kilpatrick, waving his hand. "You can let yourself out." He stood standing, swirling his whisky. Bass nodded.

"My boy, wait," said Kilpatrick. "Close the door."

Bass felt like he was falling through slow motion and on repeat. The door popped closed as loud as his heart was beating. Adrenaline pulsated through him. He knew what was coming.

Kilpatrick stood to his feet. "How about some extra cash for you, dear boy?" he said. Plucked at his dressing gown belt, it draped open. His naked black flesh reflected the TV. Bass studied his saggy chest, patches of black brillo hair, a bloated pot belly, his semi-erect penis, swinging like a circumcised donkey's. He swayed his hips and sipped his whisky. Sitting back in his leather seat, shuffled his shoulders, moulding his neck into the cold leather and closed his eyes. He fanned wide his gown.

Bass smirked as Dylan's face beamed from the TV screen. Zoe, naked, rubbing her hands over his back. Bass released his backpack. The tapes inside clattered. He inched over to Kilpatrick, stepped in between his open legs, took hold of his whisky tumbler and downed it, crunching on ice cubes.

"Cheeky boy." Said Kilpatrick, clasping his hands behind his neck. As if in coincidental timing of the action playing out on TV. As Zoe rolled Dylan over, her blurred bobbing head concealing Dylan's excitement. Bass dropped to his knees.

"I'm not gay." Said Bass, closing his eyes, imagining sounds of Snuff's Blue Gravy dub album.

"None of us are, dear. Nothing beats being fucked in the arse."

Bass shoved a handful of paper notes in his back pocket. Snapped at the door handle, hallway light broke through into the apartment. Bass slammed the door behind him. He saw the chandelier. Reached up and pulled off a large dangling piece, ripping it free. He dragged the sparkling cut glass along the bannister, scratching a perfect gauge through the surface, all the way along. He circled down the winding staircase. Flat-footed, he jumped onto one of the black linoleum squares, dropping the glass on the floor. It shattered at his feet. He alternated his feet from one black square to the next. He left the front door wide open, descended the stone steps, tapes rattled in his bag. The door clicked shut behind him. He scuffed the pavement, looking back at the lagoon blue strobing light from Kilpatrick's window on the second floor.

"Guilt is a wasted emotion," said Bass. "Transition emotion."

21

dOgHoUsE bApTisM

Moira brushed the shoulders of a fluffy jacket, flicking the loose arms over a wooden coat hanger. She ripped a pink number from a book of raffle tickets and passed it over to a red-haired girl through the cloakroom hatch of the Union club. She acted the part of a servant. The girl hoisted her ice white dress up plumping her milky breasts with cupped hands. Moira's face dropped to bored impatience as the girl snatched for the ticket and clipped her stiletto heals away without a word of appreciation. Moira slammed open a closed paperback, folding it along the spine, one leg crossed over the other, resting on her elbow. Praying for time to pass.

"Excuse me, sweet cheeks." Said a disguised, familiar voice. A clenched fist knocked on the edge of the hatch. "Can you retrieve my sheepskin, please. Lovely Jubbly."

Moira looked up, concealing a huff of impatience. She smiled, realising it was Dylan poking his head through the hatch, rubbing his palms together like a baby faced Del-boy.

"Thank god, it's you. I almost didn't recognise you."

"I'm taking that as a compliment," he said.

"You should. Loving the new hair and it's blue," she said. "You've pierced your lip too. All very drastic. How long is it since I last saw you?"

"Not long, seems like ages."

"Short sleeved band t-shirt I see, is that to show off your—," Moira leaned forward, squinting. "Your new tattoo. Check you out, bad arse. I'm trying to read it." She took him by the wrist to read the words on his arm. "I Am the Resurrection. You're changing overnight. Who you trying to impress?"

"I think this is who I am," he said.

"Yeah, all right Sandy, you better shape up. You're a walking conformity."

"What d'ya mean?"

"You're subscribing to an image you've been told to indulge."

"This is punk."

"Punk's a mentality," she said. "You don't have to shave your head. You've got it all wrong. Studded belts, spitting lips and The Clash are a convention. Living your truth and voting, despite the contradictions, is truly who you are."

"I'm not a stereotype?"

"Look around this place. It's too easy to relax into a slumber of ignorance. All these bitches pushing out their tits and flapping their fannies. And for what?"

"I assumed you loved working here."

"In a cloakroom?"

"Kind of a joke,"

"If I didn't have to, I wouldn't. It's the tragedy of life. I can't stand working here, especially on a Friday night. Everyone's so vapid."

"What book you reading?" Said Dylan.

"The Day of the Triffids." Moira flapped the book for him to read the blurred cover.

"The one with the plants? Howard Keel's in the film."

"I've never seen the film. I don't have a TV, remember?"

"I still don't understand how that works."

"It's one of the Penguin classics. I do my best not to end up like the rest of these fools. Give me a good book and the Eden project, and I'm merry."

"That bio-dome place in Cornwall?"

"I haven't been yet—, It's hard to see you under your new punk image, but yeah, near St. Austell."

"You'll get used to it. The last time I went to St. Austell, there was nothing but charity shops. Watched The Matrix at the cinema. I say cinema, more like someone's front room."

"Just so I know, do all your chats reference films?"

He thought for a moment. "It doesn't define me. It's what my degree's in."

"Your degree is in film? I thought you were in Kilpatrick's for the gender and race module. I didn't even know film studies was an actual thing."

"You're talking to the future, Kubrick."

"Now, I know who that is. I've read A Clockwork Orange."

"Interestingly, it was Kubrick himself who withdrew that. It wasn't banned."

"For your information, Mr. Mohawk. Real punks, don't give two hoots. You may have to rethink your definition of interesting. You don't have to try so hard with me."

"I'm searching."

"Give it up, no need. Since you asked, I'm doing English Lit."

"I could've guessed. What time do you have to sit here til?"

Moira folded back the long, stretched sleeve covering her palms. Looking at her watch. "Ten," she said. "Then, I'm free. But I want to get the hell outta Dodge. I can't stand the cheesy white people drivel they play here on a Friday. No offence."

"None taken. I'll wait for you to finish in that case."

"I don't want plans. I'm for spontaneity tonight," she said.

Sitting on the bank of the fast flowing River Rye, trainers tangling off the bank, scuffing the retaining wall leading to a lock, the white tipped balance beam reflecting moonlight. Cars passed in the rubbery distance. Blurred lights drift with time. Clouds of condescension escaped their mouths.

"Sometimes living this studious persona is tedious, ya know? I wanna feel numb. Really poke a stick into the midst of my grey matter. Stop myself from thinking every minute," said Moira.

"It's like you're after my own heart," he said.

Moira slammed her hands down beside her, jerked down, splashing knee deep into the shallow river below. The water filled and weighed down her Converse, made her skin contract. She waded out to the middle, stumbling on loose rocks. She steadied herself with hands like paddles, pushing forward through the water. Dylan was powerless to act. Unable to speak. He sat stiff, watching as she threw her arms wide, stiff like a crucifix. She fell back; splashing, disappearing under a wave of freezing dark water, her eyes closed tight as water washed over her face, slimy leaves sticking to her forehead.

"Moira." Said Dylan, jumping in, the cold made him want to urinate. He hopped over breaking peaks of water like an Artic fox, wading out to reach her, hobbling over the uneven stony river bed. He took hold, under her arms, a dead weight. She wasn't helping. The water cascading over her shoulders. She laughed, a maniacal laugh mixed with a burp. Flipped over, rising to her feet. Water dripping from her hoodie sleeves as she flapped her arms. She coughed a chesty dry rattle from her lungs. Pulled herself up on the wall, Dylan heaving with his shoulder to help as she climbed out. She dripped from head to toe, fully clothed. Every white highlight of her clothing was now dark, sodden with water. Moira crouched, resting on her heals, shook her hands dry, reached for a packet of cigarettes, retrieved one, sparked the tip, her eyes bloodshot. She left the orange flame burning, as a cloud of white smoke teased. She smiled at Dylan. The lighter clicked off as he waded back up the bank, water squelching from his trainers.

"You didn't have to rescue me," she said.

"I think I did."

"Too many secrets and lies in this life. Sometimes I just want to push myself. That was my baptism," she said. "You were here to experience it with me."

"I'm so glad. Fucking hell, Moira, don't do that again."

"It's outta my system," she said. "For now, I can't promise the urge won't take me later."

"Non stop Mardi Gras with you." He said, ringing water from his scrunched up hoodie. "Come on, we need to get you out of those clothes."

"Is that a promise?"

"You're unbelievable."

"And don't you forget it." She held out her hand for Dylan to drag her up. His hand grabbed her wrist. "Cliffhanger," she said. Wrapped her hand around his wrist. "That way, if I let go. You've still got hold of me. I won't plunge to my death."

"I've got you," he said.

"For now, for now. You think I'm a freak, don't you?"

"Trust me. I don't think you're a freak."

"I don't trust people who use the phrase, trust me."

"Funny, I know people who say the exact same thing."

"Loose pronoun. I'm assuming your girlfriend. I won't ask." Said Moira, removing her glasses. "I can't see a thing."

Dylan studied the teardrop shape of her face, her hazel eyes staring at his lips. His warm breath on her wet nose, eyes closed. Touched her thick lips on his, feeling silky fluttering butterfly wings. She nuzzled her wet forehead into his cheek, forced her arms under his, wrapping them around his waist, and shoved her body into his. Dylan nuzzled his chin on the top of her damp hood.

"I'm freezing my tits off," she said. Her tight grip became loose. She backed off, took a deep drag and flicked her flaming cigarette into the river. "You walking me home?"

Memories of Laura standing in front of him, gesticulating and stamping her feet, tears rolling from her cheeks. He felt the pain in his knees as he remembered begging on her driveway, pebbled shingles digging his kneecaps. Dinner with her parents, around the table, explaining and pleading that he wasn't a bad guy. That he could be trusted. Promising to make an effort to keep their daughter happy.

With Moira stood before him, her hand waiting to be held. Resistance was pointless. He wanted her the moment they spoke. Every elegant touch from her chocolate fingers, her skin dark against his. He held their hands up, seeing nothing but Spike Lee's Jungle Fever video sleeve.

"I'm not ready for this surreal night to end," he said.

22

lOvE iS pArAnOiD

Charlie thumped his BMW up on the curb. Laura rattled in her seat. She gazed from the passenger window at the porch light of her parents' house. Their heads jolting forward as the car halted.

"I feel like I don't belong here." She said, swivelling in the passenger seat. "It's my house, but it's not. I just live here. I have to do as I'm told when all I want is to be left alone."

The engine shuddered to a standstill, fan humming alive. Charlie yanked on the handbrake, flicking the interior light on.

"You OK—," he said, tutting. Spinning the volume dial, lowering the blare of Def Leppard's, Pour Some Sugar on me.

Laura flipped her phone over in her lap. "Why hasn't he text me?" She slammed it back, screen down.

"The better question is, why are you still with him?" Said Charlie, unclipping his seat belt.

Laura couldn't take her disappointed eyes from her phone, hypnotised, staring back out of the window at the long pebbled driveway, looking up at her bedroom.

"I never cheated on you," said Charlie. "The hair and lip ring sentiment is weak, it's juvenile. Who does that, gets a tattoo?" He flailed his hands in the air.

"I like the lip ring. No, I love it. I like it on my lips." She said and pressed her index finger to her mouth. "And, not these lips."

"Filth. You say all this to tease me. He's not you, he doesn't fit, I still don't know why we spilt up? You know we're destined to be together, right?" Charlie reached for her hand. "It's inevitable, the whole thing, house of our own, our own porch light, kid in one of those shoulder sling things—,"

"A baby carrier."

"Exactly, you complaining your feet hurt because you insist on wearing heals hiking over Cheddar Gorge. We'll get married in a barn, heavy metal on a cello."

"Shut up. I'm not gettin' married in a barn, my hayfever."

"It'll happen, I mean it—,"

"There'll be no heavy metal anywhere near my wedding."

"Our wedding. Soft rock only, ballads, maybe Alice Cooper, at a push, Motorhead."

"You're living in a dream world, nothing beyond a live band playing The Beach Boys."

"And don't I know it." Said Charlie, cupping her hands in his. "Laura, you're my great love, my first love. We're each other's first love. I don't want you to slip away from me, not for someone like Dylan. I don't want to tell people you're my ex anymore."

"You'll always be a part of my life, somehow." She said and kissed his hand. "What you said was sweet and I don't mean to rub it in or anything, but I think I love him."

Charlie tutted, almost roaring it from his mouth like a belch. "Someone's got to."

Laura squeezed his warm hand between hers. "Stop it."

"You do what you have to do. Sow your wild oats, experience someone else. You know, as well as I do. When summer rocks around and he's over there gallivanting with hot, blonde, American girls, groping up on 'em in the back row of the movies." He squeezed the air as if honking two imaginary breasts. "Living his best life. We'll be together, passing the time, sat having our picnics, dreading the second he comes back. That'll be our own little story, right there, a story of resentment. He'll be the jealous one when he comes to pick you up and we're sitting in the back garden, on a blanket, sharing flutes of Appletizer and egg and cress sandwiches."

"You know how to paint a picture, I'll give you that."

"Because I know it's our truth. I know you too well. There's no way, not a chance in hell, you'll maintain a long distance relationship with him. Not for nine weeks, no way you will. I mean, why waste your time?"

"You know you're gonna be mine?"

"See, right there. That." Charlie said and pointed, smirking with excitement. "That's our thing." Laura couldn't help herself laughing. "Seriously," he said. "Every couple has to have a thing, something they share." He poked her in the ribs , doing his best to appear playful. "What's funny about that, wiseguy?" He said, using a mafia style voice.

Laura snorted laughter into her sleeve. Her unintentional pig sound made her laugh louder. Charlie shook his head, playful annoyance, she was in hysterics. He tapped his forehead off the steering wheel.

As she took a deep breath in, her laughter stopped, she wiped a tear from her eye with the back of her nail.

Charlie slid his hand on her neck, under her ear. "What do you share with him?" He circled his thumb under her earlobe. She tilted her head into his hand, her eyes rolled and closed, giggling them open again.

"You're a bastard."

"I just know how to push your buttons," he said.

Laura thumbed the electric windows down. "Warm suddenly," She said. Whistling air from her lips as she fanned her face.

"See, we discovered your steamy zones together." Said Charlie, walking his stiff fingers along the inside of her cool, naked thigh. "Inch by inch."

Laura's eyes followed his exploring fingers, grabbing his wrist. "If you're gonna do something, you better do it right." She said, forcing his hand between her parting legs. Their foreheads squeezed together, as heavy breath resisted their touching lips. She slapped his hand away.

"I'm not ready to go home yet," she said. "Drive somewhere." Her hands rearranged her skirt, smoothing it over her thighs.

Charlie smiled, tugged on his seat belt, it snapped back refusing to click into the buckle. "I thought you'd never ask." He smiled, turning and fumbling the key in the ignition, checked his rear-view mirror and screeched away, bouncing off the curb. Laura flicked off the interior light as their bodies pushed into the seats with the speed of acceleration. Laura held the power button to her phone and turned it off.

"I don't want to be disturbed," she said.

The radio played. Laura clapped her hands.

"You remember this song?" Said Charlie, turning the stereo up. His concentration switched back to driving, winding country roads, headlights bouncing off green twinkling leaves and cracking tree bark.

Laura chuckled and said. "Of course I do. Even though." She notched the volume louder. "It's played to death. Yellow will always be all I hear inside a freezing tent."

"Jesus, that was a Coldplay night."

"They say you never forget your first time. To me, that was perfection. 'I only have one sleeping bag', yeah right."

"A guys gotta try and it worked. You know, we had to throw that tent out," said Charlie.

"The black and gold one?"

"You squirted in it. My dad thought it was rain damage, there's no way he'd believe a human made those stains."

"He didn't say anything, did he?"

"He was fine, relax. He described the smell as a mix of Guinness and sauerkraut."

"No, he didn't, tell me he didn't."

"No, he didn't. But, that's all I could smell." Charlie looked over his glasses, slowing at a junction.

"You're disgusting,"

"I'm disgusting," he said. "It came out of you." He fanned his upturned nose.

"I didn't have Guinness *or* sauerkraut."

"It was more the folding it away, still wet."

"This conversation is making me suitably moist, so keep it up, big boy." She said and tapped his knee.

"Sarcasm is the lowest form of wit, or so they say."

"Was that sarcasm though, more like double entendre, don't cha think?"

"I can never remember the difference." Said Charlie, squinting at the road, lit by full beams.

"Shit, where are we? Just pull into that road there." She said, pointing.

"All right, I know. I'm irresistible when I get started."

"Are we in Overdales? These houses look familiar, bloody expensive."

The car rolled past grand, electronic gates with custom initials on most, eight foot high walls protecting perimeters backed with tall evergreen bushes.

"That was Beaumont House, Yeah, this is Overdales."

"Do you want me to stop here somewhere? Maybe down the end —,"

"Pull over here," she said.

Charlie's wheel rims crunched against the curb.

"Shit, that's gonna leave a nice scratch."

"Don't worry, it's just a car."

"It's more than just a car."

He flicked off the engine, the interior light pinged bright. He poked at it. Laura swung her legs over the central console, kicking the gear stick. She straddled his lap, hitching her skirt up.

"Hold out your hands." She said, squeezing her closed fists shut. "Go on, hold out your hands."

Charlie cupped his hands in preparation, his eyes wide as Laura's lacy white thong floated down.

"That was fast, I didn't even see you do that."

"I'm full of surprises," she said.

His vision full of her smile, her nose in his face. Lips sucking, heavy breathing with tongues squeezed between teeth. She clambered to unclasp his jeans. Took hold of his face and bit his bottom lip. Flinching, he pressed his finger against it, leaving blood on his skin.

"You know that drives me insane," he said. He grabbed for her naked arse cheeks. The windows steamed. Laura's head bumped off the ceiling.

Charlie peeled his eyelids down and examined his pupils in the rear-view mirror.

"Does it smell like weed in here?" he said. "Can't believe I let you smoke."

"All I can smell is sex. And, if I swallow. I deserve a smoke."

Charlie laughed, starting the engine.

"What the hell was that music playing?"

"You mean the one song you managed to last through—,"

"All right, I put on a good show."

"It was that girl band, Dream. He loves U not. Oh, I hope it wasn't some kind of artistic omen.

"This is just between you and I, right?"

"Isn't it you and me, between you and me, you and I, isn't it something to do with the object?—,"

"Relax," he said. "We're not getting back together?"

"You relax. For now, I'm with Dylan—,"

A thump on the passenger window, a blurry commotion like a seagull caught in a desk fan.

Bang.

Bang.

Bang.

"On yer way." An aged voice shouted, fist wagging.

Charlie shoved the gear stick into first, zipping away from the curb.

"Dirty cretins, shagging outside my…" The voice faded away. Charlie shifting his eyes between the road and looking back in the mirror.

Laura laughed, her hand over her mouth. Charlie trying to get his breath, looking right, leaning forward to look left around Laura. He turned onto a main road.

Laura held up a flapping condom. "What should I do with this?" She said, waggling it in Charlie's face, not being able to stop her giggling.

"Getting it away from me would be thought one. I'm driving. Toss it out the window."

Laura pressed on the automatic windows, opening halfway. She poked her fingers out. The balloon like condom vibrated in the wind, letting it go.

"Magic," she said. "Sucked out like a toddler on a jumbo jet. I hope you made a wish." The window closed shut with a clank. The roar from the passing road outside stifled. The radio kicked over to a new track. Ten Storey Love Song by The Stone Roses.

"Good song." Said Charlie, indicating right, the click almost in tune with the opening bars of the music.

"The Stone Roses are Dylan's favourite band."

"What Roses fan has a mohawk?"

"We know he did it for me," she said. "He's playing at the whole thing."

"With or without the mohawk, he's still a dumb arse. Cutting his hair because he knows you like 'em, pathetic. Seriously, you need to get rid of him."

"And be with you, you mean?"

Charlie didn't answer.

Laura flicked her phone over, brought it to life with a jab of her finger.

'1 message received,'

'Love you, little lady. G'nite X'

Laura pushed her head back in the seat, staring at the ceiling of the car. She burst forward, flicking the power button of the radio, the car humming along the road, silence between them.

"You gonna reply with; love you too, little boy?" said Charlie.

"Shut up and drive. I got mine."

23

gAlLoW fInGeR bAnG

Dylan counted the black pixel squares making up the text message composed to Laura. Hoping by initiating contact, she might respond. No longer as fast at replying, that she once was. He sat on the floor of Moira's bedroom. Opportunity and deception forcing his pores open with sweat. Leaning against her single bed, knees hitched up. The shower finished cascading water. The bedroom door opened, Moira wearing a pair of purple baggy tracksuit bottoms and a hoodie with the cover of Disintegration by The Cure adorning it. Her hands adjusting a grey shower cap, purple framed glasses steamed up.

"You staying here tonight?" She said, stretching the cap free. Her black afro, purple ends, voluminous with heat, now curly, popped around her head, framing her face.

"I probably shouldn't."

"There's myriad of selfish acts we shouldn't partake in life, and it's those things we should take a chance on."

"Aristotle added of desire," said Dylan.

"I don't business what Aristotle said. The Republic is over there, somewhere." Moira pointed. "But not tonight. I'm asking you to stay. You need to. I want you here with me."

"Chill Winston, I'm staying."

Moira draped her wet towel over the computer chair, swivelled it around, shoulders slumped. She pushed the monitor power button on. With a humming click, the screen shone. A black cursor flashed on and off, teasing her creativity. She typed on a blank document, her fingers gentle, crunching, and gliding over keys.

"What are you doing?" he said.

"It may sound crazy." She said, her fingers stopped typing. "I'm making a note of how I felt when you dragged me outta the water. It's what I do."

"Well, how did you feel?"

"That's what I'm trying to write." Moira spun in her seat, ruffled her hand through her hair, messing it up. Eyes wide like Jack Nicholson, her best impression. "Dylan, I'll explain it to you. You're breaking my concentration, distracting me." She slapped her forehead, recreating the familiar scene she was acting out. He smiled, recognising the reference. "When I'm in here, it means I'm writing. Understand?"

"Very good," he said.

"Thanks. So, I could taste ice cube metal on my tongue," she said. "I had this falling sensation, like disappointment and excitement, all shredded up with relief." She stopped typing, turned again in the office chair. "You could have left me, ya know?"

"I wouldn't have left you, not laying in the water."

"Some people would. Don't you find that interesting?" She clasped her hands together, inspired by her own contemplation. "The way we inherently react to different things."

"My instinct was to get you out."

"Why though?"

"Are you really asking me this?"

"Tell me what you thought."

"I don't want to be some scene in your book."

"You chill, Winston. I'll change your name. Tell me what you felt."

"You're mad. It scared me, the thought you might drown," he paused. "I didn't wanna see that. It was dramatic, dramatic for drama's sake, ya know. When you didn't help, I thought you were unhinged."

"Unhinged?"

"Sorry. Not unhinged, vulnerable. You looked weak."

"I'm far from weak. I'm using unhinged though. The bravest thing you can do is control your own destiny."

"I do enjoy our self-help sessions, most insightful. I will say, you were a passenger on that water, you weren't controlling anything. It's far braver to stand on your heals, roll your shoulders and jab a crashing wave."

Moira edged her finger along the plastic cases of CDs above her computer and said.

"My dad was always more impressed with everyone else than me." She pulled a case from the shelf.

"Then don't worry about seeking his approval."

"I don't, now. I need some Maxinquaye," she said.

"You've lost me."

Moira flicked the CD case on her shoulder, like a parrot, exposing Dylan to the front cover. "Tricky," she said. "I've spent my life being told what to do, at home, at school. Then college, now University. I escape to this room just to feel sane. All this shit around me makes me feel like I'm still clinging to being an eight-year-old. I'm not sure what I'm doing here. It's like I'm having to live up to the bored expectation of my parents. All because it's what they did. Half arsed and God fearing. Out of sight, feigning interest. Aren't you worried what you'll do when all this is over?"

"Everyone is. That's the challenge. All this is about discovering who you wanna be. There's no time limit, no rush. You just have to be patient and live your truth."

"Yeah whatever, Tony Robbins. I'm not paying for your advice.

There's always a rush. I'll wake up tomorrow and be sixty."

"So, you threw yourself in a river to experience life?"

"To experience you," she said. "Ya dumb arse."

"Not sure I understand how your mind works."

"Even I've given up trying. Big D can't lace me with enough weed or pints of vodka to turn my brain off. I hate waiting for things to happen. I just wanna watch the world burn."

"I'm not being funny or taking the piss—,"

"Just say it. You think I should see a doctor?"

"No, I was gonna say, have you considered just talking to someone, anyone?"

"I'm talking to you."

"I mean like a professional."

"Been there, done that." Moira hopped from her chair to the bed. "Waste of time. My parents paid for therapy." She sat crossed legged, tucking her ankles in. "Made me more self-conscious that something wasn't right with me. The whole thing became this excuse for me to explain away my emotions."

Dylan sat up on the edge of the bed.

"It never set me free. It made me fade behind my demons. That worked wonders for my parents. Seen and not heard. They could save face in front of the neighbours," she said.

"Lay down. Try to relax," said Dylan. He guided her to rest her head on the pillow.

Moira resisted. "That's the problem, right there. You're like everyone else. It's too easy for me to be quiet. I've been quiet for most of my life. I don't want you to be someone else who tells me to disappear into the background. Forever reminded, you'll see my teeth in the dark."

"I'm not doing that, Moira. I'm staying with you." Dylan stroked her bare feet.

"You'll be gone tomorrow," she said.

"I'll have to leave at some point. I'll stay tonight, but I won't be able to stay forever."

"What's forever, anyway?"

"Whatever makes you happy. Try to rest."

Moira stared at the ceiling. "Come here," she said. Patting the mattress. The duvet folded back, her legs elevated, resting on top of it. Dylan examined his phone. A wave of nerves engrossed him. He shuffled his hand, scrolling through contacts, finding 'Laura's' name. Moira tickled Dylan's back, from shoulder blades to where his jeans met his shirt. She gripped his waistband, pulling him back. He supported himself on his elbows, refusing to lay flat. The fear of premature embarrassment, heavy in his stomach.

"Make me numb," she said.

"Moira." Said Dylan standing up, his hands shuffling.

She sat up, grabbing his crotch, sitting up on her knees to join his eye line. "It's important to do what you want to do."

"I have a girlfriend," he said.

"I have a boyfriend. We like each other. I wanna feel you. Don't you wanna know we've slept together?"

"But, Laura."

"Don't call me, Laura." She laughed. "You'll always have this experience." She slapped her palms on the side of his face, sucking at his lips. Dylan held her hands in his.

"Moira. It's OK. You don't have to do this. I'm not saying we never will. We could still have our moment together. All I'm saying is, not tonight. Not whilst you're like this. I feel like I'm taking advantage."

"Fuck off. I'm offering you sex here. I know you've never gone black."

"You don't know that."

"Believe me, I know. I can see it. You've never tasted the juice."

"I've never had the opportun—, Anyway, lay down. You're fine. I'm staying." Dylan tried to help, laying her flat. Moira fought back, shaking her shoulders. She laid back, a distant promise of tears in her eyes. Dylan covered her, adding pressure around her shoulders to tuck her in. He snapped off the bedroom light.

"You want me to turn this off?" said Dylan, pointing at the stereo.

"Just turn it down a bit."

Dylan hopped over to the bed, getting in, fully clothed, socks still on and joined alongside her. Covering his own body with the edge of the thin duvet. She turned, nestling her chin into his chest. He wrapped her up and held her close. His eyes wide open, exploring the lumpy bumps in the Artexed ceiling.

"I love this track," she said. "Suffocated Love. Story of my life."

The bedroom silent, a glow of kiwi green from the stereo. Moira's stiff, trembling hand unclasped Dylan's jeans. They popped open as if she had blurted a magic word. Her hand inside, cupping his genitals over his boxers, a handful of peeled lychees. She squeezed. Pushing her hand between silk material and pubic hair like razor wire. She gripped the shaft of his floppy penis, began pumping. His groin felt heavy, twisted inside. Laura appeared in the corner, sat naked on the desk. An upside down book, she turned over in her hands from cover to cover, end to end. She opened it with childlike intrigue. An erect, throbbing, veiny penis extended out from the pages like a pop-up book.

"Mmmm, Jewish balls." Said Laura in an Irish accent, high pitched, crazed leprechaun delivery. Her eyes rolled back in her head as the penis evaporated into her black hole mouth. Charlie straddled Dylan's chest, his balls presented in his palm, like a quality bottle of red. Dylan thrust his needle arms out to fight him off. His arms felt heavy, floating noodles, having no effect. They couldn't even touch him.

Dylan sprang up, his eyes banging open. He stared around the room, heart beating. Light cracked through the edges of the blinds. The room appeared still, much like his dream. Everything in its place. He felt a pressure on his bladder, the need to make it to the bathroom.

His jeans still buttoned. He tiptoed, used the toilet, peeing quiet against the cistern, not allowing for water explosions. He waited for the water to refill, to avoid the rattling noise being heard as he opened the door. Consideration he thought would buy him personality points. He closed Moira's door, holding the handle to silence the click from the bolt as it rammed into place. Intrigued with his back turned, he heard scratching, a shuffling sound of tickling material. Moira laid flat on her back, eyes closed, her features lost in the shadows. Her left-hand limp behind her head under the pillow. Right hand under the duvet, legs spread wide as if pitching a circus tent. A delicate, suppressed windy moan whimpered from her lips. Back arched, shoulders raised. She ripped the duvet from her legs; it rolled to the floor. Naked, stretched legs, waggling toes. Dylan lost himself in desire. Her chocolate skin required whipped cream. Wet fingers glistened between her legs. He considered looking away, only his eyes refused to listen. What if she wants me to watch?

A bashful rumble from his throat would let her know he was present. Standing still, his mind leaned to the predestination of his vibrating tongue inside her. Leaning against the door, crotch stretching jeans. He held his breath. Air sizzled from his lips, forced his hands behind his back, and pressed himself into the door. Watching was fine, he concluded. If she caught him touching himself, end of play.

Moira's eyes closed tight. She teased her lips with her finger, sucking it dry. Dylan breathed heavy through his nose, creating a whistle. Moira licked her finger, traced her body, ironing her trimmed black pubic hair with hot hands. Dylan lowered himself to the end of the bed, doing his best not to disturb her. Moira's legs trembled and shook. She pushed a finger in her anus. White eyes flashed.

"I'm coming, Dex, I'm coming," she said. Spitting and crackling from her throat. Her eyes opened, she took a deep breath. Noticing Dylan sat looking at her. He couldn't hide the bulge in his jeans.

"To spare embarrassment further. Come here to me," she said.

Dylan crawled up the mattress, adjusting his jeans with his hand. He perched on the edge of the bed, feet not touching the floor. Moira kneeled behind him, flopping and draping herself over his shoulders. Her hand dropped in his lap.

"Put my finger in your mouth, suck it clean," she said.

Dylan thought to argue for a moment. He groped for her wrist, lifting it to his mouth.

"Not that one."

"I knew which one you meant." Dylan squirmed. "Am I right in saying that was up your——,"

Moira nodded. "That's right. Swallow it deep."

Dylan swallowed, refusing to breathe through his nose as Moira poked her little finger into his mouth. He sucked like an infant on a teat.

"Quite the experience," she said. "One you won't forget and one you won't share."

Dylan gagged. "I wouldn't have, anyway." He carried on sucking.

"You wanna see how sick I am? Come around at feeding time. I want music for this." Said Moira, bending, naked from the waist down to turn on the stereo. Her round bottom tensed. "Aftermath." The music teased from the speakers. Hips joining the beat. Moira lifted her hoodie up over her head. She draped it behind Dylan's neck. Black cherry nipples poked his eyeballs, he sucked them slow.

Moira shook her Afro, straddling his lap. Their bodies entwined, not taking his mouth from her skin.

"Feed me," she said.

24

sTrAiGhT eDgeD miTrA

Bass lugged his guitar case through the open front door, clunking it on the floor in front of the sofa in the living room. Hearing the band practice replaying in his head. Descending bass lines; C Bb Am Gm F Eb Dm C. Gary's drum thumping, coming in after a stick count of four. The lyric about Brighton didn't work. The consensus being 'it sounded too much like The Smiths'. Eddie, with his leather jacket, impressed himself with his new approach to vocals.

Bass's backpack inched from his shoulder. He stood still for a second, listening for movement from within the house, an expanding creak of floorboards, the love tap of a headboard, nothing. His bag dumped on the sofa. He unclasped the guitar case. The metal clips rattled. Spun the guitar around, perching it on his knee. He thumbed the top string, alternating his stiff walking fingers over the other thick strings and frets, jamming to his own spontaneous tune. He stopped, his fingers screeching. He stood the guitar upright against the sofa. Hopped over, checking the kitchen, no one there. Dylan's door, wide open. The TV playing on mute. No sign of him. He edged side footed to the top of the stairs, looking through the spindly, chipped balustrades. His own bedroom door closed tight, a shaft of sunlight bursting through the keyhole, reflecting specks of floating dust. Yestin's door was wide open, the room dark, curtains drawn. Florence's room was the same. Bass released a roaring belch, forcing it free to have anyone around reproach him. There was nothing. Confirmed as being alone. The house empty. He peered through the net curtains, looking out to the stretching road, parked cars on both sides. He shot a look up at the other end. The road ascends into a hill, the semi-detached houses, a reflection of a reflection. Bass threw himself onto the sofa and unzipped his backpack. Wrestled and removed Dylan's Sanyo video camera. Unwrapped the aux cables. Powered on the VCR, jabbing at the inputs. He hit play on the camera. A white triangle appeared on the small television screen. He trailed the cable to the sofa, sitting, his knees cracking. The room filled with a blue illumination. Then, the image played out, a grainy, static shot of Dylan's single bed, the room obscured by strategically placed books and a crumpled t-shirt, restricting some of the frame. Bass pushed on fast forward. White lines scratched across the image until, fast moving, gesticulating arms flapped like ostriches. Bass squeezed his finger from the button. The video juddered, playing out in real time. Laura removed her brown corduroy jacket, flicking her blonde hair from her collar. Dylan kicked off his Converse All Stars, standing on the heals. He walked out of frame as music played in the background. Bass leaned forward to identify the tune and hear what they were saying. He thumbed the volume button, increasing it, the blue line stretching across the screen as The Stone Roses got louder, and the familiar soft voices of Dylan and Laura became clearer from the speaker. Laura sat up on her knees. Dylan perched on the edge of the bed with her. They kissed. Laura's hand tight behind the back of his neck. Bass licked his tongue over his teeth. He dropped the camera to his side, sat back and watched Laura lay curled up on Dylan's chest, his legs yanked up. Bass listened, his head tilted as Dylan jumped up, excusing himself from the room, jogging to the door. Laura rested on her elbows, a smile befell her face as she reached for her bag, retrieving her mobile phone. She stabbed fingers into the keypad, smiled to herself, letting her phone flop to her chest.

"Don't worry about it." Said Laura, off into the distance.

Bass giggled to himself, shaking his head. "Yeah, don't worry about it. Now, don't bore us." Bass hit fast forward. "Get to the chorus."

Laura stood naked in front of Dylan as his feet dangled from the bed. She obscured the camera's sight of Dylan's modesty with her shoulder. Bass urged her to move out of the way. He fanned his knees as Laura slipped on to her back, her hand disappearing between her legs. Dylan rolled on top of her. Bass hit pause, sitting up on the sofa, peering out over the windowsill, listening, anticipating silence to make a noise. Nothing. Exhalation, his unspoken relief. The innermost cogs of the camera cranked forward again as he resumed play. Laura exhaled, her gasp of air popped from the television. Bass studied Dylan's naked back, shoulders tense. His eyes explored the stiff, straight dip of his spine, to his white, peachy clenched naked buttocks. Dylan's hands collected and clenched at the duvet. Bass rolled his shoulders into the sofa, relaxing into the cushion. Dylan ran his hand over his nipple on-screen. Bass then pushed his own hand up and under his hoodie, hand over his erect stiff nipples and squeezed, emulating the movement of Dylan's hands. He ran his hand over the smoothness of his belly, forcing his hand under his DC belt and clasped his semi-erect penis. His cords bulged and rolled as he massaged himself. Laura's legs were wide open. The quality of the video, not clear enough for Bass to squint to see the delicate, fleshy intricacies of her vagina. Dylan kicked free the duvet from his ankles, letting it slide and drop to the carpet as his hips rolled between her thighs. Bass rubbed himself in time with Dylan's thrusting motion. He grabbed for the remote control, his thumb pushing at the volume button, turning the sound up to maximum. The sound of the creaking bed rang out. Laura's whining orgasm whimpered free, echoing tinny from the hissing speakers.

"I wish you'd shut up." Said Bass to the TV.

Dylan stopped pumping, sat up between her knees, taking his erect penis in his hand as Laura placed her hand on his and squeezed her breasts.

"You want me to try from behind?"

"God no, you're not doing me like a dog."

Bass scoffed to himself. "Boring bitch."

"I'll ride you." Her voice said loud, reverberating off the walls from the speakers.

Dylan laid on his back, Bass stared at the fleshy pink shaft of Dylan's penis, flopping and hitting below his belly button. Laura straddled him, guiding his penis inside her like a magic trick, now gone. Dylan's hands on her hips. Bass focused on the base of Dylan's penis as it disappeared, her tight cheeks bouncing off furry testicles. Heavy breathed agreement, moaned from the TV. Dylan's deep voice covering Laura's panting. Bass stroked himself, building in rhythm, matching the speed of climax from his unwitting television sex prisoners. His back arched, ejaculating inside his trousers. He wiped his palm on the side of his thigh, and slid it on the cushion of the sofa. He examined it was dry, sniffing his palm. An odour of butcher bleach. Sitting forward, he sparked a cigarette, and watched as Laura swung her legs off over Dylan's. They both laid naked, uncovered on their backs. Bass sat forward, trying to look closer at Dylan's weeping, flaccid penis. Laura scratched her flaxen landing strip with her fingernails, then waggled his shaft like a cocktail sausage.

"He's a grower, not a shower." She said, giggling to herself.

Bass laughed out loud at the television.

"Is that Dylan?" Shouted Mr. Mitra, from the doorway of the living room. Bass spun around. His throat heavy, bile scratching to escape. His heart pounded in his chest, every emotion felt contrived. Not able to grip his sense of rationality. Mr Mitra's screwed-up face stared back at him. His moustache wriggled with snarls. Then to the television. Tracing his eyes along the knotted liquorice like wires to the Sanyo 8mm camera. "What are you doing, you filthy one?"

"It's not what it looks like." Said Bass, he fumbled for the camera, jabbing to turn it off.

Mr. Mitra grabbed for the camera, knocking Bass's cigarette from his mouth. Mitra's shoulder smacked his chin, Bass landed on his back on the floor.

"You stay there. Don't you move." Said Mr. Mitra, holding the camera at arm's length above his head.

Bass's icy hand wrapped around the alder wood guitar neck. He swung it like an Olympic hammer, cracking it off the side of Mitra's head. The camera dropped. Plastic pieces broke free, scattering under the sofa. Mr. Mitra's eyes closed, slits of moon white. A groan escaped his mouth as he fell back through the living room doorway. Bass vaulted the sofa, slamming down the guitar. The strings vibrated. The wood spread Mitra's nose across his face, blood plastering the walls in Jackson Pollock splashes resembling Number 48. Mr. Mitra held his stiff arms straight, shielding his face. Elbows flopping, broken forearms, his wrists limp to defend. Bass jumped to the bottom step of the stairs, thrust the guitar on his bloodied head, like a pile driver. Slammed it with a crack. Biting on his lip. Nostrils quivering. In it 'til the end', he thought. He crunched it into Mitra's bald skull again, tearing at his scalp. Thumped it down again. And again. Bass closed his eyes. Hit down again. Mitra's distorted face, his lips gasped for breath, thick blood bubbles blocking his airway. Bass smashed it into his cheek, a pink gash opened below his eyeball. Mitra didn't move. Bass backed away, dropping his guitar to the floor. He leaned on the sofa. Mr. Mitra's eyes stared open. Lip swollen. Eyes dribbling blood. The lacerations and grazes amazed Bass, he couldn't recognise him. No longer identify he was Asian, except for a patch of brown skin through blood on his hands. Bass noticed his cigarette, embers burning a pound size hole in the carpet. He picked it up. Placed it in his mouth and inhaled, wiping his wrist across his face, smearing blood like war paint over his cheeks.

"I really like sex." Said Dylan's voice from the TV.

"You really like sex with me, you mean?" said Laura.

"Of course, that goes without saying. I think I'm obsessed with your pussy."

"Don't say pussy. It's so crass. Use something sweeter. She's, she's my Newt."

"This may be the best night of my life."

Bass remembered his loud banging on the bedroom door. Now he was seeing it from their side. The way Laura jumped up, covering herself with the duvet. Bass laughed, knowing what was coming. His voice reassuring them he wasn't entering the room. He waggled Grand Theft Auto two through the crack in the door.

He snatched for the video camera, ripped the cables from the side, launching it at the TV. It cracked the screen, turning navy blue. He fell back on the sofa, wiped his blood stained trainers on the arm. Inhaled on his cigarette and blew smoke rings toward the ceiling.

25

hAnDwRitTeN miXeD cD

Converse trainers removed. Good job too as Laura blocked the stairs. Her eyes speaking without voice.

"What's the matter?" said Dylan.

"Make sure your feet are clean. I don't want my dad kicking off again."

"That wasn't my fault."

"You traipsed mud through the house. He doesn't need another excuse to cuss your name."

"He never calls me by my name. I don't think he knows it."

"Well, he does, and it's hard work having to make him tea all the time."

"Right, they're off." Dylan presented his sock covered feet, pointing to his canvas trainers, flopping in front of the shoe rack. "It was only a bit of mud. I apologised."

Laura turned on her hands and knees, crawling up the stairs. "Even I could tell you didn't mean it." She reached the landing, standing upright. "Mud is one of his pet peeves. It's gonna take a while for him to forget." She said, out of breath.

"It's not all that radical, mud is frowned upon, I get it, and on carpets no less, raging," he said.

Laura sat down at her desk, held out a CD. Sean Paul's, Dutty Rock.

"I want you to take this with you," she said.

"To camp? I haven't even left yet."

"I was gonna keep hold of it, because the damn thing reminds me of you, anyway. But, I want you to listen to it every day. Knowing, that album is one of the reasons I love you. I can't bear you singing along and doing that dancing you do."

"Are you crazy, I've got rhythm." Dylan bent his legs, crouched and weaved his knees side to side. "I can flap a good dutty wine with the best of 'em. "

"If that's what you call it. Looks like you're having a stroke."

Dylan reached inside his pocket and pulled out his own CD. He passed it over.

Laura read the handwritten title. "Toothpaste memories," she said. "What does that mean?"

"You're always doing those yoga poses in front of the mirror, brushing your teeth."

"You're a dick," she said.

"It's a compilation of our songs. The soundtrack to our relationship."

Laura flipped the case over, hand drawn hearts, a track listing that included:

1. Cyndi Lauper - Time After Time
2. Billy Bragg - Shirley
3. Across the sands
4. Bronski Beat - Smalltown Boy
5. Venus - Frankie Avalon

6. The Cure - Love Cats

7. Prince - I would Die 4 You

8. All Saints - Pure Shores

9. Billy Bragg - The Tatler

10. Beautiful South - Song for Whoever

11. Uncle Kracker - Follow Me

"You haven't labelled track three."

"I don't need to, you know it, and more importantly, the night we listened to it."

"Very true," she said. Her eyes continued to explore the list. "Love cats?"

"Our picnic on Desborough. Rice cakes and peanut butter by the river."

"Wow," she said. Her eyes scouring through her vivid memory. "I'd forgotten that. It's called The Dyke—, We still haven't gone swimming at the Lido. I promised we would." Laura turned her face away, hiding her want to cry. She couldn't stand the embarrassment from her weakness for him.

"We will. If only to convince me a Lido is a real thing," said Dylan.

"There's no time, I forgot," said Laura, a tear forcing to trickle from her eye.

Dylan absorbed it with his soft thumb. "It's OK, little lady. We'll go when I'm back," he said.

"I think the realisation just hit me, it's nine weeks."

"It'll fly by. We'll be fine. I filled this little red book." Said Dylan, holding out a red, pocket notebook.

Laura snatched it, flicking over the front cover to read Dylan's handwriting.

"Chicken Scratches," she said. "God, you really have filled it." She fanned pages, trying to find bright spaces of white. "You've filled every page, how long did that take you?"

Dylan closed the book in her hand. "Don't read it now," he said. "It didn't take long, all came naturally. It wasn't hard work. I've been writing it since we got together. I wanted to look back and feel those feelings again. If you were to lay down in a river—,"

Confused, she said. "Lay down in a river?"

"Yeah, ya know, something dramatic. I wanna be able to hold on to the way I felt at the time, not just remember. Memories lie to you."

"There you go again, coming off with all this new philosophy. I hope I'd swim but, I also hope I still make you feel those things you're trying to capture in words."

"Well, I hope this book will let you know just how much I adore you."

"Don't go then."

"Little lady, part of me doesn't want to go. I've been dreaming about this for so long. I'd only regret it if I didn't see it through. I don't wanna resent you, thinking you were the reason I didn't live it."

"I don't want you to resent me. Things change though. What if you fall out of love with me?"

Dylan pulled Laura toward him by her hips. "Mary, you wanted the moon. I gave you the moon," he said. Impersonating James Stewart.

"That one still needs work. You sound like John Wayne gargling Sean Connery," she said.

"Maybe, but short story long, with areas of scratch and sniff for the kids." He planted his lips on the tip of her nose. "There's no chance of me not loving you."

"You say that now." She said, looking away. "With all those hotpant wearing mallrat girls, being 'like, can't you say more, Mr. Englishman, like I just love your accent. Like, do me, like, go cougars, go'."

"And you're cussing my James Stewart impression. You need to work on that one. They don't all talk like that."

"Don't defend them. It'll be like a lifetime of Clueless. Reading your emails, 'I'm butt crazy in love.' Tell me that's not gonna happen, that you won't forget me."

"I don't have to. You know it won't happen. You're my little lady, and that's the only thing I'll be thinking about. When you see the moon, I'll be right there, tugging on that lasso."

Laura rolled her eyes. "Bollocks," she said.

"You see." Said Dylan, squeezing his arms around Laura's shoulders. "I'm gonna miss all this."

"You're gonna miss my vexation at how much of a prick you are?"

"Exactly that, Little Lady."

"You better come back." She said, fluttering her eyebrows.

"Of course I'm coming back." He pressed his lips on her eyelids. "Nine weeks, gone in a flash."

"You've got your head in the clouds."

Dylan's mobile phone rang in his pocket.

"Who's that, your girlfriend?" Said Laura, her mouth open, forever playful.

"Shut up." He said, giggling, looking at the screen flashing. "It's Yestin. He never calls me."

"Answer it then," she said. Flicking through pages of the red book and flipped the back of the CD, listening to hear Dylan's phone begin connecting.

"All right bud," he said. "How's it going?" His face turned to frowning concern.

Laura held her palms out, as if to say, 'what's wrong?'

Dylan shook his head, confused. "Right. No, I haven't. No, not since yesterday." He said, into the mouthpiece.

"What is it?" said Laura.

Dylan shrugged, sticking his finger in his ear. "He would have said something," he paused. "Yeah, I know, right." Took a breath. "I'm with Laura at the moment. No, the van's coming tomorrow. I leave after. Nah, that's cool. I'll head back now. No. Yeah. Oh yeah, no worries. In a bit." Dylan ended the call.

"What's the matter? You're not leaving me?"

"Bass," said Dylan.

"You mean Mark, what's he done now?"

"Apparently his stuff's gone, like he's moved out."

Laura tutted. "He's such a drama queen. It's like he's in love with you, always wants your attention. He sees more of you than I bloody do."

"We should go back. I need to know what's going on."

"Are you kidding? My parents are in Bournemouth." She pressed her body into his, acting seductive. "We have the house to ourselves." She planted her lips on his like a temptress. "I want a bath. We were gonna make love in their bed."

"I wasn't ever keen on that idea. It's weird," he said.

"It was gonna be my middle finger fuck you to mud on the carpet."

"Since you put it like that. But, seriously, I need to find out what's going on."

"Well, FYI. I'm picking up later—,"

"Again, you've got through that bag already?"

"It was only a twenty. Anyway, I have enough for one smoke. Tonight was gonna be our last night together, alone. Now, you've ruined that. Well, Mark has ruined it, yet again."

"You stay here. I'll get everything I need for tonight and be back later."

"How do you suggest I collect?"

"Can't you give Charlie a call?"

"Oh sure, now you're encouraging me to contact my ex-boyfriend. Sure, I'll call him, rely on him instead. Since he's more committed than you are."

"I can't do this now," said Dylan.

"Fuck off and do what you have to do."

"I'll be back, little lady."

"I'm not your little lady until you're back here."

"I won't be long." Dylan kissed her on the lips.

"Suppose I should get used to this." She sat down on her desk chair and looked back over the CD. Dylan poked his head back round the door. "You can't listen to that yet. It's for when I leave," he said.

"Look up the definition of can't. Get gone."

Dylan blew a kiss and made his way downstairs.

"Notice how I didn't catch that one." Laura shouted off after him.

"Love you," his voice travelling from the staircase.

"Whatever." She said, standing, opening the little red book. Laura watched Dylan jog down the driveway. He waved up at the window. She stuck two fingers up at him. He laughed, shaking his head. She sat back down at her desk, pulled the bottom drawer out, laid it flat on the floor. Pulled a red, locked safety box out from underneath. Inserted a key stuck under her windowsill with Velcro and unlocked it. Rifled her fingers between loose packets of Durex condoms and three naked Polaroid pictures of her breasts and a veiny erection. Her finger tips brushed and landed on a small plastic baggy with flakes of ground marijuana inside. She took a single Rizla. Opened the 'Get well soon' card she had given to her grandmother and read.

"Dearest Nan, you are my Opal. Praying for you to get better. Manifesting only positive thoughts. Keep eating your blueberries." She said and laughed. "We've Californian Jumbo berries coming in on import, especially for you. Get well soon. Love you. Your Lapis Laura. Kiss Kiss." She studied the card in her hands. "RIP." She said and tore the card in two. Took a pair of office scissors and cut a small square from the card, making a roach.

Perched on her windowsill. The main road outside was silent. A manual lawnmower being pushed and pulled off in the distance. Laura exhaled smoke out through her open window. Wendy from fifty-seven, walked her French Bulldog, Stanley, past their driveway. The dog squatted, spine arched, in the middle of the pavement. Laura swallowed her outrage. If Wendy saw her smoking or stayed long enough to smell the weed soaked air. She would be in more trouble than dog shit on the drive. Wendy held her nose high, looking off in each direction. She nodded with the 'all clear' and tugged on Stanley's collar. Laura heard piano keys accompany Stanley's scamper after his owner. She giggled to herself, thinking how cute. She inhaled deep, holding the smoke, and eyeballed the pile of mess from her window.

"There you go, dad. Little gift from Nan, you bastard." She said.

26

lEaViNg oN A sHaDoW

"Friggin' hell. It's warmer outside than it is in here." Said Dylan to himself, smacking his hands together to generate heat, musty cold air filled his throat in the hallway of the shared house.

Yestin looked up. With a flapping, loose wrist wave, he gestured Dylan to join him in the kitchen, still talking on the phone, his hand flat on top of his head, a pensive concentration.

"Sup, Bud." Said Yestin, hanging up. "He's still not answering. Have you tried?" He tossed the phone, it rattled and clacked until it settled on the kitchen counter.

"I haven't. But he wouldn't just leave. Not without saying anything, unless something happened."

"What d'ya think could have happened?"

"No idea, he's not Charles Manson. There's no one out to get him. Not that I know of."

"See, that's the thing, you never know with Bass," said Yestin. "He's into all kinds of shady shit."

"True, since he dropped out of uni." Said Dylan, reaching for his mobile phone in the back pocket of his jeans. He found 'Bass' within his Nokia contacts. The phone rang.

"You never know, he might pick up for you."

"I doubt it," said Dylan. The phone ringing.

Bass sat alone, head down. Baseball cap pulled low, the peak touching his eyebrows. Sitting in a window seat. He faced the wrong direction. The train zipped through the green, flashing countryside. His phone vibrated in his pocket.

'Dildo' flashed on the screen. He watched it vibrate, flash twice, vibrate, flash a third time, and vibrate again. It finally stopped. The phone screen turned black. Bass steadied his bruised hands, shoving them deep inside his hoodie pockets, not able to stop them shaking. His knees trembled. He felt cold and intoxicated by the smell of BLT sandwiches and engine oil. He concentrated and planted his trainers on the carpet of the train carriage. The bass guitar case jolted up and shifted along the baggage rack. He flinched, looked up at the train behind him, from under his cap. A bearded man, four rows back, sat resting his arms out straight, pushing on the seat in front. His arms clenched, pursing his lips, spitting and struggling for air. His cheeks patchy red. As Bass squinted to focus, he could see the man's eyes were shaking in his head. No one else was paying attention. Bass sprung to his feet, shifting along the carriage, pulling on alternate head rests to propel himself forward. Rushing alongside the man.

"Everything good, mate?" Said Bass, putting his limp hand on the man's tense arm.

The man's beard appeared to dance and rattle. His hand gripped Bass tight around the wrist. Bass dragged himself free, pawing from his clutches. The furry necked man banged his chest with his palm. Three women shifted their attention, drawn to the commotion, turning around in their seats.

A heavyset blonde woman shouted. "He's choking, he's choking." She smacked a paperback off her knees.

The man patted himself on the shoulder blade. Bass locked his arms around his waist, under the diaphragm, measuring just below his rib cage with a fist. Remembering the manoeuvre, having been made to watch Mrs. Doubtfire. He squeezed once, thrusting his hips from behind. The man struggled for air. Bass pulled and squeezed tight, the well-built man was airborne off his feet. Bass closed his eyes, held his breath. He knew this attempt could be the last. One more concerted effort. The man gargled, then coughed a blue pen lid free from his throat. It bounced off the forehead of a beaky nosed woman with a tight, grey ponytail. She rubbed her head, picked the lid up from the floor between her naked toes. Her socks balled up inside sliders.

"I thought they put holes in em' so you didn't choke." Said the woman, moving her foot above the man's hand as he remained on all fours, gasping for air. She opened her toes like a grab machine and the lid fell in his open palm.

"I was chewing it," he said. "Thanks, man. Shit, it's hard to talk." He pulled Bass into his body, as he raised, pushing on his kneecaps for leverage. Bass struggled, now himself having difficulty breathing under the smothering of the stranger's embrace.

"We're good, man. No problem." He said, patting him on the shoulder with an insistent conclusion to their closeness.

"I'll sit with you," said the man. "I owe you at least my time to get to know ya."

Bass grimaced a polite smile, moving back along the train carriage to his seat beneath his bass guitar case, pulling his hat back down low on his face.

"I'm Luke," he said. Luke presented his hand. Bass gripped hold, a strong prolonged introduction. One shake shy of being uncomfortable but sincere enough for Luke to offer his appreciation.

"You can call me, Bass."

"You play, is that yours?" said Luke, pointing at the case. His eyes wide with intrigue.

"Yeah, I'm in a punk band. Well, punk rock band."

"That's so cool. What's the name of your band—, Mind if I

look?"

Luke bounced up, arm stretched for the case.

Bass bolted forward, pushed himself between Luke and the baggage racking, like he was blocking a basketball. Bass saw in Luke's eyes. It was too late. Luke felt wet, slimy syrup drying on his skin. He rubbed the liquid between his sticky fingertips. He turned his hand, already knowing it was blood. When he saw the riddled guilt in Bass's desperate soft concealed eyes. He was looking in the face of a murderer.

"I think you should take a seat, don't you?" said Luke.

"It's not what it looks like." Said Bass, a petrified tremble in his voice.

Luke dropped one hand, like an anchor on Bass's shoulder. Moved his other blood stained fingers to his nostrils. The stench of rust contaminated his throat. He felt anger and fear coarse throughout him, a power without force struck his muscles. He pushed Bass in his seat. Luke was doing the right thing, protecting the public. Imagining the headlines, he considered himself a hero for the day.

'Luke Ledger saves train from Maniac Punk'. He pictured the spinning newspapers. The story bought by Hollywood. Maniac Punk, starring Brendan Fraser, coming to a cinema near you. Luke's grin was hard to hide. His excitement lost in the daydream.

"We'll wait for the police," said Luke. "It's not safe until you're in handcuffs. Ya see, someone's gotta take responsibility of this situation."

Luke slapped Bass on the knee. "Are you scared? What might happen to you—, I mean, that's what I'd be thinking about, where I'd end up."

"I'm not scared what'll happen to me. I'm scared for everyone else, I enjoyed it too much," he said.

Luke stood up, stretching. "Proper hard man, innit." He said.

Bass, side swiped Luke, planting his elbow to his groin. Luke coughed, trying to yelp. Winded, he collapsed in a heap between the seats. Bass bolted up the aisle, hopping along, using the head rests, firing himself along the train carriage, so fast his baseball cap ripped off with the gusts he created. His nose bounced off the carpet, his eyes began to water. The barefoot woman tripped him, she landed dead weight on his back, locking his wrists behind his back.

"Would you believe I'm a pacifist?" she said.

Bass cowered, his mouth open, dribbling spit. His eyes clenched closed, cheek rubbing on carpet. A group of female have-a-go heroes yanked him to his feet, arms pushed up into his shoulder blades, bent forward at the waist. Forcing him along the train as if readied for public humiliation in the town square stocks. His phone vibrated again in his pocket. The phone dropped to the floor.

"No calls for you." Said a woman. She clicked 'reject'.

Dylan stabbed his reluctant index finger into the red cancel button on his phone.

"Nope. He's not even answering for me. No idea what he's up to," he said.

The front door slammed shut. They both stretched their necks to see Florence, carrying her usual hessian bag, resting on her forearm like she was carrying a punnet full of fresh strawberries.

"Ayubowan. Ayubowan. It's so cold." She said, dropping her keys on the counter. "You hear anything?" She said, looking at Dylan. Then kissed an expectant and reciprocating Yestin on the lips.

"What we gonna do?"

"Don't worry, he'll be fine," said Dylan.

"I'm not worried about Bass so much," said Yestin. "It's more, what we're gonna do for three months without his rent coming in. You're paid up 'til September. But Bass, he's paying Mitra month by month. My loan won't cover his rent."

"I hadn't think of that," said Florence.

"Thought. You hadn't thought of that."

"That too. I need toilet. Hold your thoughting. I'll be back." Florence jogged up the stairs. The bathroom door slammed shut behind her, the bolt clicking locked.

"I'm leaving tomorrow morning, whatever happens. I'm thoughting of nothing else," said Dylan.

"Shut up," said Yestin, laughing. "She's cute. No, don't change your plans, Bud. You've got nothing to worry about. Mitra's got your money. It just pisses me off he's gone and said nothing. I'll have to beg my mum for money, if he doesn't come back, bastard."

Dylan looked at his phone again. "I can keep trying him, but I've got these last few boxes to pack. Then I'm getting a taxi to Laura's. Little shin ding before I depart, tomorrow."

"Are you saying we're not invited?"

"Not deliberately. It's at Laura's. Her parents are away. It's more *her* friends than mine. You're welcome to come, both of you. We can share the taxi."

"I'm only joking. My head's all over the place, Bud. I can't tonight, anyway. We've got this call with her parents. They're insisting we meet. Flor is on about us having to go over there in the summer. They hate that I'm not Muslim. They're trying to marry her off to a family friend. Ultimatum being, I meet them, prove I can convert and then she won't have her hand forced."

"I thought they were trying to leave, anyway. Since it was so unsafe over there."

"You know more than me," said Yestin.

"Yest, come upstairs. My room stinks," said Florence. Hanging over the bannister, covering her nose.

"All right, babe." Said Yestin, feigning interest. "Bud, if I don't see you tomorrow morning before you leave. Seriously, it's been such a laugh. You're a good guy and I hope all goes well. Should be a blinding summer for you."

"Cheers, bud." They shook hands. Yestin patted Dylan hard on the shoulder and joined Florence upstairs in her room. Dylan looked up as the floorboards creaked. He glanced around his room with forgotten romanticism. The room that had acted as his sanctuary for a full term. He flicked through the panels of his flat pack desk, his unplugged computer on the floor stacked ready to be collected. He pictured himself sat upright, stretching between pauses of typing. He spun on the office chair, stopping and facing his single bed. He thought of the occasions he shared the bed, snuggled up to Laura. She insisted she faced the wall, her back arched into his naked groin. He pictured the first time they had sex. Laura on her back, him nervous to disappoint, his erect apprehension in his palm. Tickling his silky foreskin on her lips. So uncertain of what to do and working himself into a stupor, he would fail himself in copulation. He pulled the top drawers of the dressing cabinet open, checking he had left nothing in the back. The cupboard empty of clothes. The top of the wardrobe, empty of his suitcase, now stacked in the corner, stuffed to the brim, zip stretching. The books he relied upon for personality were taped shut inside boxes stacked on top of one another, lost for a summer. The Sanyo camera shut away in its green turtle shell case. He picked up his backpack, filled with clothes he planned on wearing tonight at his makeshift leaving party. He felt reassured that everything was ready for the moving van. He thought he only had one last night to survive.

Dylan sprang to his feet, his eyes peering out of the living room window.

"Guys, my taxi's here," he said up the stairs. "I'm leaving now."

A crack and squeak of floorboards above. Yestin and Florence stood at the top of the stairs. Yestin nodded, not making eye contact, adding a subtle, almost distracted salute, studying a worn eraser on the end of a pencil he turned between his fingers. Florence side stepped down the stairs, holding a yellow and green wrapped square box, checking her footing as she descended.

"It's Sri Lankan etiquette, not to open a gift upon receiving it," she said. "So, you wait until you arrive home tomorrow before doing so."

"Bohoma istuti, Shreenika." Said Dylan, taking the wrapped box in his two hands, rattling it for a clue as to what it contained. He placed it on the windowsill and moved in for a tight armed hug. Florence rested her head on his shoulder and he took the back of her head in his hand. Yestin looked on from the stairs, a raised eyebrow of unspoken disapproval.

The hug continued.

"All right, that'll do." Said Yestin, chuckling with jealous authority.

"It's been a pleasure." Said Dylan, breaking away from their embrace.

"Good luck." Said Florence, holding her soft eyes on his over the top of her glasses. Sharing words without speaking. Hearing The Karate Kid soundtrack, Young Hearts by Commuter, playing on repeat because Florence and her cute, round, chubby cheeks couldn't stop smiling at the chorus, doing her best to sing along, only to get the words wrong. Any embarrassment morphed into giggling, faces concealed by a pillow. It was as if they both explored what could have been between them. All the things they should have said. How things may have been different if they were forced together. Dylan contemplated Florence shouting at him instead of Yestin, all because he misunderstood something she said.

Dylan grabbed for the bag at his feet, waved his hand. "Take care, both." He said.

Florence waved as he got into a taxi at the bottom of the driveway. Yestin joined her in the doorway, resting his arm around her shoulder, claiming ownership. She clutched his hand in hers as they both waved Dylan off.

"Why does it feel like we'll never see him again?" Said Yestin, closing the door behind them.

"No idea. I know I'll see him in my future."

"Don't say it—, Cosmic synergy," said Yestin.

Florence made her way into the kitchen. He followed. "If it gets worse. I'll get hold of Mitra," he said.

"Your nose is weak. How can it get any worse? Ya know, I'm gonna miss Dylan."

"Too much, by the looks of it."

"Oh, is Yesty Yesty jealous." Said Florence, poking him in the ribs with stiff fingers. "You know, I only have heart for you." She tickled his belly as they embraced in the middle of the kitchen, kissing.

Dylan checked his phone again, expecting to see a message or some form of contact from Bass. Nothing. The screen blank, except for the name of the network. His signal bar dropped from four rectangles to two as soon as he reached the curb outside of Laura's house. Poor internet connection in the cusp of the country. Dylan grabbed his bag, handed over a twenty-pound note, insisting the driver keep the one pound eighty change as a tip. His suspicious eyes signalled he was less appreciative than he was insulted.

Laura opened the front door, loose pebbles kicking up under his feet.

"No one's arrived yet," she said. "It's just you and me. We can have some fun."

"Hungry Hippos?"

"You need to come up with your own lines."

"Duly noted, little lady. Duly noted," he said.

Dylan pulled on his jeans. Laura sat up in bed, lifting the duvet as she searched for her bra. She ran her hand under the pillow, finding it, holding it proud. She clasped it closed at the front of her chest. Dylan studied her breasts.

"Wait." He said, lurching forward and placed his mouth on her left nipple, sucking. Moved to the right, kissed and sucked from his lips with a slurping pop.

"You're welcome." Said Laura, as she spun her bra between her fingers, lifted her slight breasts into place, and adjusted the straps under her shoulder blades.

"So, who's coming tonight?"

"The usual," said Laura.

"Right, and who are the usual?"

"Tilly, Henry, Lizzie, that lot. Still haven't heard from Sofia, she's being so weird."

"And?"

"Cheryl maybe. Oh, and, Charlie."

"Why do you insist on inviting him to everything?"

"He's my friend."

"If there is one thing Charlie ain't, and that's your friend. Men and women can't be friends. One of the two always, and that's no exaggeration. One will always want the other."

"You're so cynical,"

"It's true. Always sniffing around, trying to get the other one drunk. Forever hopeful, they'll flop into each other's arms and finally give into temptation. Too much repressed, fiery passion to think about protection, until it's too late and the polite friendship turns to regret and resentment."

"How romantic," she said. "Thanks for that. You're thinking about his balls, aren't you?"

"I still don't know why you had to tell me that. I already think he's a cock. Now I picture him with massive King Kong balls. You really know how to make me suffer, don't you?"

"Charlie and I are just friends. No one tries to get the other drunk. There's no repressed lust from either of us. It didn't work, us being together, we tried, it didn't, and that's that. We can still be close, though. We've known each other for too long. What do you care anyway? You won't know what's going on from tomorrow."

"What does that mean?"

"It means, whilst you're away, you'll have to trust me. Just as I will you. Knowing full well that you've cheated on me."

"Always that hierarchy of illicit mistakes."

"I'm only counting when you fuck up," she said. Pulling her skirt over her hips and peeling a silk black top over her black bra.

"Bit revealing," said Dylan. "I can see your bra."

"Shut up, ya girl. No, you can't. You know they're your tits."

"I love you. I know I shouldn't say it." Said Dylan, grabbing Laura by the waist looking her deep within her blood-shot eyes.

"I know you do." She said with a fake smile, refusing to make eye contact.

"What's wrong? Tell me you do too." He said, trying to catch her eye line as she shifted her head away from him. "Why can't you look me in the eye?"

"I can," she said. She stopped moving her head. "It's you who needs to remember you just said that. Hold on to that feeling. I don't want you coming home after all this, getting on your knees, begging me for forgiveness because you feel guilty about fucking some all-American girl."

"Never gonna happen."

"Forgive my scepticism."

The door bell rang, amplified from the plugged in extender. "I'll let them in," said Laura. Dylan didn't let go. "That's the front door." She said again. She broke free from his hands. "I should get it."

"Laura," he said, she looked up through moist eyes. "I love you," he said.

"There you go again, poor timing. Forever breaking the rules. But, ditto," she said.

Dylan smiled as he heard her thumping down the stairs to unlock the front door.

"Nazdar." She said, in a fake European accent. The roar of laughter and passing salutations travelled up the stairs, piercing Dylan's ears with the cacophony, making him shake his head.

"One more night," he said in a whisper, encouraging his public persona to breathe to life.

27

cHiCkEn tAlOnS

Red wine pumped into a glass like the aorta being severed. The last drops rolled from the depths of the bottle. Laura passed the glass by the stem to the clutches of Tilly, licking her lips. She held it above her head, examining the claret in the pristine kitchen light, turning it like a kaleidoscope. Dylan gave Laura a peripheral glance, enough to non-verbally express his disdain.

"Looks like a good one," said Tilly.

Dylan raised his eyebrows, suppressing a yawn.

"My rents brought it back from France, it bloody should be." Said Laura, kissing her finger dry of spilt wine. She turned her back to Dylan and Tilly, fidgeting with something on the long kitchen table, grabbing for her own glass of wine, gulping at it and setting it back down, not savouring the contents.

"So, Dylan." Said Tilly, loud enough to be heard over the stereo, blaring the original soundtrack from Human Traffic. "You ready to go on your American adventure?

Dylan prepared his voice with an exasperated huff. "If I've forgotten anything, then it's not worth taking." He looked around the kitchen for distraction, to escape the tedium of conversation from Tilly.

"Aren't they gonna be livid?" she said.

"Livid with what?"

"When you arrive on camp with that garish blue mohawk?"

His eyes pinged with realisation, having never considered it. He touched the peak of his Dax Wax erect hair, smoothing the stubbly number one sides through his palms. "I hadn't thought of that—, Garish?" he said.

"You know what I mean. It gives you this; dismissive attitude." Said Tilly, leaning into him, pressing her soft breasts hard into his shoulder, and whispered. "I'll shave it, if you'd like?"

He chuckled, but didn't dare look at her cleavage. Silently channelling Laura for help failed to work, with her back turned, not paying attention. Tilly gave a soft eyed look of authority, slapped her hand on Dylan's chest, pushing him back into a dining room chair. He steadied his wineglass in his fingers.

"Lau, you got clippers here?" She said, taking his glass in her hands. She held her eyes on his, put her lips on the glass, sipping.

"What d'ya want clippers for?" said Laura. Her back stiff, not turning around.

"I'm giving Dylan a haircut."

"You're what?" Said Laura, wiping her hands dry, her face as scrunched as the tea towel she dropped to the table. "You want to shave it off?" She said, now looking at Dylan. "But, you did that for me."

"I know," he said. "Tilly's got a point though. What if they kick me off camp? I don't want to create the wrong impression."

"Screw their impression," said Laura. "That's what the hairstyle says, and it's another reminder of me. The reason you did it. If you get rid of it, you'll get rid of me."

Tilly unravelled the stiff, stubborn rubbery cable, wrapped around the clippers. "It'll grow back." She said, plugging the clippers into the wall socket. She thumbed the power button. The clippers buzzed and vibrated, sparking a glint in her eye. "Take a seat." She said and pressed Dylan on the shoulder to sit, pulling a plastic cape around his neck. "Like a superhero." She said, flashing a wink.

"You don't listen to me, anyway." Said Laura, turning her attention away again. Taking a large egg-shaped bud of marijuana in her palm, inspecting it like a delicate, precious stone. "You're not taking that lip ring out. You know how much I like that."

"We've all heard." Said Tilly, cocking her head at Dylan.

He scowled, realising Tilly's covert attempts at underage seduction.

"What can I say? I've created an animal." Said Laura, as she filled a large novelty shot glass with green luminous absinthe, shifting around to the other side of the table. She sniffed the bud between her spinning fingers, held it for a moment over the surface of the still absinthe, then released her fingers as she watched the bud sink to the bottom of the glass, resting still. She moved to eye level as it drifted to the surface, floating.

Dylan looked on from his seat, his girlfriend's blue eyes magnified through the glass.

"Here we go." Said Tilly, using a number two plastic hair clipper blade. She ran the blades through the middle of his hair, the motor whirring and struggling to slice and cut its way through greasy wax. Blue dyed hair dropped to the tiled floor between his legs like straw. Tilly smiled, grabbing Dylan's hair between her fingers. Warmth ran through his scalp, pins and needles pricked him as she yanked. The snapping sensation of excitement made him gasp. It was too late to hide his squeal. The depraved devil in Tilly, smirked, holding his head back. He tried to glance for Laura, searching for silent help. Tilly tugged harder. She pressed her knee into his groin, her dress riding up. She side stepped over his thigh, yanked his hair again. He exhaled, his mouth tight shut, a whistle from his nostril, settled his urge. She lowered herself. Her dress ravelled further up like a theatre curtain. She rubbed herself back and forth along his thigh, still holding his shaking head, as he concentrated on not becoming aroused. Tilly held her smile, mouthing, 'It's OK.'

"I have no idea how it'll turn out." Said Laura, flicking the shot glass. Ripples of absinthe covered the iceberg peak of green bud.

Tilly flicked the clippers off, bounced up and acted like she was deep in pensive observation, having to concentrate on where to cut next, concealing her own aroused breathlessness. The clippers covering her beating heart.

"How long is that taking you?" said Laura.

Tilly held one eye closed, shifting her head from left to right. "I want to get it right."

"Give it here." Said Laura, snatching hold of the shears. "You're shaving it off. He's not the Mona Lisa." She slapped Tilly's hand from gripping his remaining hair. Tilted his head up from the temples, his eyes still meeting Tilly's. She refused to look away. Laura shifted between them, snapped on the shears and moved them from his forehead, down his neck, clumps of hair blanketing the floor. "See, nothing to it, front to back. No time at all." Laura removed the number two cutting guard, pulled back on the adjusting arm, the blades moved to the shortest position. She moved her head closer to his face, inspecting the top of his scalp, and pressed the blades in hard, intricately creating two parallel lines.

"Two chicken scratches," she said. "So you can't forget me. Now, you're done." Laura stood back, admiring her intricate addition to the all over buzz cut.

"It look all right?" Said Dylan, running his hand backwards and forwards over his head, minute splinters of hair flicked into the air like a mist.

Laura yanked a swollen pine drawer open, removing a paddle mirror, presenting it in front of his head. He took hold, pulling it closer to focus on his hair. Tracing two fingers through the bald lines now in his head.

"I look so ill," he said.

Dylan sat on a cold concrete step, illuminated by the bone white glare from the moon. He passed Laura a half-smoked cigarette. She collected it between pinched fingers and pulled her in close, keeping her warm against his body, as she shivered.

"We probably shouldn't sit here for too long. We could get piles."

She exhaled smoke and said. "Piles is the last thing on my mind. Surely that's a myth?"

"Could be. Have you cheated and read some yet?"

"I've read a few pages," she said. "I thought I was supposed to wait."

"I knew you couldn't resist." He planted his lips on her hairline. "Each page tells our story. Read it from start to finish. It'll tell you everything you need to know about how I feel about you."

"I'd feel much better if you showed me, instead of having to read it in those silly little letters you write."

"I do show you. But, my my words reiterate it. We're not over because I'm going away. Far from it, this is only the beginning."

Laura passed the cigarette, almost to the filter. "I hope you're right, I really do. I wrestle with this every day. I'm not sure if it's that thing of infatuation. You going away isn't something I can imagine. I think of what I'd do and I know I wouldn't leave you. But you're leaving me. It's irrational on my part, I know. It's my problem. I thought this would be one of those normal boy meets girl things. That's all I hoped for, all I ever wanted, at least. I wanted to be applauded, end it with happily ever after. I mean, shit Masugar, you're a poet, you know what I'm trying to say."

"You're saying it better than I ever could," he said. "I'm not looking for attention. I want you to believe you have me. I wasn't sure I could feel this way about myself, let alone anyone else. But I do, you've proven me wrong. You're all I care about, genuinely. Like I said, this is only the beginning. It'll be nine weeks and I'll be back laying in your arms. My travels will be our poetry."

"I hope you're right, I really do."

"You've got the CD. Listen to the Roses and you'll feel me." Dylan slid the spent cigarette under his trainer, rubbing it extinguished against the concrete step.

Laura pulled her knees into her chest. "It hurts, just how much I'm gonna miss you. I hate myself for admitting it, like I'm lying. You've been such a bastard to me. My parents worry I've let you off. They can see, and my dad especially, he hates how submissive I've become, letting you drag me through shit. I've become this weak little girl for you."

"Little Lady." He said, wrapping his arms around her. "I'm gonna miss you so much. Before you know it, I'll be back, I promise. I won't be doing anything to make you hate me whilst I'm there. I only want to make you proud. I'll come back and convince your dad of that, too."

"You better. Your biggest adventure is with me. Just you remember that."

Their lips touched, eyes closed. The moon acting as voyeur.

"You don't have to worry," he said. They stood, knees cracking. "Shall we get this party started? I'll prove to you my eyes are yours."

"You talk a good talk, Mr. Nemerov. It's time to prove it."

"Lasso the moon. It's all for you, Damian," he said.

Laura tutted, pushing him away. "Don't leave that there." She pointed at the squished yellow dog end on the step. "My Dad sees that, he'll go mental." Dylan picked it up and tossed it in a large evergreen bush. "What's the matter with you?" said Laura. "My mum toes egg shell into the dirt to keep that alive. Don't roll your eyes. We buried Jan and Dean underneath it. Pick it up."

"Jan and Dean?" Said Dylan, separating branches, sweeping his trainer through dry mud, scouring for the discarded cigarette.

"Our Guinea pigs, my first official pets. My mum only got them because I stole the school's and hid it in my underwear drawer. She was more upset I was feeding it Skittles."

"Found it." Said Dylan, pinching a dog end between muddied

fingertips.

"Put that deep in the bin bag in the kitchen. I'm leaving no clues," she said.

Glasses chinked. The music banged from the stereo speakers. No official DJ, party goers would wait for their chance to rifle through the available CDs and hit play when it was their turn. A mix of genres from Miles Davis to Cypress Hill. Every track chosen, motivated by individual poignant nostalgia, sharing the feeling with those shuffling their hips and tapping their feet. The patio doors were open, outside lights sprinkling white out across the artificial lawn, edged with railway sleepers around rose gardens, scattered with organic blue, egg shells.

Dylan stood outside, under a gazebo, blowing smoke rings into the night sky. A tumbler in his hand. Puzzled why no one had asked what he was drinking. Discovering it an unimportant detail, contrary to novice social convention.

"That blonde girl's giving some guy a blowy in the bathroom." Said a voice from the shadows.

Tilly, with a look of 'I told you so', woke Dylan from immature introspection. He glanced up at the bathroom window, the yellow light casting two figures through frosted glass. It could have been Laura. She had long hair. Tilly slid her hand inside his and squeezed.

"You should check. Might decide where you sleep tonight," she said.

"I don't need to check." He shook his hand free. "I know she wouldn't do that. Not to me."

"If Charlie's involved," she said. "I'm never confident about what goes on. He has this hold over her, ya know, I can't explain it. None of us can. We all see it. I bet if you asked her, she doesn't even understand it."

"For fuck's sake, Tilly." He said, jerking forward, stomping toward the house. "Now I have to check, don't I?" He sidestepped shoulders, avoided smashing into Laura's unsuspecting friends. He grunted to excuse himself, forced articulation of archaic words only they would understand. Dodging and swerving, weaving through people gathered throughout Laura's party house. The floor unsteady, a fun house travelator. He hand planted the bannister, gripping for support. If it was indeed Laura, behind that locked door. He felt rage kick through his vibrating bones. Everything within him tensed. Heart rate thundered with jealous speculation. What if she was on her knees? The next concentrated step made the stairs stretch out like a mountain. The bathroom door at its peak, fellow adventurers with their kit and caboodle, felt heat from his heart. I could do with some oxygen, he thought. Breathless, reaching the top of the stairs. Looking back down as Tilly arrived at his side. Struck with wobbling vertigo, he teetered on the edge of the chasm.

"Deep breath," he said. "Deep breath." He inhaled slow, his eyes closed, held it, one, two, three and four. Exhaling.

"What are you waiting for? Kick it down."

"Tilly, this isn't The Bill. I'm not gonna kick down the door, retard." He said and tapped one finger three times off the door.

Tap.

Tap.

Tap.

No answer. He pressed his ear flat.

"See. You're gonna have to kick it down," said Tilly.

"Shut up. If they cussed me for mud on the carpet, can you imagine if I smashed down the door?" Dylan tapped again.

The bolt clicked, a guy with blood-shot eyes, wearing a t-shirt with an animated toaster on the front, flapped his arms, wafting the air. "Sorry mate," he said. "I don't envy you right now."

Dylan stuck his head inside the toilet, quickly jerking back out. His eyes struggling to open, nostrils expelling stinking air. He closed the door behind him.

"They're definitely not in there." He said, fanning the air.

"I made that smell in one." The guy said as he shuffled down the stairs, retrieving his beer bottle from a windowsill at the bottom.

"That stinks," said Tilly. "Check her bedroom." She pinched her nostrils.

Laura's box bedroom door was closed. Dylan rushed in, grabbing it to stop from smashing into her bedside table. He stepped inside, saw his backpack on the floor. His coat on the back of her chair. Everything appeared normal, the way they left it.

Tilly pressed the bedroom door with her bottom, closing it with a click.

"Not here either. Weird, don't you think?" she said. "Funny, when Charlie's around, she can't be in two places at once. Magic, just disappears."

"Tilly, what're you sayin'? She's not Supergirl. I thought you were supposed to be best friends."

Dylan sat on the office chair, reached into his coat pocket, pulled out his mobile phone. No messages or missed calls.

"I am her friend," she said. "Sometimes I wanna be bad."

Dylan distracted, glanced at Tilly, performed a nonchalant double take. She appeared shorter. Now she had removed her heels. She stretched on tiptoes, folded one leg at the knee, resting against the door.

"Are you trying to be sexy?" he said.

Tilly brushed her fingertips over her bosom, stretching her dress, exposing her black, lacy bra.

"It's not working." He said, looking down at his phone. "You look ridiculous."

"I'm like a female James Dean," she said. "You want to carry on from downstairs? I've been waiting months to get you alone." She walked with seduction, her best attempt at catwalk sex appeal. She straddled Dylan's lap, her finger between her breasts, pulling on her dress, exposing ample blushed flesh.

"Get off me, seriously." He said, wafting his hand like she was a winged, picnic annoyance. "What are you doing?"

Tilly fell back on the bed, bouncing and arranging herself into an open legged position on her back. She walked her probing fingertips up the inside of her chunky thighs, hoisted her tight dress up, and tapped two fingers off her thong underwear.

"I know you want this too," she said.

"I really don't," said Dylan, turning away. "One day, you'll get some guy into trouble with your hidden innocence. You're everything Gary Puckett was warning against. If ever I've seen a set up, this is it. Where is she, in the cupboard?" He swung the cupboard doors open, lunging forward, messing up the hanging clothes.

Tilly hopped from the bed, grabbing at his arms, spinning him around. "This isn't a setup," she said. Her eyes glimmered with mischief. She pressed into him, the bedroom door appeared miles away. She held his face in her hands, squeezing his cheeks to hold him in place.

He squirmed, dodging her lips.

"Take advantage of me. She's not here. Charlie's only doing to her what you should to me."

Dylan pushed her away, reached and rattled the door handle, dragging it open and rushed out, holding her back with helicopter arms.

"She'll be bent over the bonnet of his beloved BMW, doing her super charged and fuel injected. Faggot." She said, leaning over the bannister, her breasts pumped up to her neck. Flustered, red face embarrassment blotched her cheeks, like chicken pox.

Dylan stared up at her from the safety of the stairs.

"Tils, I haven't got any morals." Said a voice from the landing. "I'll do you a solid. Give you a quickie. I'm here for you, girl."

"Oh, fuck off Jason." Said Tilly. Her clawing fingers smoothed down her dress, back into place.

Laura staggered up the driveway, carrying a twenty-four crate of beer in her arms. Charlie behind her, laughing, knocking into her, making her shift faster to the open front door. School yard flirtation.

"Where you been?" said Dylan.

"We went to get beer." Said Laura, avoiding making eye contact.

"And lemonade." Said Charlie, holding up a four pack of lemonade in his arms, two blue plastic bags hanging from his wrists, bulging with confectionery. He wiped his mouth with his wrist.

Tilly nudged into Dylan's back, watching Laura and Charlie walk to the kitchen.

The thoughts whirled round and round, repeating over and over. Laura held her nerve, looking straight ahead. Not flinching, giving him anything to clutch for a clue.

"See, guilty," said Tilly.

"Oh, shut yer mouth, Lolita."

"You need to keep your eyes open and your nostrils sniffing for sex sweat. All this is a game," she said.

"There's nothing going on. I'm not a fool," said Dylan.

"You're a fool for love. She'll always know you're a cheat. All because you couldn't keep your mouth shut. Now, you've given her a lifetime of free passes. Plus, you don't get red raw rug burns, buying lemonade. Check her knees out." She said, nodding beyond the kitchen counter.

Dylan rushed forward. His legs became pillars, refusing to move. He watched as Charlie laughed. That familiar shoulder nudge. The way he whispered in her ear. His lips always too close. Especially with him there, present in the room. Who's saying what goes on without eyes of fidelity casting judgement. Laura snorted, pressed her shoulders into her earlobes. Dylan's head throbbed with music blaring. Bubbling to the point of insanity. Laura stepped out from behind the island counter. Dylan dodged heads and limbs, blocking his view. Laura turned, two symmetrical red grazes on her kneecaps. Dylan's eyes cut through Tilly's. She smiled with, ' I told you so,' smugness. Dylan stomped over, thrust into Charlie's shoulder. His shocked face moulded to surprise as he ducked Dylan's swinging fist. Off balance, Dylan spun on the spot, face planting the fridge. Mayonnaise and gherkin jars rattled as it rocked back upright. Charlie pushed Dylan's face into the fridge door, his forearm pressing on his neck.

"What was that, coming out pitching, mate?" said Charlie.

"Both of you, relax." Said Laura, forcing herself between them. "Charlie, let him go. Dylan, whatever you think is going on, isn't. This is a party for you."

Charlie relaxed his arms, backing away.

Dylan, red faced, shook his arms free, pulling on the collar of his shirt, letting it flop down into place.

"Come running at me like that. I'll defend myself," said Charlie.

"If nothing's going on, why have you got skinned knees and shit?"

Laura looked down. Her eyes exploring her knees, then back up, meeting Tilly's. She thought for a second, side eyeing Charlie. "I fell over," she said.

"Yeah, fell on his cock," said Tilly.

"Outside the shop. Before we went in—," said Laura.

"It was my fault. I was trying to be funny. Nudged her a little hard," said Charlie.

"From behind. Took a run up, more like," said Tilly.

"Tilly. You and I are gonna fall out if you carry on," said Laura. She lurched forward. Tilly coward out through the crowd of onlookers. She escaped to the living room, out of sight.

"I can see she's trying to stir shit up." Said Laura. "Never happy unless she's the centre of a drama."

"I don't know why you still hang with her," said Charlie. "She shows her immaturity, every opportunity she can. I'm putting this stuff away." He gathered items from the counter. "Dylan," he said. "Shake my hand. No hard feelings."

Dylan shook Charlie's hand, gripping hold of it, begrudging and concealing behind his reluctance, an obvious pinched, supplicating fake smile.

28

wEeD sOaKEd aBsIntHE

"I've let this dry out on the radiator." Said Laura, grinning. She held up a broccoli sized sprig of green marijuana. The bud spun in her fingers like a flawless diamond. "Should be ready to smoke. I soaked it in absinthe." Her eyes shimmered with transfixed delight, throat primed for floral smoking. She longed for a gacky, dry mouth, that imperfect heart rate, reminding her of life's subtle vulnerabilities. The familiar feeling of her back loosening, that fluffy, loose, marshmallow head, the whoosh of dopamine surging, setting her free from social anxiety. Letting her forget.

Lizzie gathered her blonde hair, scrunched in her fist, flicking it over bare shoulders. They really did look like one another. The thought ignored as fast as it interrupted.

"Let me know when you spark it," said Lizzie. "It's been a long time since I've had a puff on the old ganja." She smoothed her palms over her hips, freeing wrinkles from her tight plum dress.

Laura's eyebrows meandered with boredom. "Puff-puff pass, for sure. But, don't call it ganja," she said.

"That girl Kia," said Lizzie. "Does a BTEC in Social care. She always chirps on about how her name means marijuana in Barbados."

Laura huffed. "Jamaica, it's Jamaican slang."

"Aren't they the same place?" Said Lizzie, pouring wine from an almost empty bottle.

"I'm not sure you deserve this, with comments like that," said Laura.

"Tilly said something to him, ya know?" Said Lizzie, and studied her reflection in the kitchen window, posing and pushing out her buxom breasts.

"That bitch is always meddling," said Laura. "Too much vino and her mouth doesn't belong to her." She sniffed the bud again, holding it against her nostrils, rolling her eyes in orgasmic frenzy.

"He wouldn't believe her anyway, would he?" said Lizzie.

"I can sweet talk him. She can be persuasive. We both know that. She still tries it on with anything walking. I could always accidentally let slip to Henry's wife."

"You wouldn't?"

"No, I wouldn't but she needs to live with the threat I might. Anyway, I've only got to get through tonight, then I've got nine weeks alone with…"

Lizzie listened, leaning in, waiting to hear a name from Laura's lips.

Laura realised and said. "How are things between you and Charlie, going good?"

"Can I ask your opinion?" Said Lizzie, looking back over her shoulder, not wanting anyone to overhear.

"Of course. What's up?"

"It's not normal, is it?" whispered Lizzie.

"What's not?" Said Laura, lowering her voice.

"After we have sex. Me and Charlie. He—, Well, he asks me to sleep the other end of the bed."

"The other end of the bed? What d'you mean, like top and tail?"

"My feet by his head. His feet by mine."

"Yeah, top and tail." Said Laura, holding back a giggle. Trying to sniff the bud to hide her amusement.

"Out of interest, not to be weird or anything. I just know he wasn't that up for it with me. Couldn't keep up."

"What, Charlie?" said Lizzie. "Nah-uh, I can't keep up with him. But, you're right, that is weird, talking about it with you."

"It is," said Laura. Pressing her nostrils harder against the bud. "Must be the rowing. Built up his stamina. It's not weird to ask the last time you slept with him?"

"He came to mine Tuesday. No, Thursday."

"Last Thursday?" said Laura.

"Yeah Thursday. Pretty late or early I should say. After midnight, for sure. Why do you ask?"

"Nothing, nevermind."

"He said your name the other night," said Lizzie.

"He what?"

"I wasn't gonna tell you," she said. "Saying it makes it real, ya know? I wouldn't have minded that much, but I was riding him. He was sucking my neck, giving me a love bite."

"Chavy," said Laura.

"Nah, I loved it. As he came, he squeaked your name. He didn't even try to disguise it. He just laid there and apologised. He must have felt guilty because he spooned me all night. No verrucas in my face that night."

"You're being safe, though, using a condom?"

"You know what it's like. Sometimes the moment takes ya, he'll make sure he comes on my back."

"Not a thought I want, thank you."

"That's tame. I'll be nervous now, the next time we, ya know, just in case he says someone else's name."

"It's nice to be wanted."

"It's nicer to share sex, without fantasying about someone else." Said Lizzie. "You and Dylan worked everything out?"

"Yeah, for now. But, do you ever really get over something like that? All I know is, one of two things will happen this summer. Either Dylan and I survive, or we don't. If not, I'm sure I'll have other options. Keep their balls sauna warm. If I have my way, though, Dylan ain't going anywhere tomorrow."

"Wait, why, what d'ya mean?"

"He can't refuse a challenge. He's like a schoolboy." Laura nodded at the green liquid. The bass rumbled from Looking for a Kiss by The New York Dolls, creating a ripple across the surface.

Lizzie shook her head. "The absinthe?"

"You bet."

"That'll knock him on his arse."

Laura smirked, shrugging. "Maybe we'll have to wait and see." She said. Her fingers plucked and grabbed for the shot glass from the kitchen counter, being careful not to slosh the contents.

"Guys," said Laura. "Guys," she repeated. "Can you shut the music off for a second?"

"You can't interrupt the Dolls," said a hollow voice.

"In my house, you can." She said, holding the absinthe above her head like the ten commandments, a disguised trophy offering. "Dylan," she said, standing on tiptoes, scanning over the top of people's heads in the kitchen. "Anyone know where he is?"

Apathetic shoulders bobbed, lips upturned and heads shook.

Dylan appeared confused in the doorway.

"Here you are," said Laura. "Quick one, everyone." She cleared her throat, fist to her mouth. "Everyone, we're here to give Dylan a good send off."

"That's not why I'm here." Said Charlie, in a whisper as he scoffed into his tumbler of golden spirits.

"He leaves me tomorrow, for the United States of Advertising, I jest. The land of the free. Going away for nine weeks. I'm gonna miss you like crazy. We all are." Said Laura.

"Speak for yourself," said Charlie.

"To send you on your way, as good luck goes. I propose a toast. I've got your shot ready here, Masugar." Laura flapped her eyelashes.

"What is it?" said Dylan. He took hold of the glass between his fingers, sniffed the surface, closing his eyes as if nearing magma. "Absinthe?"

"We hold these truths to be self-evident," said Laura. "To Dylan, and the republic for which he stands. Play ball." Laura raised her glass.

Dylan held the shot glass to the light. Thick green liquid with flaky floating residue. He put the glass to his lips, and in one, gulped it down, gasping for air. "Whoa, that's strong." He said, struggling for breath.

"I'll miss you, baby." Laura kissed him on the mouth. The crowd in the kitchen cheered and clapped. The music kicked back in. Shoulder shuffling and head bobbing returned, one hand in jean pockets. One, two, step.

Sofia crashed and staggered through the open front door. Banging herself from one wall to the next. Eyes streaming, black mascara smudging her dirty face. Her tights ripped and shirt torn. She wailed and screamed.

Laura waved her hands. "Luke. Turn the music down. Luke," she said. She tapped shoulders for people to move. "Can you turn the music down, Connor." She flapped her arms. "Get Luke to turn it down."

"Laura!" Screamed Sofia.

The noise cut through the house. Consumed everyones panicked attention. Sofia sounded like a pig dying into a distorted microphone. A screech, the smack and gurgle for another breath. She managed to expel another cry for help before collapsing to the floor. The music stopped with her body thudding in a heap.

Laura skidded to her side, dragging her limp body into her arms.

"Oh my god, Sofia." Said Laura, slapping her cheeks. "Sofia. What's happened—, Dylan. Charlie. Someone help."

Dylan dropped the shot glass, it smashed on the kitchen floor.

Charlie bolted forward. They ran through the kitchen, dodging the concerned onlookers. The only noise was Laura, crying and sniffing through her dripping nose. She rocked Sofia's body in her arms.

"Get her some water," said Dylan.

Charlie grabbed a litre bottle from the sideboard, passing it to Dylan. Water trickled over Sofia's cracked lips. Her eyes crusted and gunky black. She coughed for air, shaking herself upright. Laura wrapped her arms around her waist, holding her between her legs.

"It's OK. It's us." Said Laura, pulling her in tight. "Shh. It's OK. It's Laura, Dylan and Charlie. You're OK. You're safe."

Sofia settled, nodding for the water bottle again. Dylan lifted it to her lips and poured, slow into her chattering mouth. She gulped, nodding for him to stop.

"What's happened to you? Where have you been?"

Sofia whimpered. "Bass, that bastard. He took me to the Pot." She cried, hiding her damaged face in Laura's chest, smudging stains across her dress.

"It's OK. You're fine, now." Said Laura, stroking her fingers through Sofia's greasy hair.

"He kept me in his bedroom—,"

"What, in our house?" said Dylan.

Sofia wiped her eyes, sniffing up tears. "He put a choker on me, chained me in his cupboard."

Dylan tried to hide his disbelief. The scoff convinced Laura he thought this was a bullshit story.

"There's no way." He said, shaking his head.

"Look at me. I'm tellin' ya. What they've done to me. I wish I was dead."

"Charlie, call the police." Said Laura.

"No." Said Sofia, her hand waving for Charlie to stop. "I don't want the police. Traveller Crumble will find him. He's already sorting that landlord out."

"You wanna eat anything?" said Laura.

"I need a shower, then I'll be able to think straight."

Sofia gorged on sausage rolls, handfuls of honey roasted cashew nuts and Chinese spare ribs. She continued to nod for a glass to be filled with orange juice, with extra juicy bits. Her preference over other varieties.

"Last I heard," said Sofia. Her tongue flicking the back of her teeth, swallowing flaky pastry. "He was picked up outside Cambridge."

"By the police?" Said Dylan, stumbling. "I'm going away tomorrow. I can't be dealing with the Police. What is all this?"

"He was bailed, not enough evidence. I told you. It's being dealt with in our own little way. Ya see, my community sticks together. Bass, ain't getting away with anything. I knew he wasn't right. It was his eyes, nothing there."

Dylan's face faded to a pale white.

"Masugar, you sure you're OK?" said Laura. "You don't look right."

"I'm gonna be sick," said Dylan. He pushed himself through the kitchen, almost knocking Laura over. He bowled to the toilet under the stairs, forcing himself past the previous startled occupant, pulling them out by the collar of their shirt.

Dylan stopped, stared at the see through toilet lid, seashells embedded. His vision blurred. Burping, he vomited and spewed cloudy pea coloured puke all over the cistern, bouncing off the floor, covering his dripping socks. He collapsed over the bowl, head hanging, forehead touching the water. Tilly arrived, rubbing his back.

"Let it go. That's it," she said. "Keep breathing, let it go." She rubbed his back along the spine, then cupped his buttocks in her hands. He groaned, too distracted to recognise her voice or even fight her off.

Laura arrived at the door, clicking her fingers, shooing Tilly to scatter. "We don't need anymore drama," she said. Tilly spun, squeezing past Laura in the tight doorway.

"Charlie, Jason. Help me get him upstairs." Said Laura.

Charlie tutted from the kitchen, his foot stopped tapping to Lene Marlin's Sitting Down Here as they both dragged Dylan under his crucifix stretched arms, head drooping forward and pulled him up the stairs, unconscious, his head flopping, one step at a time.

"Is he all right?" said Sofia.

"Just the worst whitey ever," said Laura.

"I'm jealous—, Isn't he heading to the airport tomorrow?" Said Sofia, reaching for another sausage roll.

"I'm almost regretting this now," said Laura. "He is, and he will. He can't miss that flight. One drama after another. I'm knackered."

"We have to sober him up," said Charlie. "He needs to get on that plane, babe."

"I'm not your babe. I know what I'm doing," said Laura.

Laura fluffed a pillow, stuffing it under Dylan's loose head.

"Turn out the light, give us a second," she said. Charlie left, the bedroom faded to dark. The hallway light sliced along the wall until the door was closed. She listened for footsteps to disappear up the landing. She rested her head on Dylan's chest. His head flopped to the side, unconscious.

"You probably can't hear me, Masugar. That makes this easier. Sometimes I hate you. I can really detest you. You annoy me to the point of wanting to stab you. I think I'm joking, I hope I am. But, then you make a noise like a lobster boiling, even do the face, the weird arm thing for claws. Then I'm giggling all over you again." She turned his face by the dimple in his chin, held his lips pert and kissed him. "That's what I'm gonna miss about you the most. I need you to change me from angry to stupid. I'm ready to let you love me." She pressed her lips soft against his.

"How's he doing?" Said Sofia as she sidled into the room.

"He'll be fine," said Laura.

"You say it was absinthe?"

"Not just any absinthe. I soaked a Henry in it. He's having a blast."

"I wish I was," said Sofia. "There's so much I wanna forget."

"You're telling me,"

"What do you need to forget, babe?" said Sofia. She took hold of Laura's hand in hers.

Laura sniffed a tear and said. "I'm late."

"I take it I'm not congratulating you two just yet then?"

"I'm not sure who you should be congratulating."

Dylan snorted, rolled over and pulled his knees up into the foetal position.

29

gUiLtY oF bEiNg vAniLlA

Florence and Yestin lugged heavy, full supermarket carrier bags, stocked with 'store cupboard staples'. Yestin huffed with a chuckle every time Florence referred to their weekly shop as such.

"Why have you got all this stuff, anyway?" Said Yestin, switching bags between hands. He dropped back behind Florence as she waddled along the pavement, scuffing to an impatient halt.

"It's for us. I don't want to go back through the town." She said. Her arms dangled like an orangutan's, weighed down by the bags.

"I can always pick anything up on my way home. This seems excessive."

Florence sighed. "I don't like you walking here on your own. We're almost home now. Keep going."

"It's not that bad round 'ere," said Yestin.

They paused, looking back down the street of Semi-detached houses.

Florence took a gulp of stale traffic air. She noticed three men blocking the pavement further up the hill. "We should cross," she said.

Yestin spotted them too. Two black men, hoods up, and a spindly Asian, sucking on a shared cigarette. "I'm not crossing the road," said Yestin. His shoulders popped back, gritted his teeth, and he strutted with defiance toward them.

"Babe, it's worth not, cross road with me." Said Florence from the middle of the road, checking for cars as she double stepped to the curb of hopeful safety.

Yestin shook his head, refusing to hear. He wrapped his fists tighter around the handles of the bags. His eyes narrowed to a hero's performance of nonchalant confidence, a whistle, he considered too obvious. The three intimidating men parted, leaving Yestin to walk between them like the red sea. Their peering eyes scoped him as he passed. Yestin nodded, holding himself stiff. A polite, silent display of street respect. Relief swept through him, grateful he had so far survived as he passed them.

"Best place for her." Said the Asian, flicking his cigarette at Yestin's feet. "Keep her in place."

Yestin's trainers scuffed to a stop, trampling the cigarette. He glanced at Florence, she had stopped the other side of the road, shaking her head, her eyes pleading the encounter not to escalate.

Seeing her reminded Yestin of her love, the reason for defence. 'Honour. I am a warrior. My purpose is real'. The unspoken mantra repeating in his head. The choices flinched through him. Use the bags, swing them, you idiot. Run. Get out of here. Respond. Say something. Don't let him get away with that. It was derogatory. No shit. Battlefield tactics and strategy imparted realism. Three against one. I don't stand a chance; he thought.

"You wanna say something, bruv?" Said all three of them, encircling Yestin on the pavement, gathering around. Filling his vision, close enough he could examine the smoke stained plaque built up between each of their bottom teeth. A white head in the crease of one black guy's nostril.

"All right guys, not looking for any trouble," said Yestin. He edged backwards on the balls of his feet.

"Ya see, we are looking for trouble." Said the Asian, as the trio matched Yestin's steps. "And we tend to get our way. An elbow to your face is my Sunday morning stroll. Breathing carbon monoxide and tasting blood on my tongue. I can't get enough."

"We just wanna get home," said Yestin. The ability for him to conceal his fear was fading.

"Live up 'ere do ya pastey, boy?"

"Yestin. Leave it." Shouted Florence, as she skipped back toward him.

"Yestin," said the Asian. "What kind of foreign name is that shit? Yestin, booby, let me ask you. Who d'ya think y'are fucking our sisters?" He jabbed Yestin in the chest with a straight finger.

The shopping bags spilt, a box of washing powder scattered and snowed across the pavement.

Yestin turned his body, feet apart, left shoulder blocking his chin. Head down. He brought his fists up. The seven-year-old in him remembered the summer of boxing lessons on Townhill Road, back in Swansea.

"What's your problem, bruv?" said Yestin.

"I ain't yer bruvva."

Florence darted across the road, not checking it was safe. Instinct or luck caused her to stop as a Honda Civic beeped past her. She waved her hands. "Don't do anything, don't you do anything," she said.

"Need your whore to protect ya, do ya, bruv?"

"She's not a whore," said Yestin.

"She's your little Chinky whore," said the Asian.

"She's from Sri Lanka."

"You trying to make me look stupid, pal?"

"You're doing a good job of that yourself," said Yestin.

"OK. It's OK. We leave now." Said Florence. She grabbed up the ripped shopping bags, thrusting the contents into Yestin's chest.

"We're leaving, we're going, it's OK." She backed into Yestin, pushing him along the pavement.

"Bitches like you, get yourself raped for being with a vanilla cunt like him."

Yestin stepped forward. A fist struck him in his right ear, his neck flopped and deflated, like a giraffe thumb puppet, ringing with a crack. The pavement slanted, his knees stiffened. White light flashed through his vision. Confusion, his tongue flapped to form words. Nothing came out, not coherent.

"No more," said Florence. She backed Yestin up, trying to steady him, and ushered him along the pavement. "We're leaving, we go."

The three guys giggled into closed fists.

"Stick to your own shade, vanilla." Said one of the black guys, pulling his baby blue hoodie over his head.

The spilt and ripped supermarket carrier bags were dumped on the kitchen counter, some on the floor. Florence covered herself in Yestin's dressing gown. She pressed a frozen box of Mr. Brain's pork faggots against his ear.

"He hit me in the ear," he said. "I tell ya, if I see them again, catch 'em on their own. Well, then they'll know."

"I know, babe. Don't worry. Does it still sting?"

"Not as much now. Can't believe he got my ear. I could have blocked that."

"I know, babe. We're OK. Just keep pressing that against it. You need to hold it. Why is it so cold in here? I freeze?" Said Florence, shaking her shoulders. "Jesus, bloody ridiculous."

"You can call me Yestin." He laughed, then winced in pain, adjusting the ice covered box against his red ear. "Turn the heating up, if you want."

"You're going shop if we've run out of gas again," said Florence. Her feet tripped, she fell up the stairs.

"You OK." Said Yestin, out up the stairs. "Dylan put twenty quid on it, only the other day."

"What is that smell?" said Florence. She coughed, gagging, fighting not to vomit. The sleeve of the dressing gown covered her nose.

"You choking?" Said Yestin, still leaning in the kitchen.

Florence gulped for air, covering her mouth again. "Oh my god, you gotta come up here. That smell. It's got worse. Come up here, serious." She said.

Yestin shuffled up the stairs, one step at a time, pressing the chilled box against the side of his head. Reaching the landing, the frozen faggots dropped to the floor, landing like a brick. Yestin squinted and pinched his nose.

"Holy shit, that's disgusting," he said.

"What the hell is that? My eyes are burning. It stinks like dead egg and cabbage."

"Where's that coming from, the bathroom? It's like rotting shit."

"No. It's coming from in there." Said Florence, pointing, stuffing her nose into the crease of her elbow.

"You haven't left some weird packaged fish to rot, have you?"

Florence couldn't breathe to utter a word, her cheeks full of air, holding her breath. Sleeve blocking her mouth.

Yestin shook his head. His eyes narrowed, fingers still pinching his nose. He took a quick deep breath, stooped over and nudged the bedroom door open. Preparing himself as if he were a fireman entering a burning building.

Florence scrunched her shoulders into her neck and wrapped her dressing gown around her cold body.

"It's coming from here," mumbled Yestin. His feet creaking on the floorboards. He jumped on the spot. The floor felt unsteady and loose.

Florence stood in the doorway, nodding.

"What is that?" Said Yestin, his eyes almost closed.

"That idiot, Bass. That rat he trapped must have died under here."

Said Florence into her elbow.

Yestin backed out of the bedroom, dragging the door closed tight behind him. He rushed to the landing window, bursting it open on its hinges.

"I've never smelt anything like that." Said Yestin, sticking his head out the window. "It reminds me of when this fox died in our garage, back home, its carcass stuck to a garden cushion. Mitra needs to come sort that shit out." He searched contacts on his phone, found 'Mr. Mitra,' listed. Hit call, put his mobile against his ear, wincing, Swapped hands and used his good ear instead. "We set fire to it in the end."

"What you talking about?"

"The fox. The fire didn't get rid of it. We were left with its skeleton, tail still poking in the air—,"

"Shush a minute, you hear that?" said Florence. Her head tilted, concentrating, looking around, listening out. Yestin stopped talking, the tinny, stifled sound of his phone calling, the melodic ringtone of Ghalla Gurian by Punjabi MC came from behind the closed bedroom door. It stopped, rang again.

Confused, they screwed up their faces. Yestin lurched forward, pushing the bedroom door open. The ringing louder. A female, computerised sounding voice cut in, suggesting to leave a voicemail. Yestin ended the call. He thought for a moment. Hit call again. Hoping he was wrong. The same tune started again from under the floorboards. He looked at his phone, then at Florence. His eyes back to the floor. He clicked off the phone. The melody stopped.

"I think we should call the Police," he said.

Florence squeaked into the dressing gown sleeve, mumbling. "Because of a rat?"

"Yes, yes, because of a rat. What are you talking about? Stop being dense. Catch up."

30

iT'lL bE wORtH iT

Dylan's heavy head pressed into the headrest of the passenger seat. He flopped himself forward, a bubbling, unsettled sensation rumbled through his gurgling stomach. His finger snapped off the radio as the lyrics from Gorillaz, Clint Eastwood, made his skull hot. He checked his phone in his lap. No text messages. His massive travelling backpack was on the back seat of the Ford Fiesta, a blue sleeping bag wrapped tight on top, Sanyo video camera snug inside. He dabbed his moist forehead with a scrunched up piece of toilet tissue and fanned the collar of his grey t-shirt. The rosary beads rattled against his throat as he jerked the window a crack, cool air whistling inside.

"How's your head?" said his mother. Her eyes on the road, looking left, then right as she fed the steering wheel between her hands like a learner.

"Banging, I feel so rough."

"Should have been more sensible. You knew how important today was. You need to be at your best and you go and blow it. You need to grow up. Thank god you got rid of that stupid hair."

Dylan sank his shoulders, exhaling as he tried to focus his eyes. The road ahead zipping him to motion sickness.

"Look at the state of you," she said. "What are they going to think?"

"It's Laura's fault, giving me that shot."

"Don't blame Laura, poor girl. Take responsibility for yourself. No one's going to be there to make sure you get back to your cabin safe. You'll be on your own if you drink too much over there. Don't go embarrassing yourself. You're supposed to be setting an example for those kids."

Dylan rubbed his temples. "All right, you're making my head hurt."

"Good, you need to hear it. You've been working toward this for so long. I can't believe you drank yourself stupid, not the night before."

"It's all a learning curve."

She tutted and said. "Now, we're late too. If you miss this flight, it won't be my fault. You need to eat something. You look green."

"Funny that. I can't eat. I won't hold it down."

"We need fuel. When we stop, I'm getting you a large coffee. If we hit traffic—, God, you're so stupid sometimes, you really are."

"We'll get there. Think positive. What would Pooh do?"

"You'll be walking in a minute. You've stressed me out."

"Walking on water." Dylan flipped his phone over as it vibrated in his lap.

'1 message received,'

He thumbed for the 'read' button. Surprised to see 'Coconut'. Assumed or hoped it would be Laura, Little Lady.

'You better keep your promise. Nine weeks and I'm taking you to a free party x'

He sniffed a stifled laugh. The blurred vision of dragging Moira from the river. Her smile, flinching nostrils.

"That Laura?" said his mother.

"Laura—, Yeah, I mean no, just a girl from uni."

"Rarely, with you, are they just a girl from uni? Don't go messing Laura around. She's a lovely girl."

Dylan concealed his uncomfortable laugh. "She is a lovely girl and I'm not messing anyone around."

"Yeah, well, make sure you don't. You don't wanna end up like your father."

"Horror show."

"Exactly, just remember that. If you can't control yourself, at least make sure you're safe."

"Mother, there's really no need for this conversation,"

"There's always a need. Look at Arnold, had Russell, now he's got another one on the way. Couldn't carry on with his massage therapy, had to get a proper job to support the family. Don't go kissing your life away for two minutes of pleasure. That's all I'm saying."

"I hear you," he said.

The shiny, speckled airport floor reflected Dylan's sunken, puffy eyes. Travelling with heavy, dark bags under his eyes along with his backpack. He traced his fingers through the two shaved chicken talon lines in his newly trimmed hair. It helped with his nerves. He saw Laura adding the finishing touches. Is it possible to already miss her? He thought. He moved the wooden rosary beads around his neck, stopping them from pitching finite, wispy hairs. His tongue rolled his lip ring.

"You look so lost. You sure you'll be OK?"

"I'll be fine, mother. I can't wait."

"I know. I know. I just worry."

"I should go."

"You got everything, passport, money?" she said. His mother stood with her fingertips to her mouth, pride and disquietude. "Got your phonecard?"

"It's in my wallet. I'm good."

"Off to America, on your own. All grown up."

"I've been at uni for two years."

"I know. This will be just another adjustment. It's not something I would have done on my own. You're braver than me."

Dylan embraced his mother, pecked her on the cheek. Conscious people around would judge. He readjusted his massive travelling backpack on his back, leaning forward and jerking up.

"Be good. Do as you're told."

Dylan shook his head. A cheeky smile filling his face. Childish disobedience. He waggled and waved at his mother. His body joined the end of the line. No turning back now. He waited to check in. The 'Sleepaway America' representatives, orientating the disorientated with instruction and commands read aloud from a clipboard.

Sweat beads formed in his hairline. He steadied his breathing. Taking a mouthful of air-conditioned breath in, holding it, then releasing. The girl in front of him stepped forward, as if uncomfortable. She side eyed him from behind her straw brown hair. He forced a subtle nod. She didn't reciprocate. The girl disappeared over to the makeshift registration desk. The three representatives sat beaming fake smiles, going through the monotonous motions.

"It'll be worth it, it'll be worth it," he said.

"Next," said a woman with a double chin, from the table, beckoning him forward from the queue. "What's your name and what camp you assigned?" she said.

"My name," he hesitated. Coughed and cleared his throat. "Dylan Nemerov. N-e-m-e-r-o-v. I'm heading to Red Oak and Silver Wood. Surrey, New York, apparently."

Her finger rolled sheets of paper. "Apparently, you're right. Lucky you. Here." The woman said, holding out a handwritten name badge. 'Dylin' written on the front in black Sharpie. "Put that on. Go to the

Virgin desk, thirty-seven. Next," she said. Her hand waved in the air to get the attention of the next person stood in the queue.

"You've spelt my name wrong," he said. "It's Dylan, with an A, not an I."

"Don't worry about it. No one cares," she said. Her wrist watch jangled as she continued to wave, insisting the next person step forward.

"Just a name on a list," he said. Veins popped in the back of his hand as he scrunched the name tag, tossing it in a nearby bin.

"Remember Dylin," he said. "It'll be worth it. It'll be worth it."

The Next Books:

Flagpole
Autumn In Georgetown

*If you enjoyed this book and would be so kind, I would truly
appreciate your words in a short review.*

Neil Hall was born in England.
He is a writer of fiction.
Simple as That.

Tallbluemidget.com

Shattered Vanilla

Neil Hall

Printed in Great Britain
by Amazon